LOVE RULES

Book Seven in the *Beach Reading* Series

Part of the appeal of...the series is that Abramson sticks close to the reality of San Francisco—the Castro, in particular. He writes what he knows, drawing on his experiences in the community and as a waiter-bartender. Local readers can recognize the stores and bars they frequent; Abramson even features a few San Francisco celebs in cameos.

The idea is to draw readers into a world they know. The series is both familiar and escapist. It's aggressively unpretentious, because that is the kind of book Abramson wants to read.

—Louis Peitzman, *San Francisco Chronicle*

...the author creates one heck of a suspenseful page turner, featuring the characters already endeared to those of us who read the earlier books in the series. (While reading them all in order is not a must, as Abramson provides sufficient detail for "newbies" to catch up on what they need to know, I do indeed recommend reading them all, as this is absolutely the best gay mystery series to come along in at least a decade!) As always, the writing takes you to the Castro instantly, and you can almost smell the sourdough bread!.

—Bob Lind, *Echo Magazine*

LOVE RULES

Love Rules

BOOK 7
IN THE
BEACH READING SERIES

Mark Abramson

Lethe Press
Maple Shade, NJ

Book Design by Toby Johnson
Coverman credit: shutterstock photograph: DmitriMaruta
Author Photograph by David K. Bruner
    davidkbruner.com

Published as a trade paperback original
by Lethe Press, 118 Heritage Avenue, Maple Shade, NJ 08052.
First U.S. edition, May 1, 2013
ISBN 1-59021-161-8 ISBN-13 978-1-59021-161-8

*Special thanks to Toby Johnson and Steve Berman at Lethe Press
and to Brian Butler for his expertise in the Queen's English.*

Library of Congress Cataloging-in-Publication Data

Abramson, Mark, 1952-
 Love rules / Mark Abramson. -- First U.S. edition.
   pages cm. -- (Beach Reading series ; Book 7)
 ISBN-13: 978-1-59021-161-8
 ISBN-10: 1-59021-161-8
1. Snow, Tim (Fictitious character)--Fiction. 2. Gay men--
California--San Francisco--Fiction. 3. Castro (San Francisco,
Calif.)--Fiction. I. Title.
 PS3601.B758L68 2013
 813'.6--dc23
                              2013014961

*D*espite any resemblance to living and/or historical figures, all characters appearing or mentioned in Love Rules are fictional except(in order of appearance:) Reverend Cecil Williams, Amanda Blake, Rachel Maddow, Jackie Kennedy, Judy Garland, Tony Bennett, Jake Gyllenhaal, Sue Grafton, Jan Wahl, Johnny Mercer, Henry Tannenbaum, Donna Sachet, Harry Denton, Peggy Lee, Keely Smith, Billie Holiday, Margaret Hamilton, Julie Brown, Officer Jane Warner, Albert Camus, Aimee Semple McPherson, The Radio City Music Hall Rockettes, Claude Monet, Dan Anderson, Joe Mac, Leah Garchik, Florence Nightingale, Billie Jean King, Andy Roddick, James Blake, Roger Federer, Pat Montclair, Amy Vanderbilt, Liza Minnelli, Carol Channing, Bea Arthur, Sylvia Browne, Joshua Norton, Jose Sarria, Gladys Bumps, KC Dare, Marcus Schenkenberg, Brett Stewart, The Brown twins, Marian and Vivian, Reese Witherspoon, Adam Sandler, Cameron Diaz, Ben Stiller, Matt Dillon, Lady Gaga, Michael Reno, Sharon McNight, Bill Clinton, George W. Bush, Bette Midler, Frank Lloyd Wright

An ambulance screeched through the swirling fog of 18th and Castro Streets, crossroads of gay America for generations of gay men and lesbians, queers, fags, dykes, clones, cross-dressers, snappy dressers and all sorts of misfits in search of a place to fit in. The sounds of sirens in San Francisco were as common as the cries of seagulls along the city's waterfront. The fire department was on the job whenever a cat climbed a tree, but this time the loudest wails came from police cars. An officer was down.

Birdie Fuller opened one eye at a time. She was on the floor just inside the doorway of Cliff's Variety store. Her vision swam into focus and landed on a rack of children's books spinning above her face. Pain made her glance down and notice the blood staining the carpet below her left foot.

"Don't try to move. The ambulance is almost here. You're gonna be fine," said George Tavares, her new partner on the beat. Birdie had asked to be assigned to another lesbian, but ended up with George, a rookie who filled out his uniform better than most, according to the guys in the Castro. Many of them swooned at the sight of him and some even gave up their places in line outside the Badlands on a busy night to follow him when he and Birdie walked by on their way down 18th Street.

George enjoyed the attention and sometimes gave the lucky ones a special business card—*Officer George Tavares* plus an e-mail address and phone number printed in silver ink to match the six-pointed star that took up half the card. Birdie scoffed the first time she saw it and told him it looked like a cartoon sheriff's badge.

"Never mind me…"

"But you're bleeding, Birdie. You must have taken a bullet to bleed like that."

"Where did the robbers go? Was anyone else hurt?"

"Stay calm. Don't try to talk."

"You let them get away, didn't you George?"

"I was busy cuffing the pickpocket. He came off the escalator at the MUNI station, ran across the middle of the street and tried to blend into the crowd outside the Castro Theatre. He had eight wallets in the lining of his coat. Nobody wears a coat like that in San Francisco. He's in the back of the squad car now. Did you get a good look at who shot you?"

"Nah, there were two of them and they both had their faces covered."

"Ski masks?"

"More like nylon stockings…dark ones…"

She felt a scream building. "Shit. I can't believe you let them get away!"

The EMTs had arrived and Birdie moaned as they lifted her into the ambulance.

"But at least I nailed the pickpocket, Birdie."

A half hour later and a block south on Castro Street, Tim Snow served drinks to his first table of the evening at Arts restaurant. He'd slept past noon today, yet he still had a hangover. The smell of food left him nauseated. Artie and Phil were performing out of town again this weekend, so a fill-in was playing the piano, an unsmiling young blonde woman. Arturo had made some kind of an arrangement with the music academy, but most of these students they sent had never set foot inside a gay bar before and they didn't know what to make of drunks requesting show tunes.

Tim's Aunt Ruth had cut back to working Sunday brunches—and then only rarely—so Scott was alone behind the bar tonight. "Hey Tim, did you hear all those sirens on the street earlier? I wonder what happened."

"Yeah, my customers were just telling me that Cliff's got held up by a couple of armed robbers."

"Wow, that's the second one this week. They robbed Catch the other night at the end of the dinner shift. Most of the meals went on credit cards, but the bartenders had a lot of cash in the registers. I wonder if it was the same robbers."

"Could be. Two guys with their faces covered, gloves too, so no fingerprints anywhere." Tim would rather stand around and dish the dirt with Scott tonight than wait on tables, but a group of six preppy-looking guys bustled in all the while giggling and chattering an octave too high for Tim's taste.

"Hey Jake, these guys must be your birthday party of six," Tim smirked at the other waiter. "They requested you, according to the reservation."

"I don't recognize any of them. I should have known with a name like Bip, they'd be the skirt and sweater crowd."

"You better be on your toes. Bip might be a trust-fund heiress..." Tim let the esses hiss through the air above the sound of the student pianist plunking out *Fool on the Hill.*

"Sure hope so." Jake took the stack of six menus Tim handed him on his way to greet his customers. "And I hope whoever's picking up the check is on a fat expense account."

Chapter 1

Always toward absent lovers love's tide stronger flows.
—Sextus Propertius

A few hours later that night, Tim was half-drunk and fumbling for his house keys when the stranger beside him asked, "You don't have a partner, do you?"

"He's out of town."

"But you're bringing me to your house?"

Tim blinked at such an obvious question. "So?"

"I'm just sayin'…some couples have rules; that's all."

"What kinda rules?"

"You know, like…no hosting, no unsafe sex, no French kissing or whatever…don't you guys have any rules?"

Tim shrugged. Inside, he almost fell down while pulling off his shoes at the top of the stairs. He wasn't a fanatic about shoes in the house, but the vacuum cleaner tracks were still fresh from this afternoon's house cleaning. Tim thought that he and Nick must have had a conversation about this at some point, but he'd forgotten if they came to any conclusions. Did they have any rules or not?

"It's not *our* house," Tim said by way of dealing with one of them. "It's *my* house and I can do whatever I want. We don't live together…at least not full-time."

"What about safe-sex?" The guy sat down to unlace his Doc Martins. "Do you guys use condoms?"

Tim tried to remember why he'd let this stranger follow him home in the first place. "I *have* some condoms, sure…for times like these. My partner and I are both HIV positive, so…I mean…we used them for a while when we first met, but after a couple of times of them breaking, we just figured…there's nothing we could give to each other at this point. It's not like we fuck around that much, but he's out of town, like I said."

The stranger looked around. "Nice place. You lived here a while?"

"A while…yeah."

"What do you do?"

Who did he bring home, a game show host? Tim missed the good old days when you brought someone home and all he said was, "Oh, my God, you're hot!" or nothing at all.

"I'm a psychic and I moonlight as a waiter. No, I don't work for the government. And you?"

"Nothing right now. I'm between gigs." The guy took off his gloves, stuffed them in his leather jacket and slung it over the back of the couch. Tim noticed the crude blue-inked tattoos across his knuckles and wondered whether he'd gotten them in prison. It seemed like it would only be a matter of time.

"Rents must be high in this neighborhood, huh? How much does a place like this set you back every month?"

"My house, I already told you."

"You must do all right as a waiter. Or as a psychic." The man grinned but the smile held little warmth. Or even lust.

Tim was growing less interested in this guy by the minute. Just because Nick was out of town, he'd felt like he had to go out after work and see what it felt like to cruise the bars again, to make sure he still had it, whatever *it* was these days, but the more this guy talked the less interested Tim became. He'd seemed kind of hot at the upstairs bar at 440 and then he'd mentioned when they were out on the sidewalk on Castro Street that he was from out of town, so that made him a safe bet, free of any entanglements later. Now that he was inside, Tim felt like he had to at least be polite. "Hey, you want a beer or something?"

"Sure." He followed Tim into the kitchen. When Tim stood up from pulling a couple of beers from the vegetable crisper, the guy leaned in, placed his hands on Tim's hips and ground his pelvis against Tim's ass.

"Umm, one rule." Tim turned to face him. "What did you say your name was?"

"Carlos."

Tim thought it had been Carl back in at the bar. "I don't just bottom on a moment's notice, Carlos."

"Had you figured for a total bottom."

Tim brought the beer to his forehead, reminiscent of Carnac the Magnificent. "Sixty-nine," he said. "And the answer is, Carlos, from the way you sucked on that cheap cigar outside 440, I figured you only knew how to blow."

The guy didn't laugh—must not have been a Johnny Carson fan. Jay Leno kinda sucked, in Tim's opinion. Carlos stomped back to the living room and picked up his jacket.

"Jeez, Carlos…sorry. Look, I already opened the beer; you might as well finish it. Do you want me to call you a cab?"

"I can walk back to Beck's from here. And I don't need your beer either, asshole! Cigar smokers are *real* men!"

"What-ev-er." Tim followed him to the top of the stairs and yelled down after him, "Goodnight, Carl…er…Carlos… er…Carlita. Hope you enjoy your stay in San Francisco!" But the would-be trick was already out of ear-shot, headed back toward the bars in the Castro. Tim still made a point of slamming the door.

Buck came running to see what all the noise was about and Tim knelt down to scratch between the puppy's ears. "You didn't like him either, did you boy?"

Tim dead-bolted the front door, not because he was afraid of anything. It was merely a symbol, the way slamming it had been. "Damnit, Nick. I miss you."

Tim walked down the hall to the kitchen and poured both beers down the sink. Then he dropped a couple of ice cubes into a fist-sized glass and covered them with good scotch. It was the bottle Nick had bought several weeks ago to celebrate a big business deal at the nursery. Then he'd left it at Tim's place for special occasions. Tim rarely drank scotch and this wasn't exactly a special occasion. It was a lousy occasion, if Tim was honest with himself. This was the first time it really sunk in that Nick was going to be out of town for a long time and tonight he missed him like crazy.

Tim put the bottle back on top of the refrigerator and carried the glass to his bedroom, finished getting undressed and slid into bed alone until Buck jumped up to join him. Tim lifted the glass to his lips, wet his tongue, but the fumes caught him by surprise and he started coughing. He set the glass back down on the bedside table beside a picture of him and Nick that his Aunt Ruth had taken. They were in swimsuits, holding hands, lying in the sun beside Ruth and Sam's pool in Hillsborough. "What *are* our rules, anyway?"

Tim had been having clairvoyant dreams for as long as he could remember. Sometimes they foretold the future and sometimes they helped explain his past, but this wasn't either. It was just weird: Tim was walking down a long white hallway. His shoes clicked on the shiny floor and someone in slippers materialized beside him, shuffling to keep up. It was his doctor, dressed in a hospital gown, panting and out of breath.

"Dr. Hamamoto, what's going on? Where are we? What are we doing here? Where are we going?"

Tim's doctor had recently switched his HIV medications. He'd stopped taking Neutriva, which had made his dreams more vivid, more unsettling. Tim and several other psychics had been recruited by a fraudulent group of scientists who upped their dosage and used their subconscious powers for identity theft. Tim had almost gotten used to the Neutriva dreams when his doctor thought it was time to switch to something else entirely. Now Tim took three fat pills from three different bottles, once a day with breakfast. Dr. Hamamoto told him not to expect any sudden changes from the new regimen, but Tim's Technicolor dreams with lush movie soundtracks and choreography were fading back to normal…or whatever passed for normal in his case.

The Walgreens print-out with Tim's new drugs listed a slew of possible side-effects: nausea, diarrhea, vomiting, dizziness, muscle pain, swelling, numbness, rash, trouble breathing, sleeping, eating, urinating and operating heavy machinery. Dr. Hamamoto said that none of those symptoms were likely and the only machinery Tim ever operated, besides his car, was the coffee maker at work, the DVD player at home and the vacuum cleaner. Tim half expected some sort of life-altering revelation whenever there was a change in his medication.

This dream was strange, but it didn't feel important or scary. Tim could usually tell whether a dream was born of his "gift" or just an ordinary dream. Sometimes he thought he was having Neutriva flashbacks and this time he was almost disappointed that his dream wasn't a blockbuster musical.

Doctor Hamamoto had a coughing fit and held onto Tim's arm until it subsided. "You're going home today. You're getting out. I'm going to sign the papers right now and then I'll go back to my cell. Wanna smoke?" They'd been walking past hospital rooms, but now Tim realized they were on Alcatraz back in the days when it was still a federal prison. Their footsteps echoed through the main cellblock. Dr. Hamamoto reached into a pocket of his gown for a pack of Camels, non-filtered. He lit one with a shiny Zippo and offered the pack to Tim.

"No thanks. I only smoke pot. When did you start smoking cigarettes?"

"Just today."

"But you're a doctor, You know they'll kill you, right?"

The man shrugged. Even smiled with nicotine-stained teeth. "We've all gotta go sometime."

Chapter 2

Ruth would never say so—especially to her friend Artie—but she didn't want to be working behind the bar at Arts bar and restaurant that day. There were so many more important things she could be doing, like having a soak in the hot tub in Hillsborough or finishing that article on gun violence in America that she'd just started reading in the *New Yorker* yesterday or painting her toenails. At this point in her life, she didn't *have* to work.

Ruth Bergman Taylor Connor had an inheritance and she'd married into more money—twice! So how did she ever get stuck behind a bar on Castro Street slinging drinks at Sunday brunch for drag queens and their fans? Yes, she wanted to be close to her nephew Tim. And all the other gay "boys" had taken her in, adopting her as the warm and loving, totally accepting mother, sister, aunt or "real-girl" girlfriend some of them had always wished they had when they were growing up. Owners Artie and Arturo treated her like family from day one, but they were that way with all their employees.

Artie felt like family to her. He could come across as just a fussy old man, but when he disappeared into the back room and came out in drag, transformed into Artie Glamóur, he became another person, an exotic creature filled with good humor and raw talent. He was as free-spirited as Ruth's mother had been and as full of life and confidence as Tim ought to be.

Ruth hoped that her nephew would realize his own confidence one day. If only his parents hadn't done everything they could to sap it out of him.

But Artie wasn't here today. He had been out of town a lot lately; his drag persona had finally caught on again for the first time since Finocchio's had closed years ago and his act was getting too big for San Francisco to hold him. This weekend he had a live appearance in Los Angeles. Ruth heard them mention the name of the nightclub, but it meant nothing to her. That was on Saturday night and then he had some kind of taping or recording on Monday morning. All Ruth knew was that she'd agreed to be here, so she and Sam decided to spend the weekend in the city.

"I could have flown back in between," Artie had told Ruth when he talked her into working, "but Monday mornings come so early, especially when I have to bring *her* along. Ruth was getting used to Artie referring to his alter-ego in the third person. "I have to shave again, you know, and then I have to do her hair and make-up all by myself. It's not that they're being cheap; I'm sure they would have hired some local queen to do it for me, but I just don't trust anyone I don't know…"

Customers arrived and took her mind off Artie. She looked up and recognized one of them as her hairdresser. "Rene, how nice to see you."

"Hey there, Miss Ruth," said one of the two tall black men. "I thought I'd better come by and see how your hairdo is holding up in this lousy weather."

Ruth did a pirouette and glanced at herself in the mirror behind the bottles on the back bar. "It's doing just fine, I think. "She smiled at the man behind Rene. "Who is your…?"

"Miss Ruth, I'd like you to meet my twin brother, Antoine."

"How do you do, Antoine." Ruth shook his hand.

"Pleased to meet you, Miss Taylor."

"Please call me Ruth."

"All right, Miss Ruth," Antoine kissed her hand, smiled and sat down. Rene beamed.

"Antoine is visiting me from New Orleans. We're fraternal twins...not identical. You can tell because I look younger."

"By two minutes," Antoine said and they all laughed.

"I'm showing Antoine around town a little. He hasn't been to San Francisco in a long while. We just stopped at Walgreens after Glide and then we thought we'd grab a bite to eat. I was going to take him to Harvey's, but there's a wait a mile long for a table and then it occurred to me you might be working today and I haven't seem Miss Timmy in ages."

"I'm so glad you did. There's been a full house since we opened this morning, but it's starting to slow down a little now." Ruth still wasn't used to Rene's habit of referring to everyone as *Miss...something or other* and especially not her nephew. "Tim must be in the kitchen but it looks like one of his tables over by the far wall is getting ready to leave soon. Or you're welcome to eat right here at the bar if you're in a hurry."

"There's no big hurry," Antoine said. "We're on CPT."

"I'm afraid I don't understand," Ruth frowned.

Rene laughed. "Miss Ruth, you might need a translator for my brother. He lives in the south. That means 'colored people's time.' It's even slower than gay time."

"Oh, I see," Ruth smiled. She didn't think that anyone used the term "colored" anymore, but slang always escaped her. "So, you went to Walgreens to buy some air freshener?"

"Huh?" Antoine was bewildered.

"You said you were after some Glade at Walgreens, didn't you?"

"Oh, Miss Ruth, you *are* for real, aren't you?" Antoine smiled and shook his head. "We stopped in at Walgreens so that Rene could pick up a prescription after we went to church at *Glide*…Glide Memorial is a Methodist Church down in the Tenderloin."

"Oh, I know that place," Ruth said. "Tim took me there once. Reverend Cecil Williams even stopped in here one time when I was working. He was with a young fellow who was running for some kind of city-wide office. I don't remember the name, but he was charming."

"Cecil was all wound up today, let me tell you," Rene said. "He was really cooking. We just made it to the last service because we went out last night."

"Did you take your brother to some jazz clubs last night, Rene? Where did you go, Yoshi's? North Beach?"

"No, Ma'am, but we probably should have. We went to a couple of clubs in Oakland I'd heard about, but most of the brothers there were on the down low."

"Is that anything like getting the 'low-down'?" Ruth asked. "I love mysteries—"

Antoine piped up, "No, Miss Ruth, this time it's Rene that needs to be translated into English for you. 'Down low' is when black men get it on with other men, but they call themselves straight. I *am* straight, so that *sure* wasn't my scene. They even have wives and girlfriends at home to convince themselves it's okay."

"Do you mean that they're in the closet?"

"Sort of like that, yes." Rene said. "I, however, have always known exactly who I was. When I run into the dude who suggested that club to me, I'm going to give him a piece of my mind."

Antoine laughed. "When Rene came out of the closet he tore that closet door right off its hinges!"

"You've got that right. But it's sad, really. Those 'down-low' brothers go out and catch who-knows what-all diseases to bring home to their unsuspecting women-folk." Their conversation was cut off by the phone. It had hardly stopped ringing all morning. By the time Ruth turned back around, the twin brothers had moved on to a table in Tim's section.

Tim didn't feel much like working either. He could hardly believe he poured himself that scotch last night, on top of what he'd already had to drink at 440. Sometimes a hangover didn't hit hard until later, after he'd been moving around for a while. It was mostly dehydration—someone older and wiser had said to Tim once. It was one of those things that stuck in his head like "A stitch in time saves nine" and all the state Capitols, though he always wanted to say Kentucky's was Louisville instead of Frankfurt. He stood at the sink in Arturo's kitchen at Arts restaurant and glugged down a tall glass of water. Even though Arturo was out of town, his assistant chef was so well trained to do everything exactly the way Arturo did that it still felt as if Arturo was there. The customers would certainly never notice the difference and that was Arturo's intention.

"Thirsty, huh?" Someone asked.

Tim looked up and saw that it was the new dishwasher, waiting for Tim to get out of his way. "Hung over," he muttered.

"No, Artie won't be here today, but the show must go on." Ruth was speaking into the phone behind the bar. She might as well make a recording; every caller wanted to know the same thing. Better yet, Artie should make a recording before he leaves town next time. What a good idea! She'd try to remember to suggest it to him. "Artie will be back here doing Cabaret Brunch at Arts a week from today. Last week he was performing in Orlando. Yes, the Parliament House...I think that was the name of the place. This weekend he's in Los Angeles, but taking his place here at Arts today we have Rochelle and Roxeanne. They're a delightful duo from Chicago who are appearing here instead of Artie."

"Four Bloody Marys please, Aunt Ruth," The caller had already hung up, so Ruth replaced the receiver and made the drinks. Tim reached for the soda gun at the waiters' station and filled another glass with water. "I'm so thirsty today."

"What did you and Nick do after work last night... anything exciting?" Ruth asked.

"Nick's out of town, remember?" Tim didn't want to talk about what he had done, picking up the Latino stranger who didn't exactly work out. His Aunt Ruth wouldn't understand.

"With his grandmother...Amanda...of course I knew that. It just slipped my mind. She's on a book tour. Artie's on a singing tour. And *I'm in the mood for love*," Ruth began singing.

"You sound chipper today," James appeared at the station as soon as Tim backed out with his tray of drinks. "Two Ramos Fizzes, please."

Ruth smiled. Seeing her nephew always perked her up. Tim was gorgeous, sweet, good-hearted. Besides, there was no reason to bring anyone else down. "Coming right up, James!" She cracked and separated an egg into the blender and went back to singing, *"It's a lovely day today, and whatever you've got to do..."* she flicked on the blender to drown out her voice and her thoughts, "and I'd rather be doing it anywhere else but here..."

Teresa came in about 2 p.m. when the brunch eaters were winding down. It was time now for the brunch drinkers and Teresa looked like she would fit right in. "Where's Birdie today?" Ruth asked. "I haven't seen her on the beat lately. Is she working?"

"No she's still out on sick-leave. Didn't you hear about it? She took a bullet in that hold-up at Cliff's the last week."

"No!"

"I guess you don't get the *B.A.R.* down in Hillsborough, do you. It's on the front page."

"Is she all right?"

"She's fine. It just grazed her ankle and it swelled up a little. She's on antibiotics. Make me a tall gin and tonic, wouldya Ruthie? Make it a double! Birdie's carrying on like she's at death's door or something. What a terrible patient! I'm not much of a cook, you know. Arturo's been bringing

things over from across the hall and taking stuff home from
the restaurant for her, but Birdie's so fussy! She'll thank him
like crazy and then as soon as the door is shut, she'll hobble
out to the kitchen to taste it and add her own spices...or throw
it away!"

"Sam is a terrible patient, too. He doesn't have the
patience for it...no pun intended...Tim was a lousy patient
too. Remember when he was laid up after that accident with
Nick's truck."

"But it's easier with guys," Teresa said. "They'll say
what they mean, right Tim?" But Tim was out of earshot.
"Birdie can never make up her mind. I'll ask her, 'Do you
want some ice cream?' It should be yes or no, right? Not with
Birdie. It's always, 'Not unless you're having some. I'd hate
for you to go to all that trouble.' Hey Tim! Is Nick like that?
I'll bet not."

Tim poured himself another glass of water at the station.
He didn't have a drink order. "Is Nick like what?"

"What would Nick say if you asked him...oh...how
about...whether he was done eating? Would he hand you his
plate and say 'Sure, thanks' or would he fuss about it? With
Birdie, it can be the middle of the afternoon and the eggs from
her breakfast are dried up and stuck to the plate, but if I try to
take it away she's all 'I'm still working on that.'"

"No, Nick's not like that at all. He always cleans his
plate right away. I have to keep him talking during meals to
slow him down."

"See what I mean, Ruth? Guys are different."

Tim was still thinking about Nick and missing him.
Last Sunday they'd spent the day together. Tim had taken
the day off work and they'd slept in, made breakfast at Tim's,
watched an old movie, made love on the living room floor...
"Last Sunday I asked him if he was finished with the Sunday
paper and he said, 'all but the pink section.' I was about to
toss the whole thing, so I was glad I asked."

"At least you got to toss the rest. Birdie's never finished looking at the advertisements, even after the coupons have expired!"

"I asked Nick if I could throw away his old ski boots or if he planned to use them again. I don't know how long they'd been in the trunk of my car."

"What did he say?"

"He thought he'd already thrown them away. One sprung a leak. He forgot they were in my trunk. He says we're both getting new ones this winter and he's gonna drag me up to the Sierras every chance he gets. I don't know about that. I don't want either of us to break a leg. He's not afraid of anything, but I've had more experience on crutches then he has."

Teresa laughed. "Birdie would have said we had to fix up the ski boots so that we could donate them to the missionaries or something. For such a butch little cop, she sure has a thing about missionaries. Give them to the homeless or some poor starving heathen in Africa whose soul can't possibly be saved until they get a pair of used ski boots? I tell you…"

Ruth laughed. She was glad her former neighbor Teresa had come in. Maybe this was what she needed to cheer her up and distract her.

"It's kinda slow in here today, isn't it Ruth? I thought this place would be crawling with Catholics right after the last mass let out at Holy Redeemer."

"We were very busy earlier," Ruth tried to keep the smile in her voice, "right up until just before you got here. A lot of people left when the entertainers finished their set. That's how it goes. You never know. I thought with Artie out of town the place would be empty all day, but I guess this act they booked to take his place must have a following of their own."

"At least these two new drag queens are more entertaining than the piano player they had last night," Tim said. "I never thought I'd miss having Phil around."

"I don't know much about drag queens," Teresa said. "I just come in for drinks and for Arturo's food."

"Arturo's out of town too," Ruth said. "He's in L.A. with Artie and Phil and the rest of the band."

"Artie's got a band now?"

"Well, there's Phil on the piano and a drummer and a bass player. I think they were talking about adding a saxophone, maybe more for some of the bigger venues."

"Arturo didn't mention leaving town. He brought over some soup for Birdie yesterday afternoon."

"He flew down to L.A. last night to catch Artie's show. Artie had to be there earlier for a sound check or something. They'll come back tomorrow morning after the taping. That's how they talked me into working today. I'm trying to wean myself away from this place, at least the work part, but they practically begged, saying they needed a *grown-up* to keep an eye on the kids, as if Tim and James and Scott would get out of hand. Jake is off until the dinner shift tonight. I told them I'm no manager, but they ought to hire one. I'm getting too old for this."

"Maybe it's time to sell the place," Teresa said. "It must be worth a fortune, prime real estate on Castro Street, plus the reputation it's got. Artie could still appear here I'll bet and they wouldn't have all the headaches."

"What a good idea, Teresa. I'll bet Artie would love nothing better than to just perform. It's Arturo you'd have to convince. I think he has a stronger attachment to the place than Artie does. He's a sentimental old guy beneath that masculine façade."

"Yeah, you're right, Ruthie," Teresa laughed. "Arturo is an old sweetheart. He'd be lost without his kitchen here. You know the size of our kitchens on Collingwood! He'd probably never sell."

"No, but it's still a good idea. Maybe I'll mention it to them both when the time is right."

Chapter 3

Ruth set down her fork and had another sip of wine. She and Sam were at their favorite table at Farallon. "Amanda who?"

"Amanda Blake. She played Miss Kitty on *Gunsmoke* on television. She died of AIDS, you know. I was just reading an article the other day about.... Hello. Earth to Ruth. Are you still here with us?"

Ruth had a glazed look on her face, but she snapped back to attention. "This sea bass is delicious...have a taste. You just reminded me...I wonder how Amanda Musgrove's book tour is going. I hope Tim can manage to stay out of trouble with Nick gone to Europe for a few weeks. I know Tim misses him terribly."

"They must talk on the phone."

"It's not the same. Every time you go to Europe without me, I try to stay very busy so I won't miss you too much."

"Or so that you can manage to stay out of trouble?" Sam winked at her. "Which is it?""

Ruth just smiled.

"And here I'd pictured you lolling beside the pool all day whenever you weren't having your hair and nails done or being pampered at the spa with a hot stone treatment. You know you're always welcome to come with me to Europe. But what were you saying earlier, about the restaurant?"

"Well, I am trying to get out of there, trying to wean them off depending on me so much. I love seeing the boys and I adore a lot of the regular customers, but my feet get tired and my back aches. It would be a lot more fun if I did it less often. They need to hire a manager if they're going to be gone so much. Artie's got his *show biz* career going now, just what he's always wanted, and Arturo is involved with that all the time. He doesn't have time to be in the kitchen anymore. He's too busy making bookings, hiring musicians, signing contracts; Artie needs a manager, too."

"So you think they'd actually sell the place? It's hard to imagine, after all it's meant to them over the years."

"Oh, no; I don't think so. Teresa thought of it, actually. I have to give her the credit, but it's not a bad idea. I'm going to mention it to them."

Nick's phone call woke Tim. "Where are you?"

"London. You sound like you were asleep."

"No, I'm awake," Tim lied. "How is your grandmother? Does she need you to push her around in a wheelchair by now?"

"She's strong as an ox."

"How was the ocean crossing?"

"She loved it. I didn't like it so much."

"Why not? I've heard those ships are full of gay employees ready to jump your bones. All you had to do was ring for room service…or state-room service or whatever they call it."

"I'll try to remember that for the return trip, Snowman. No, I was kinda sick."

"Seasick?"

"I don't know. I've never gotten seasick before in my life. Maybe it was something I ate or something that was going around like Legionnaires' disease."

"Just so it wasn't a social disease."

"What?"

"You heard me. I don't want you to come home dripping with the clap and think you're coming near me with that thing."

"Don't worry, Tim. I've been too sick to even think about sex and besides, if I was going to mess around I wouldn't be careless about it."

"You mean you'd be serious about it?"

"No, not serious. Maybe casual would be a better word to use for sex. Casual, yes...careless, no."

"Hmmm. I was just thinking about how we've never really discussed this before, you know? I've heard about how some couples have rules."

"Where did you hear that?"

"It must have been in an article I read in a magazine. I don't remember. Some couples establish boundaries, so that they're both okay with each other getting their needs met without it being any threat to their core relationship.

"Tim, I don't think this is a conversation we should be having over the phone when we're half a world apart. This is the sort of thing people need to discuss when they're alone together in the same room, preferably nude—in bed—right after having had great sex. With each other."

"Oh, okay, I know you're right."

"What's new in San Francisco? Are the naked people still hanging out at Jane Warner Plaza?"

"Not when it rains and you must have heard Scott Weiner got that ban against nudity passed, with exemptions for the Folsom Street Fair and Bay to Breakers. The Wiener anti-weiner law. Only in San Francisco, huh? At least they used to give the tourists something freaky to look at. I'm sure the clientele at the Twin Peaks doesn't miss them."

"How are things going at the restaurant?"

"The same for me. Work is work. Artie's out of town again this weekend and next so they've booked a couple of other drag queens—Rochelle and Roxeanne—for the Sunday brunch shows. They're okay, I guess. Lots of people have been coming in to see them. What do I know about show biz?"

"I've gotta go, Snowman. I'm being summoned by the author. It's time to go to breakfast."

"Tell your grandma hi from me."

"I will. And I'll talk to you soon. Love ya. Now go back to sleep."

"I love you too, Nick," Tim said, but he wasn't sure if he got the words out before their connection cut off. He was mad at himself anyway, for trying to talk about *rules* over the phone. They should have discussed them before this separation. Nick was right. They needed to have that conversation naked together. The thing was…whenever they were naked right after sex, Tim wanted to luxuriate in those moments together. He never wanted to talk about anything serious. Eat, maybe; call out for a pizza, yes, but talk? No.

Chapter 4

Tim and Buck were among the first to arrive in Dolores Park on Monday morning. They had their pick of spots along the "gay beach"—that shelf of lush green grass below the uppermost corner at 20th and Church Streets, just above the new children's' playground. It smelled like the gardeners must have just mowed it this morning. The smell of freshly mown grass always reminded Tim of Minnesota, where people have room for lawns around their houses. He missed that intoxicating smell, but not enough to want to go back there.

Sometimes Tim liked Dolores Park when it was quiet like this, with fewer distractions than on a hot, crowded day. Today it was barely warm enough to sunbathe but the temperature was rising as fast as Tim's libido. By the time he spread his beach towel and got undressed, half a dozen other guys were settling in all around him. Tim rearranged his position to get a better look, but there was no way he could see them all at the same time.

"You're a big boy, Snowman. You know what you need," Nick's voice was in his head from some earlier conversation. Tim couldn't even remember now what they'd been talking about back then. Bits and pieces of things Nick had said rolled around in Tim's head in a jumble. "You can make your own decisions... You know I love you... Take care of yourself... and stay safe." Tim tried hard to remember what might have prompted Nick to say those things to him. Maybe it was only a dream. If it wasn't a dream, it must have been the closest he and Nick had ever come to talking about rules.

Nick saying "play safe" would mean that Tim should use condoms, even though it was more likely that Nick would say "stay safe," than "play safe." He and Nick were both HIV positive, so they had no fear of getting infected, but infecting others. Then there were those warnings about contracting a different strain of the virus. Nick had to have said those things in a dream.

Tim also replayed in his head the line with the word *need* in it. Knowing what you need wasn't exactly the same as knowing what you want and Tim wasn't sure of either, but he knew he was so *needy* right now that his teeth were about to curl up in his mouth. He called to Buck, who was running in circles with a female terrier. Damn, it looked like their baby boy was going to grow up to be straight after all. "Come *on*, Buck! Don't make me have to come and get you!"

The dog finally came running and Tim snapped his leash on him. Then they walked home to get the car.

Morning mist rose through the trees from the damp earth in Buena Vista Park, an urban paradise overlooking the Castro. Sometimes Tim liked it better here on a quiet day like this when there were fewer distractions. This used to be one of the cruisiest places in town before the city gardeners remodeled it a couple of years ago. The north side facing the old St. Joseph's hospital—now pricy condos with terrific views of Eureka Valley—and convent was a maze of dirt paths through heavy vines and bushes that created cul-de-sacs where guys could get it on with each other, day or night. A few years ago, before Tim had even met Nick, he'd come up here one day and seen people hanging something shiny from the bushes and tree branches. He assumed they must be entomologists setting traps for fruit flies or some kind of dangerous biting insect. When he got closer he asked one of the guys what they were doing and he held up one of the shining objects for Tim to get a closer look. It was a plastic bag with two condoms and a tube of lube inside. He said the city health department figured with the full moon coming that night on a holiday weekend there would be lots of action and they wanted people to play safe. Tim just shook his head and said, "Only in San Francisco!"

Now all the bushes were gone. The paths had been replaced by a fancy redwood boardwalk and concrete staircases with railings. Maybe the people in the high-priced condos had complained about witnessing one too many trysts from their dining room windows. Or maybe the professional dog walkers had put up a fuss. It seemed a shame that such a convenient place to find casual sex had to get all cleaned up, but the city was always changing. Tim figured the park had such a decades-old reputation that there still might be some cruising going on. Gay men weren't about to give up their instincts so easily when the need arose. Tim knew that all it would take this morning was to run into one other guy who was out looking for some fun. He could figure out where to take them later, maybe home, maybe not. And he could definitely think about rules some other time after Nick got home and they had time to talk.

"Hey there!" Tim heard a deep voice, but couldn't see where it came from. He turned around and saw a guy in a Prius curbing his wheels across the street on Buena Vista East. "Wasn't your name Tim?"

"Uh, yeah…it sure was and it still is, huh…"

"Yeah, I thought I recognized you."

Damn! Tim didn't have a clue as to who this guy was. He was tempted to get back in his car and go home, but Buck had already run ahead of him chasing a squirrel. The stranger rolled up his window and climbed out of the car. He was kind of cute.

"You work at Arts, right? You were our waiter at brunch a couple of weeks ago." Then his cell phone rang. He pulled it out and looked at the screen, but he didn't answer.

"Sure!" Tim was relieved that this game was over. He would have let himself wonder about it all day before he'd admit to not knowing someone who called him by name. Artie had told him lots of times, "Just get over it. When you're in the public eye, all sorts of people will recognize you." Artie ought to know. He was getting more famous all the time. But Artie had an awesome memory for names. When Artie and Aunt Ruth were working behind the bar together, Ruth remembered everybody's drink, but Artie could tell you their name, where they lived and the date of their birthday.

"Name's Howard." The man handed Tim his business card and they headed east on the wooden boardwalk.

"Sure, I remember you now. You guys ordered champagne and you paid the tab that day, right? You were there with your..." Tim stumbled on his shoelaces and Howard made as if to steady him, but Tim caught his balance and stopped to tie them again.

"With my partner, Mickey."

"Your partner..." Tim wasn't sure if he'd said that out loud or was only thinking it, so he said it again, "Your partner...as in...*life* partner?"

"We've been together almost twenty years, since college."

"No kidding."

"You married, Tim?"

"Um, not exactly...I mean, we talked about it once or twice, going to New York or Iowa or Massachusetts or someplace."

"Oh...you're talking about *legally* married. All I meant was, if you had a partner, but I guess you do. Taking some time off?"

"He's out of town for a while...business, mostly." It wasn't a total lie. It wasn't Nick's business trip; it was his grandmother's book tour to celebrate the release of her biggest sellers in translation to French, Italian and German, so far. "I haven't been up here in ages."

What was worse, Nick and his grandmother were sailing, something Tim had always wanted to do. Amanda Musgrove hated to fly, even on short trips, and she downright refused to fly over the Pacific Ocean. "I remember the park used to be pretty cruisy at night and I wondered if anything was still happening up here in the daytime," Tim added, by way of confessing his motives.

Howard laughed and said, "I'm sure it's nothing like it used to be before they landscaped everything. I've heard that you used to be able to drive to the top. I guess it was pretty wild back in the day. They used to hang slings in the trees for days at a time."

"No kidding? When was that?"

"Back in the 70s. Before AIDS. Yeah, I'll bet just about everything has happened in this park at one time or another, from childbirth to murder over all these years, but just look at that view." Howard's cell phone rang again and this time he texted a few words with his thumbs on the tiny keyboard.

Tim looked out across the Castro and Mission districts to a huge white ship on the bay. He could picture Nick right now; hauling crewmembers back to his cabin while his grandmother signed autographs and held court at the ship's gayest cocktail lounge.

"Beautiful," Tim started walking again and spoke over his shoulder to Howard, "Where's Mickey?"

"Alabama. It's his parents' wedding anniversary. His brothers and sisters had to bribe him to come home. In return, they're sending us both to Cancun for two weeks when he gets back…all expenses paid on a cruise! I'm the lucky one. I don't have to spend time with his fundamentalist parents and I still get the free trip!"

"Right," Tim wondered whether to ask if Howard and Mickey had any "rules" or whether he should try to lure Howard into a quiet place far from innocent eyes. They really had cleaned up this park. There didn't appear to be any place to go do it at all anymore.

Howard stopped for a moment at the top of a flight of stairs that led down toward the Castro. "Nice seeing you, Tim. I've gotta make some business calls before I head back to the office. The connection's not very good here. Enjoy the sunshine!"

Tim watched Howard put his cell phone back in his pocket as he headed down the stairs. "So much for that bright idea," he said to Buck, but the dog was enchanted by a little yellow butterfly. Buck wasn't the least bit concerned with Tim's needs, either.

Chapter 5

"Arturo, this looks like a recording studio. Where the hell are you taking me? I don't see any cameras. I don't know why I had to get up and put on a full face just for a radio interview. A pair of good earrings and some lipstick would have almost been enough for me to get into character if it meant I could have slept another hour!"

"It is a radio interview, but they'll want to take some still shots, too. The photographer should be along any minute. Just relax now, Artie."

Artie noticed that Phil and the other musicians were setting up in the center of the room, so they obviously intended for him to sing. "I'm relaxed, already, I'm relaxed, dangit!"

"Besides, you always sound more cheerful when you're in full costume, even over the phone."

"Arturo! I ask you...when do you and I ever talk on the phone?"

"Not you and me so much, but I hear you at the bar when you answer the phone all the time."

"I can't imagine I sound cheerier with heels on! Not unless I'm sitting down. Oh, okay, maybe you're right, but that's only because Artie Glamóur is a much nicer person than Frank Arthur Reynolds III. That old fart can be a real stick in the mud, while Artie Glamóur is always *fabulous*…"

"Atta girl!"

Introductions were made between the musicians and various sound engineers. Artie tuned down the *Glamóur* enough to give them each a matronly nod. An officious-looking woman in a suit appeared, introduced herself and explained that she'd be conducting the interview for a satellite radio station. They sat down and the room grew quiet. Lights flickered on a panel and the woman smiled, counting down from five on her fingers. Artie was only a little nervous, still wondering why he needed to be this dressed up so early, but glad to be off his feet.

"My guest today is San Francisco's very own Artie Glamóur, who has been packing them in at his Castro Street restaurant, Arts, for the past several months. Welcome, Artie. May I call you Artie?"

"Of course, but it's Arturo's and my restaurant. I wouldn't know the first thing about all the work he does to keep the food coming out and the bookkeeping in order. He's right over there…"

"Of course…so I understand you've been traveling a great deal lately. Is that right, Artie?"

"Yes, I've been invited to perform outside of Arts restaurant more and more often these days, which is quite an honor, but I always like coming back home. *I left my heart in San Francisco* and all that, you know…" Artie thought his speaking voice sounded surprisingly good and strong for so early in the morning. This radio interview wasn't so bad, after all. They talked about the restaurant some more and Artie thought he should try to get in a plug for the album he had coming out soon…or *would* have, as soon as he found the time. He and Arturo had been talking about recording one for months. Artie had narrowed down his repertoire and picked out the songs he wanted to include on his first album, mostly up-tempo standards—classics, really—with a couple of ballads thrown in for good measure, to show off his tender side.

The interviewer was obviously a lesbian, Artie decided. It seemed especially strange so early in the morning, in such a formal environment, that he was the one wearing the make-up and a dress while she wore what appeared to be a man's suit and not even a smudge of lipstick. Artie always thought that even the butchest dykes could use a little eye-shadow now and then, like Rachel Maddow, who almost went too far some evenings on her show, but he supposed that was the producers' doing. Regardless of her severely butch look, this lesbian was pleasant enough. Things were going along swimmingly until she said that the audience would want to hear about Artie's "glory days" at Finocchio's.

"Ancient history!" Artie declared as forcefully as he could while remaining lady-like. "No one else remembers those days, so why should I? If any of my old fans from the North Beach era are still alive and listening to this station, come on down and see me at Arts Bar and Restaurant on Castro Street every Sunday for Cabaret Brunch! Well, not every Sunday. We have fill-ins when I'm gone. I've been doing more traveling lately…here, there, wherever they want me."

That led the interviewer to use the ill-chosen term "come-back" in discussing Artie's recent popularity on Castro Street and beyond.

"I prefer to call it resurgence!" Artie corrected her. "Please! You make it sound like I'm back from the dead. I was never dead, just in mothballs for a few years. Are we on live right now or will this be edited later?"

"We're live *and* on tape. It will run more than once."

"I should sing then…as long as the band is here. I see they're all set up and twiddling their thumbs…something from my new album of old chestnuts."

"We're hoping you'll do more than one, actually. We've scheduled you for the entire…"

Artie had already stood up. "Then I'd better sing." Phil played an arpeggio as Artie stepped up to the standing microphone and got started. *"I'm gonna love you, like nobody's loved you, come rain or come shine…"*

Artie felt more secure singing than he did talking, anyway. And he sang remarkably well, considering it was Monday morning and he was stone-cold sober. A long-haired boy had snapped a couple of pictures while Artie talked to that woman on the microphone, so that part of the plan must be over for now. Artie kicked off his shoes before he started in on *Sing me a swing song* and when he sang *Tangerine* he was in great voice, hitting every note dead-on and feeling right in the groove. The woman in the suit made another announcement after that song. She thanked Artie for coming and thanked everyone for tuning in and then she signed off the show and removed her earpiece.

"That's it?" Artie asked. "I was just getting warmed up." Artie thought he was booked for the whole hour. She must have said half hour. Now it hardly seemed worthwhile to have stayed over that whole extra day and night in Los Angeles and miss another Sunday brunch yesterday at Arts, which he'd been missing more and more often lately. It certainly wasn't worth it to get up so early and go through his entire transformation into Artie Glamóur just for a couple of lousy snapshots of him doing a radio interview, for Heaven's sake! He planned to give Arturo a piece of his mind, just as soon as they were alone. Artie thought this appearance was going to be on television, at least.

"But now that you mention it," the woman was still speaking to Artie, "this studio is free until at least noon. You might want to do another song or two. If they turn out better than the ones we already have on the tape of the live show, we could fit them into the program when we re-broadcast…and for posterity, of course."

"Posterity?" Artie was starting to take a dislike to this dyke…and he tried to like everyone. First she had him raised from the dead, talking about his "come-back" and now she wanted to mention "posterity," as if this was the time to look back on his life. "Yes, that's a fine idea. Let's do *I'm still here.*"

And he grumbled under his breath, "I'll show you posterity, indeed!"

They went on to do *Jersey Bounce* and *From This Moment On* and all the rest of the songs on Artie's imaginary album. They had a couple of rocky starts, but since this part wasn't being broadcast live it didn't matter. They just stopped and started over. When they finished it was well past noon. The lesbian announcer was nowhere to be seen and Artie had no idea how much time had elapsed. He felt that good.

"Are you ready to go home now, Artie?" Arturo was standing beside him. "We have plenty of time to go back the hotel so you can change before we head to the airport. Are you hungry? We could grab some lunch. You sounded just great!"

Phil and the other musicians were packing up too. "Terrific session, Artie!" the bass player shouted.

"Why, thank you," Artie blushed. "I enjoyed that."

Artie and Arturo took their seats in row 6 of United flight 6519. Artie always asked for a window seat, especially when the flight was landing in San Francisco during daylight hours. He loved catching sight of the Golden Gate if they used that particular landing pattern. The view was spectacular at night, too, with the lights on the massive towers and cables, but this time of year there was usually too much fog. Even then, he loved to look out at the ship-shaped top of the Sutro Tower, sailing on a sea of white. The best part of leaving San Francisco was always coming back. Artie liked to travel even more when he was younger, before he had to take Artie Glamóur along everywhere he went. Artie was mostly glad to be out of his professional get-up and heading back home.

The flight attendant announced *"Ladies and gentlemen, in preparation for landing in San Francisco, please make sure your seat backs and tray tables are in their full upright position. Make sure your seat belt is securely fastened and all carry-on luggage is stowed underneath the seat in front of you or in the overhead bins."*

It brought Artie out of his trance. "What was the name of that radio station, Arturo?"

"What radio station?"

"Arturo, have you lost your mind or did you have a stroke? *What radio station?* What do you think, Arturo, the one on the moon? The radio station where we just spent all morning and part of the afternoon! What was the name of it? I think my voice sounded pretty good. I might like to hear that program sometime. Can we get a copy? I could fast forward through the talking parts."

"That's exactly what we intend to do, Artie. Nobody will hear those. That was just to help you get in character...to get in the mood, you know?"

"What do you mean, nobody will hear that part? What are you talking about? Not even on the radio? She said they'd rebroadcast the whole show. Do you mean they'll put in more songs and take out the interview? I thought she meant..."

"There was no radio station, Artie."

"Now I'm thinking I must have had a stroke."

"You're fine, Artie. We've been talking about you recording an album forever. Now you have."

"I have what?"

"You've recorded an album. I knew if I set everything up for you, you'd stew about it every minute until the day came and make yourself sick with worry."

"You don't mean..."

"Please turn off all electronic devices until we are safely parked at the gate. Flight attendants, prepare for landing. The current temperature in San Francisco is a pleasant 68 degrees with a trace of wind out of the northeast."

"I wanted you to be as relaxed as you are on Castro Street. At first I thought about doing a live album from Arts, but maybe we'll do that next time. The producers and I talked things over and came up with this idea. For your first album, they wanted to have more control over all the technical aspects than they could get in the restaurant with a live audience."

"Arturo, you son of a gun." Artie sounded like a cantankerous old man again. "You know me too damned well."

The flight attendants said "thank you" and "bye, now" to the two nice older gentlemen from row six. Well, the taller one on the aisle had been awfully nice. The chubby balding one had mostly stared out the window until the last few minutes of the flight and now he sounded like he was upset about something.

Chapter 6

Teresa threw a little party for Birdie Monday evening. It was partly in recognition of her birthday that had passed while she was laid up and didn't want to see anyone and partly to celebrate her return to work. She'd invited mostly "family"—all the current tenants of the building on Collingwood, plus a couple of the other lesbians on the police force, but they hadn't shown up yet.

She'd also invited Tim, but he was an afterthought. Teresa had stopped by the restaurant on Sunday afternoon to find out what time Arturo and Artie's flight was due in from Los Angeles and that was when she invited Ruth and by extension Tim...

"Teresa, shame on you for giving me such short notice!" Ruth scowled. "You know we would have loved to, but I simply can't. As soon as Scott sets foot behind this bar to replace me, I will have served my last cocktail and I am out of here. I promised Sam we'd go back home to Hillsborough tonight and stay there. He's been so good about spending time in the city with me these past couple of weekends and chauffeuring me around all by himself."

"Instead of having his chauffeur doing it?" Tim asked.

"He doesn't have a chauffeur, Tim, and you know it…
well, only on special occasions. Don't mind Tim, Teresa. He's
been out of sorts ever since Nick left town, the poor dear. I'm
sure he misses him terribly."

"Then *you* should come to the party tomorrow, Tim! I
figured you'd be heading up north to be with Nick. Artie and
Arturo are flying back from L.A. tomorrow afternoon and
I've invited all the neighbors. You'll know everyone except
the other cops."

Tim wasn't interested in going to a lesbian birthday
party, but he thought it might keep him out of trouble. That
was on Ruth's mind too, so she was glad when Tim answered,
"Sure, Teresa. I'd love to hear about Artie's show in L.A. Since
you're right across the hall, I guess you can't miss them."

Arturo and Artie were the last to arrive at the party.
They would have spent a blessedly quiet evening home alone
if Jeff from the second floor hadn't spotted them when their
cab from the airport pulled up out in front. He and Tony were
on their way upstairs to the party, but ran downstairs instead
to help Arturo carry in their bags. Artie Glamóur took up a
lot of room in the luggage compartment these days. Birdie's
lesbian co-workers had just arrived at the party, in uniform,
plus one lone gay policeman that Tim had never laid eyes
on—or laid—before. Maybe this party would be fun, after all.

"Uniforms, badges and guns, oh my!" Artie screamed.
"Just for me? Teresa, you shouldn't have!" Arturo looked tired,
but Artie, even out of drag, was as cheerful tonight as if he
were still on stage; he was that happy to be home. "I thought
this party was in Birdie's honor, not mine. My Lord, with so
many cops on the premises I've never felt so safe in our own
building…and you," Artie pointed to the lone police*man*, "are
gorgeous! You can stay as long as you want."

Marcia, formerly known as Malcolm, Tony and Jeff's
across-the-hall neighbor, hit it off with the lesbian cops,
one of whom she'd known from a panel on diversity in the
workplace at the LGBT center a few months ago. Tony's

gay cousin Eddie from Phoenix rang the bell a few minutes later and soon joined the party with his partner Clay. Once everyone was present and accounted for, Teresa propped herself in the corner of the kitchen with the rest of the lesbians and a cold bottle of Beck's beer and put her feet up on a stool.

In the living room, Artie told stories about his trip to Los Angeles to the boys from downstairs while Arturo went around freshening drinks. He stuck his head out the back door and found Tim on the deck, face to face and very close to the policeman. The pastel glow of the Castro Theater marquee lit the sky behind them. "Warm enough for you two out here tonight?"

Tim jumped, as if they'd been caught doing something besides talking. "Hey, Arturo. Yeah, it's nice out, not bad at all. Come and join us. Have you met?" but Arturo had already gone back inside.

"It's George," the policeman said.

"Huh?"

"You're Tim, right? My name is George...George Tavares. I thought you'd forgotten my name just now when you were about to introduce me to your boss. He *is* your boss, right?"

"No, I just...yes, he and Artie are the owners, but..." Tim's nervous instinct made him start to reach inside his shirt pocket for a joint, but then he didn't suppose he should light up in front of a cop, even a gay one. "...are you still on duty, George?"

"Going back on in a few minutes...just taking a break, you know. Maybe you and I should get together sometime when I'm off." George moved closer and put his arm around Tim, the fingers of one hand sliding down Tim's spine to his belt and then a little lower.

Arturo must have left the door open because Tim could hear Birdie in the kitchen, talking about the robbery at Cliff's when she'd been shot. "...two guys with their faces covered, still at large...closing time. My partner George and I were on foot patrol and I took a bullet in the foot…hey, that's not funny!"

The word *partner* reminded Tim of Nick, so he blurted out to George, "My partner gets back in town in a couple of weeks. It would have to be before then." Tim thought mentioning Nick before things got too serious was a good idea. Maybe that should be one of their "rules": You have to mention that you have a partner before you agree to have sex with anyone else.

"I'm off tomorrow," George whispered in Tim's ear as he nuzzled his neck. "Here, take my card…don't lose my number, now." The Silver Star on the business card reminded Tim of *Deputy Dawg*.

They heard Birdie still talking. "I'm going back to work tomorrow, but I'll be stuck behind a desk for a while until my doctor says it's okay. I hate that…"

When he got home that night, Tim was glad he hadn't brought home the cop or anyone else. He sat down at his computer and checked his email—nothing but Viagra ads and offers for young Asian girls and penis enlargement. The spam filter must not be catching everything. He started poking around at the sites on his favorites list until he ran across dudesurfer.com. He hadn't even looked at it since he met Nick. Tim's profile was still there, even though his premium membership had expired. There were a few messages in his in-box, mostly from guys who were trying to set something up in the middle of the night several months ago. Tweakers, no doubt.

Tim clicked to see who was currently on-line and found dozens of guys looking for tops or bottoms, vanilla or kink, hosting or traveling, oral or anal and everything else Tim had ever done or heard about or could imagine. Some of the profiles even showed faces and several of the faces looked familiar, customers at the restaurant, maybe, or guys he saw on the streets in the Castro nearly every day. Some were men he'd brought home to his old apartment on Collingwood when he was single and didn't have to worry about rules or anything else.

Tim looked at his own profile again. If the other guys' pictures were as old as his were, he wouldn't trust any of them. He'd have to get some new ones taken, but by whom? Then another screen popped open and Tim noticed that he had an instant message from someone with the screen name Britlad: <Hello. Ur really sexy! Care for a chat?>

Tim clicked on the tiny photo to enlarge it, but there was just a close-up of someone's left butt-cheek from an odd angle looking down at it, as if the guy took the picture himself by holding the camera over his shoulder. It was a nice enough butt-cheek, firm and smooth, but it didn't give Tim much to go on. <Where are you?> Tim typed back and waited, but a minute later the instant message box disappeared and Britlad was no longer logged on. Tim clicked on MAIL and wrote: <Thanks for the compliment. Got any more pics? What's your name? Mine's Tim.>

Then the phone started ringing and Tim was really glad he hadn't brought anyone home that night. It was Nick. "Hey babe, it's me. Where've you been? I've been calling every half hour this evening."

"I just walked in the door," Tim lied. He'd been home at least ten minutes, but Nick didn't need to know he'd been surfing the web for dudes on dudesurfer.com. "Where are you?"

"Still in London. Whatcha been doing?"

Tim had another pang of guilt. Tim had assumed Britlad was a British guy who lived in San Francisco, but he might be in London too. Maybe Nick was testing him. Maybe Nick knew Britlad. Maybe Nick *was* Britlad! This was ridiculous! Tim was really getting paranoid these days and for no reason. He was just horny, that was all.

"Teresa had a party for Birdie tonight before she goes back to work at Mission Station. They're keeping her off the beat and giving her a desk job until she fully recovers. It was just cocktails and munchies. Arturo and Artie got back from L.A. tonight too, so Teresa invited all the neighbors on Collingwood plus me and a bunch of cops."

"Sounds hot!"

"Mostly lesbian cops."

"Mostly?"

"All but one."

"Was he cute?" Nick asked.

"You said we'd talk about all this when we're together again, not over the phone!"

"I'm just playing with you, Snowman..."

"Well, don't! I miss you too much for that. And I've been thinking. Nick, I don't think we should be naked together when we talk about our rules. I know it sounded like a good idea at the time you suggested it, but if you're gonna tell me all about how you want to go out and fuck around with other guys, I would feel too vulnerable. I think I should be fully clothed, maybe have a coat on...yeah, a coat and a scarf and long underwear and then I can just go outside and throw myself into a snow bank and drown my sorrows with cheap whiskey from a flask like the ice-fishermen carry."

"Tim, whoa...back up. Hold on a minute. What the hell are you talking about?"

"Nothing..."

"It sounds to me like you're the one who wants to go fuck around, not me. Just remember to play safe. Use condoms. There's lots of other things out there besides HIV, you know. I don't want you bringing home any diseases we don't both already have."

"But Nick, you're supposed to talk me out of it...aren't you? Aren't you supposed to try?"

"Tim, I love you. I trust you. I miss you too, you know. I miss you like crazy, but I don't own you. I want you to be happy. I don't want to tie you down when I'm out of town. I'd rather save that for when we're together and I have rope and handcuffs." Nick laughed and made his voice real low. "How does that sound, boy?"

"Nick, I thought we weren't going to talk about this when we're so far apart."

"Hey, Snowman! Who brought it up? You did, not me."

"Well it's just that if you're out fooling around, I feel like I should be too."

"Who said I was fooling around?"

"Aren't you?"

"None of your business."

"Damnit, Nick!"

"Can we talk about something else now? How's Buck?"

"He's fine. He's right here. Buck, it's your other daddy on the phone. Come and say hi."

Chapter 7

A few miles south of San Francisco, Tim's Aunt Ruth was petting her purring cat Bartholomew while basking in the last rays of sun before it moved behind the acacia hedge. She was about to finish a biography of Jackie Kennedy that covered her life after the all too brief years in the White House. Ruth enjoyed it, even though it wasn't as juicy as she expected it to be. Ruth had always felt a mixture of pity and envy for Jackie as so many young "girls" Ruth's age had lived vicariously through those years of Jackie's elegant grace and tragic loss.

Ruth luxuriated in her own life here with Sam. The estate in Hillsborough was large enough for tennis courts and stables, a pool, Jacuzzi and sauna and the gym equipment she'd had installed especially for her morning workouts. There was even an organic vegetable garden, planted at Ruth's suggestion, where she could spend an hour pulling weeds if she ever got homesick for Minnesota. All she'd ever grown when she lived in Edina was tomatoes.

A winter snowfall would be more apt to make her homesick, though…looking out the window at it, not trudging through it. She could see snow in Tahoe every winter if she wanted. Ruth wasn't the type to get homesick anyway—not for a place. She missed some of her friends in the Twin Cities and a few of her old neighbors in the suburbs, but she kept in touch by e-mail…sporadically. The only thing she was sick about was that it took her until middle-age to move out here, meet and marry this wonderful man and find so much happiness. She wished the same for her nephew Tim, but she couldn't learn his lessons for him. She had to try to remember that.

"Penny for your thoughts, darling," Ruth's husband spoke from the kitchen doorway. The word *husband* had a delicious sound when applied to Sam, much more so than she'd ever known with Dan Taylor. This time she got lucky… or smart. "Don't get sunburned, now. Should I rub some lotion on your shoulders for you?"

"Sam, come and join me. For a penny, I'll tell you that I was thinking about another dip in the pool before I go back inside and figure out what to fix for our dinner."

"I told you to hire another cook, dear. I'll go change into my trunks."

"Doris is doing fine on a part-time basis. We don't need another live-in cook, especially when it's just the two of us. I enjoy cooking for you, Sam."

"Whatever you say, dear."

"And don't bother to change. We're all alone. Just come over here. Charlie told me he'd finished his project in the potting shed and was going home. I heard his truck drive off ten minutes ago. Come here."

Sam loosened his necktie as he walked toward her. She'd almost forgotten he'd been seeing a client this afternoon. "How did your meeting go?"

"Fine, dear…" Sam slipped off the jacket of his beige suit and draped it across the lounge chair behind Ruth's bare back. His crotch was at eye-level and Ruth could see that he already had something on his mind besides a business meeting.

Tim was staring at a bulging crotch too, at home on Hancock Street. He hadn't meant to fall asleep on the couch, but here he was and whether or not this was an important dream or run-of-the-mill, he didn't want it to stop. He recognized that it was Nick's crotch in an old pair of button-fly Levis. They were well-worn at the crotch and that was all Nick had on, as far as Tim could tell in his dream. His eyes were focused on a close-up that would fit inside a round picture frame. The top of his vision began at Nick's navel and extended down a track of brown hair that disappeared behind silver buttons. The buttons popped open with the steady pressure from Nick's thumb—two, three, four. The bottom border of Tim's line of sight was a few inches lower. Tim's lips parted as he sat up, leaned forward, closer, his tongue making circles in his open mouth.

"Yeah, take it..." Nick's whisper grew into a moan. "That's it. You know you want that, you hungry boy." The picture spiraled shut like the end of a Saturday morning cartoon, too close to focus on it anymore. Tim didn't need to see, anyway. He could feel Nick's fingers on the back of his head, his palms above Tim's ears, guiding him past that spot where the gag reflex used to kick in before he trained it not to. He and Nick had learned this maneuver together. It was a winter project. Tim would have moaned now too, but there was no air here, hence no sound, only firm fullness, even during the pull-outs and Nick didn't pull out very far. He was riding on the trained spot, punching through that deep oral sphincter at the back of Tim's throat again and again. He knew exactly how much Tim could take. Nick had learned his part too and he knew how to tell exactly how much Tim wanted.

Tim was as content as a baby with a pacifier or earlier...in the womb, safe and warm, floating in a place where breathing wasn't necessary, all existence distilled for a moment down to something as simple as two beating hearts.

Nick, thousands of miles away on his last morning in Paris, was getting a real blowjob. Masturbation was the plan when he woke up alone in another strange hotel room, even hornier than usual, but the phone rang just as he was getting started. "Nicholas, are you packed?"

"I packed last night, Grandma. I'm all set. I have my passport and our tickets on top, but the Chunnel doesn't leave for hours."

"I'm aware of that, dear boy. I need you to run an errand for me, please. Go down to that bookstore where we went last night and fetch my glasses. I remember now exactly when and where I took them off and set them on the counter."

"But I was just about to...shower. Should I hurry? Are you blind without them?"

"No, take your time. They're not my everyday pair; they're the ones I wore at the book signing."

"Why not call that woman your publisher hired to set things up...Madeleine? Couldn't she have them picked up and sent?" Amanda Musgrove's appearance last night was at one of the largest bookstores in France. Nick dreaded going back there with his nonexistent proficiency in French to try to find the right person to direct him to the lost and found department. "That place was so big I wouldn't know which floor..."

"Not that store, Nicky," she interrupted.

Nick was already pulling up his jockey shorts and reaching for the trousers of the blue suit he wore last night. He might as well get this over with. "Sorry, my friend, maybe later," he frowned down to bid apology to his deflating cock as he tucked it in.

"The other book store. Remember later, after the reception, when we stopped at the little antiquarian place down the block and around the corner? I was delighted to find them open so late and with customers inside. You'd never find a store like that in the states doing business in the wee hours, not even in San Francisco."

"Yes, I think I can find it again. You finish packing. I'll come and get you in a couple of hours and we can grab a bite of breakfast if there's still time."

The clerk at the book store was a big bear of a man in a red beret and matching apron. He glanced at Nick's crotch as soon as he walked in the door and then Nick remembered him. He'd been with another man at the larger bookstore last night. They'd both eyed Nick then, but he assumed they were a couple and Nick was usually attracted to guys his own size or a little shorter.

The glasses were ready for him, wrapped in brown paper with a rubber band and "Amanda Musgrove" written in blue ink with a fine hand. Nick smiled as he put them in his pocket, said "merci" and felt foolish that he had no more French vocabulary than the basics. It didn't matter.

The man smiled back and licked his lips. He was cute, not handsome; burly, but not fat. He wasn't much older than Nick. It was hard to tell and at this point it didn't matter. Nick looked down and felt the familiar stirring in the pit of his stomach that moved south and began to churn. Two little boys were playing with a green rubber ball in the doorway. The clerk shooed them out of the way with a few French words and pulled the door shut and locked it. Nick smiled again and slid his right hand into his pants' pocket, moving his fingers to adjust things there.

The man in the red beret gestured to a tiny office behind a row of large volumes—reference books, atlases, travel guides, coffee-table books and even a few with English titles. The Frenchman's tongue was so busy in his warm mouth that it felt to Nick like a deep dark cavern full of underwater eels. The red beret slipped off once to reveal a bald spot the size of a silver dollar. Nick caught it with his free hand and started to set it on the desk, but the man took it from him without missing a beat and set it back on his own tete.

He wasn't great, nowhere near as good as Tim, but it didn't matter. By this point in the trip, Nick was starting to think of sex as much as Tim did. The last time he looked up at the Eiffel Tower he'd pictured it in a condom. Even the women who flirted with him on the streets of Paris looked tempting and he hadn't had sex with a woman since he was in high school.

Nick wasn't one to overanalyze a situation, but knowing he was on the last leg of this trip made him homesick. At last, it was close enough that he could admit it. He started panting and sucked in his breath, then moaned as he came and thought of how much he missed Tim. The clerk pulled out a handkerchief to wipe white droplets from his face and beard, even though the sink was right there. Maybe the plumbing didn't work or maybe he wanted to save the smell on the handkerchief and savor it later. Nick wondered too whether the shop-keeper's apron was only there for the purpose of covering his always open fly.

The clerk wrote something on a notepad and handed it to Nick. It was his name, phone number and address, Rue de something-or-other. It was in the same handwriting as his grandmother's name on the glasses. Nick touched his shirt pocket. Her glasses were still there. He would hate to have to explain how he'd forgotten them.

The man in the red beret reached to shake hands. Nick lifted his right hand, but changed his mind and opened both arms, pulling the man toward him for a hug and said, "merci, merci," again. Nick wanted to feel the warmth and energy of holding another man and being held, if only for a moment. He might have missed that feeling almost as much as he missed the sex.

Outside, the door stood open again. Nick looked back toward the bookstore. A young mother with her baby was on her way inside. The two little boys who'd been shooed away earlier emerged from behind a bakery truck. Their green rubber ball rolled toward Nick and he stopped it with his foot. They pointed at Nick and giggled, "merci monsieur," and then squealed in soprano several French words that Nick couldn't understand. It didn't matter.

Nick crumpled the note inside his pocket and tossed it in a trash can. He would never call the man. If one day he returned to Paris, he might walk by that bookstore and remember those moments in the back room or he might not. If Tim ran across the man's name, address and telephone number in blue ink in a fine hand, that was the sort of thing that Tim might think had mattered.

Tim woke up on the couch in his living room on Hancock Street and reached down to find the sticky mess across his belly. He couldn't remember the last time he'd had a wet dream.

Later on that night in Hillsborough, Ruth kissed Sam goodnight and turned out the light.

Chapter 8

"*I left my heart...in San Francisco...*" Artie's second audience of his first day back at Arts gave him a standing ovation before he could even finish the line. The reservations were so heavy that day that he did two sold-out shows. Ruth had let Artie talk her into acting as hostess. Unlike when she worked behind the bar, at least she got to sit down now and then. Ruth and Sam had planned to be in the city overnight on Saturday anyway. His granddaughter Sarah had a birthday party that afternoon, so they stayed over at Ruth's old apartment on Collingwood.

"*...your golden sun will shine for me...* Thank you very much, ladies and gentlemen, and what a wonderful audience you are!" The audience had stood up again at the end of the song and Artie was thrilled. "You know...I decided to start out with that song for my first Sunday back here at Arts because it's true. My heart will always be right here in San Francisco, no matter where I roam. Now I'm starting to sound more like Judy Garland than Tony Bennett...*there's no place like home, there's no place like home*...where is that damned Toto, anyway?"

Artie wasn't used to doing two shows back to back and he was worried that he'd run out of steam, but there was no fear of that happening with this audience and so much love pouring back at him. "Sit down, sit down before I start to cry. Then I'd have to do one of Judy's sad songs, maybe *The Man that Got Away* and that's not even on my set-list. Sit down, please…sit down…"

Ruth sat down too. Her job was done. Every seat in the place was filled and people were standing at the bar and all along the open windows, inside the restaurant and out on the sidewalk on Castro Street. Ruth had reserved the big round table in the back of the room for her and Sam, Jeff and Tony from the second floor on Collingwood and Teresa from the third floor. Teresa's wife Birdie was on duty at Mission Station this afternoon, still waiting for a clue to the identity of the two armed men who had shot her at Cliff's. Marcia arrived just before Artie started singing, so it was a Collingwood tenants' reunion. Tim was their waiter and they hadn't ordered food yet, but he was busy at the bar with a big drink order for Scott. They would just have to wait.

Artie introduced his musicians, Phil, his regular piano player at Arts, plus a drummer whom Ruth couldn't see behind his drum set and a string bass player who bore a striking resemblance to Jake Gyllenhaal. Everyone had the hots for him, but he was as straight as they come, so straight that most of Artie's innuendos went right over his head and he didn't even notice that the guys were all checking him out and trying to flirt with him.

Artie was carrying on, telling a story Ruth had heard a thousand times, and then teasing one of the cute boys at a ring-side seat. Ruth had heard this all before too, so she turned to Tony and spoke very softly. "Tim tells me your cousin is visiting from Phoenix. Is he enjoying his stay in San Francisco?"

"I guess so. We haven't seen very much of them. Our place is too small for house guests. They're staying at a hotel."

"How long are they in town?"

Jeff was sitting between Tony and Ruth, so he answered, "Eddie's husband Clay got transferred here, so Eddie's looking for a job and they're both trying to find an apartment."

"Mine might be available…" Ruth started to say, but Sam poked her and gave her a stern look. Then finally Tim arrived to take everyone's brunch orders. Artie said something from the stage that Ruth didn't catch, but everyone else in the room roared with laughter, even Sam, Ruth was glad to see. She leaned over and whispered into his ear, "Is something wrong, dear?"

"No, it's just that you're too good-hearted, Ruth. I know you mean well, but you hardly know these people and you're offering them your apartment. I shouldn't butt in; you do whatever you want. Artie sounds better than ever today, doesn't he?"

Artie broke into an up-tempo *Fly Me to the Moon* and Ruth had to speak louder than a whisper to be heard. "Yes, he certainly does, Sam." She sat back and listened. Ruth always did whatever she wanted, anyway. Sam knew that. And he knew that she knew that he knew that she knew. Ruth laughed to herself. That was one of the reasons she adored Sam. Still, she tried not to be insensitive. She tried to make accommodations for his opinions whenever she could. She sometimes asked for his opinion but she almost always ended up doing things her way, anyway.

And Artie really did sound terrific, Ruth had to admit. It wasn't so much the way he sang that made him sound so good, but his mere presence; it inhabited the whole room. He radiated good times, no matter if he was singing a novelty number or a ballad. When Ruth considered that Artie had two sold-out shows today and that all of these people would come back and bring their friends, who would tell even more people to come, she wondered how much longer Arts Bar & Restaurant on Castro Street could hold Artie Glamóur.

"And this next number will be on my new album. Did I tell you all that I cut an album? Last weekend I was in L.A., you may have heard. I hope you all enjoyed Rochelle and Roxeanne here in my place. Anyway…I made an appearance on Saturday night at a fabulous gala. I only did a few numbers, not my whole act, but you should have seen the line-up! I was elbow-to-elbow with some of Hollywood's biggest stars. I won't mention any names because afterward we were knee-to-knee at the party. Oh, you'll never get me to divulge who was cruising whom and which ones got lucky that night. Well, maybe later I will. Somebody get me a drink and you might twist my arm. Thank you, Jake."

Artie reached for one of the drinks on Jake's tray as he was about to serve them to a ring-side table. "That's *not* my drink? Whose is it, then? His? *What* is it? Well, as long as there's vodka and ice in the glass, I'll drink it. Give me that! Bring him another one, on the house. Bring his friend another drink, too…he's a beauty. Are you two boys from out of town?"

The musicians continued to vamp while Artie picked on the boys at a ring-side table, asking their names and the details of their relationship. They turned out to be roommates, both single, so Artie had them stand up and made sure everyone in the room got a good look at them before he started singing *"Please don't talk about me when I'm gone…"*

Artie's second set ran a full twenty minutes longer than the first. The songs were the same but for adding an extra chorus here and there. His patter made the big difference. Artie didn't usually tell jokes, but he was very funny. Then he did two encores and the crowd still didn't want to let him go. They were on their feet cheering and whistling and stomping after he left the stage. He finally came back out and calmed them down with a reprise of his first song, but this time he began it with the entire opening verse *"The loveliness of Paris seems somehow sadly gay…"*

After the show, the tables cleared quickly as people left or moved to the bar. Sam picked up the tab for their table and headed to the men's room and Ruth turned toward Tony and Jeff. "Your cousin might like to use my apartment on Collingwood, Tony. That way they'd be right downstairs from you. Sam and I are only there on weekends, rarely, and that's going to stop for a while. I'm not going to work here regularly any more.

"Oh, no," Jeff said and Ruth assumed that he was protesting the fact that she wouldn't be around much anymore.

"I'll still fill in when they're in a bind, but I'm a married woman, now. You'll still see me from time to time. You and Jeff should drive down to Hillsborough some afternoon and use the pool, but in the meanwhile, Tony's cousin..."

"That's really generous of you—both offers, but we don't want them staying so close by. Eddy's okay, but Clay is so boring! He suits his name."

"Hey, don't go insulting my relatives. You've got some real nuts in your family," Tony said.

"I already said your cousin Eddy was fine. If Clay is your relative by virtue of him being married to Eddy, then Eddy is my relative because I'm with you. So that would make Clay my step-brother-in-law...or something."

"Thanks anyway," Tony said. "They're staying at a hotel right now. I think Eddy said his job is providing housing as part of the transfer, at least for a few months while they look for a permanent place. And their budget is a lot higher than what we could afford. They'd never be satisfied with our building. They're looking at places in Diamond Heights and St. Francis Wood."

"And Nob Hill," Jeff added. "I'd rather live in the Castro. It's more convenient. But you know how those bourgeois fags are. They like to snort their crystal off real crystal."

"They don't do drugs!" Tony scowled.

"I wouldn't be too sure..."

Ruth interrupted the squabbling with, "Well, if they're ever in a bind, let me know."

"Thanks, Ruth."

Arturo joined their table and asked how everyone enjoyed the show. "Artie's added a few new numbers to his repertoire. I thought he sounded good."

"He sounded better than ever, Arturo," Sam had just returned from the men's room.

Ruth put a hand on Arturo's arm. "I don't know how much longer San Francisco will be able to hold him. You know...I promised Sam I'm not going to spend so much time in the city, so the next time you and Artie go out of town, you really need to find someone else you can trust to be responsible. What you need is a manager, Arturo."

"I know. I know."

"Teresa had the idea that you might even think about selling the place, now that Artie's career is taking off."

"Selling?" Arturo couldn't believe he'd heard her right.

"It must be worth a fortune. Just look at the crowds you had today, two shows sold out and the bar is still busy. If you found a buyer who wanted to keep it the same and build on your success, it might work out just great, maybe add even more entertainment. Those two you had here the last couple of weekends, Roxeanne and Rochelle...they were good, not as big a draw as Artie, but I'll bet they'd love to come back."

"They are coming back," Arturo told her. "We've already scheduled them for next weekend."

"And Artie could still come and perform here whenever he wanted, I'll bet. You could stop having to worry about the whole business end of running the restaurant and you could just focus on Artie's performing career."

Arturo stared at his coffee without a word. Ruth couldn't tell whether he was considering what she'd said or if what she'd said had made him angry. "I don't mean to tell you what to do, Arturo. It's none of my business. It's just that I can't keep coming into the city whenever you two leave town. I hope I haven't upset you, Arturo. It was probably a silly thought, anyway. It was Teresa's idea. Where did she go? Oh, she's moved to the bar, I see."

"You know how we feel. You're like family to us—you and the rest of the staff. And you barely know the guys I have working in the kitchen these days. They're good workers and

I've trained them well. Whenever I need to take off, I can just pack my bags and go. At least that part is under control."

"The food was excellent while you were gone, by the way," Ruth said and wondered whether that was the right way of putting it. She didn't mean it to sound like "the food was so good they don't need you anymore." Should she have said it wasn't good? That might have suggested that Arturo hadn't organized the kitchen for his absence as well as he thought. Now Ruth wished she hadn't opened her big fat mouth at all, but she refused to be guilt-tripped into spending another shift behind that bar, just because Artie hadn't made plans to cover it until the last minute.

As if Arturo read her mind, he said, "Artie has always handled the front of the house. He'll just have to find someone to take his place. If he won't do it, I will. But sell? Look around here, Ruth. This is our family. This is our home. We're not gonna sell. Giving up this place would be like a death in the family. It would kill Artie. It would be a stake in my heart too. We'll never sell…"

"*This is a stick-up!* Put your hands in the air where we can see 'em!" The two gunmen burst in the front door and one of them ran behind the bar. "Everybody do as you're told and no one gets hurt! You too, lady! Don't try any funny business!"

He meant Teresa. She was sitting at the bar with a twenty-dollar bill in her hand, trying to order another drink, not trying any funny business at all, no sir! She dropped the twenty on the bar and put her hands in the air. A half hour earlier the place had been packed. Now half the tables were empty and the crowd at the bar had thinned out too. If they had come in to rob the place a half hour earlier it might have looked to a passerby like Artie was leading a willing group in some kind of audience participation or an exercise class for drinkers; some of them were having a hard time keeping both hands in the air. But Artie was in the back room taking off his make-up and changing out of his performance drag.

The robbers both wore blue jeans and dark hooded sweatshirts, gloves, boots and something pulled down over their faces. Ruth would later tell the police that the robbers were wearing pantyhose on their heads "...either jet black or midnight. They didn't touch anyone, thank God. The one who did all the shouting stayed in the doorway and the other one went behind the bar and took all the money out of the cash registers."

"It all happened so fast!" Scott told the policeman. "I know, people probably always say that, but it's true. They were in and out of the restaurant in three or four minutes. I was making change at the back register, so I had my back to the door. Then I opened the front register before they even told me to. I didn't want him coming after me with that gun. I'm sorry!"

"You did the right thing," Arturo told him. "We're fully insured for something like this. Nobody's blaming you, Scott."

"If you think of anything else, please give us a call." The policeman handed Scott his card and he started to read it out loud: "Office George Tavares…" It didn't look legitimate with that big picture of a tin star.

"No, not that one, sorry, I gave you the wrong card. This one has the number at the station. The other one is my personal information." George winked and handed Scott another card, but made no attempt to take back the first one.

Chapter 9

Tim opened his eyes far enough to spot the bottle of water on his bedside table. It was merely an outline in the dark, a phallic shape. He took a sip and fantasized about Nick. Then he fell right back to sleep and this time he knew he was dreaming because he was in such a bad mood. He hadn't felt such a defeatist attitude since high school when he was inched out of first place at a track meet at the very last second. This dream was disjointed, too, one of those dreams where time and space are jumbled and meaningless. First it was morning in Minnesota. Tim was in high school with a bad hangover and then there was a scene in the locker room that might have been sexy, but there was so much steam that he couldn't see the other guys.

Then the steam turned to fog and he was driving back from the Russian River with the top down on the Thunderbird. The fog was so thick he could barely see the towers of the Golden Gate Bridge even when he was right under them. They were phallic symbols too, hazy orange ones, rising up out of the damp black sheet of roadway. Then he heard the sounds of tires on wet pavement and bellowing foghorns.

Tim rolled over in bed but he didn't wake up. Now he and Nick were beside Banderas Bay in Puerto Vallarta, Mexico listening to waves crashing on the beach. The bay was so vast it might as well have been the Pacific Ocean. They were in swim suits, sun-tanned and sprawled on canvas lounge chairs, side by side and only a couple of inches apart with a table on each side of their configuration—the outside—straws keeping count of how many drinks they'd each downed. Tim heard another male couple nearby. One of them called this the "blue chairs" beach and the other insisted that it was called Playa de Los Muertos, or "Beach of the Dead." Nick kept ordering those silly umbrella drinks that always sneak up on a person. The sexy waiter had slick black hair. An iguana tattoo wrapped around his left nipple and he barely spoke English. He set down another drink for Tim and walked around their feet to bring Nick's, who lifted his high in the air and said, "Drink up! You need another hair of the donkey! Here's to the sunshine, Snowman."

A real donkey brayed in the distance and Tim lifted his glass. "Don't be such an ass!" and they laughed loudly enough that Tim figured they both must be very drunk.

Tim wanted to reach across and grab Nick's nearest nipple, run his hand down Nick's muscular chest and pull down his swimsuit. No, he wanted to wait, to go back to where they were staying and have great sex, sweaty and hot and naked, but where were they staying? He couldn't remember checking into a hotel.

Then they were beside the pool at the Highlands resort outside of Guerneville. How did they get from Mexico to the Highlands? And if they were back at the Russian River, why weren't they staying at Nick's house in Monte Rio? Tim didn't care anymore. He was drunk. He and Nick were both in shorts and tank-tops with flip-flops on their feet. Tim looked down and saw the bandage on his toe.

Now he was a little boy again. He was sitting on a blanket with his grandmother beside the lake in Powderhorn Park in Minneapolis on the Fourth of July. He was the little boy in the framed photograph beside his bed and his grandmother wasn't such an old woman, really. She was the one who was psychic. She was the relative from whom he had inherited this so-called "gift" of his, which usually only manifested itself in his dreams. Now that Tim felt that he'd gotten to know his grandmother better, he remembered that time and space were only an illusion, just like in a dream, and this was only a dream...or was it?

The Minnesota Orchestra played the 1812 Overture and they watched the fireworks, Tim's grandmother beside him and his Aunt Ruth on another blanket. His parents must be nearby too. It was dark now, except for the embers of a charcoal grill, someone's cigarette glow nearby and then the crashing colors of the fireworks, like shooting stars of green and red and gold.

Now it was morning in his dream and Tim had grown to be a very old man. He was sitting on the back deck of the house on Hancock Street and thinking that it was wonderful to still be alive. He blew on his steaming cup of coffee and a pair of noisy crows flew up from a nearby tree and scolded him. Tim yelled back at them, "Fly away, dammit! This is my house. This is my yard. These are my stairs." He felt good, but he'd always planned to work the crotchety angle if he ever got to be this old. "I was here long before you were hatched, you noisy motherfuckers!"

"Leave those crows alone, Snowman. Come in and eat your breakfast," a voice yelled out at him from inside the house. Did it really call him "Snowman?" Nick was the only one who ever called him that. Tim smiled and set down his coffee cup, reached for the railing and got to his feet. Now Tim had something else in mind besides breakfast and he was thrilled to still be sexual at this age, but he also knew that time was only an illusion. His dreams could hardly predict future events if they had already happened. Then the clang of the garbage truck outside on Hancock Street woke him for real.

Tim sat up on the edge of his bed and tried to think about his dream. It was a dud, as far as any of his psychic powers were concerned. They were so random and unpredictable to be nearly useless, especially since his doctor took him off

Neutriva and started him on another new HIV drug. The only thing he liked about this dream was the thought that he and Nick would grow old together. He hoped that part was true. And then there was the part about still being horny in his old age, just like he was now.

Horniness was a given, especially with Nick out of town. Or maybe it was just loneliness, although Tim would never admit it. From where he sat on the edge of his bed he could reach the two business cards on the bedside table. One was Howard's, the guy he met in Buena Vista Park the other day. They might have had some fun if it weren't for someone calling Howard on his cell phone every two minutes. Tim didn't even get around to asking whether he and Mickey had rules.

Tim looked down at the laundry basket full of clean socks and underwear he'd washed yesterday. He thought about going back up to Buena Vista Park, but it seemed like an exercise in frustration. He might meet someone there, but the gardeners had cleaned out all the old underbrush and destroyed his favorite cul-de-sacs where a private tryst used to be possible. Tim went to the kitchen and put on the coffee, let Buck out the back door and went back to sorting socks. He was in one of those moods where he could spend all morning doing chores, folding T-shirts to exactly the same dimensions, dusting each and every picture on the walls, detailing the kitchen stove, going over it with a scouring pad and the eye of a surgeon, making it sparkle and shine like it just came from the factory.

The other business card was from Officer George Tavares. When Tim saw him at Arts yesterday he half expected George to ask why Tim hadn't called him yet. But when Tim came out of the kitchen right after the place was robbed; George seemed to stare right through him. George had apparently forgotten all about Tim because now he was hitting up Scott the bartender. Tim was insulted that George ignored him, especially after he'd come on so strong at Birdie's party the other night.

Most places Tim went, he overheard people say things like, "Look, there's that hot waiter from Arts." He pretended that it was annoying, but he was secretly flattered and it was a whole lot better than being ignored. Tim matched another pair of socks and tossed them into the dresser drawer. It wouldn't have been so bad if George Tavares wasn't so hot, especially in his uniform. Tim would have liked to see how he looked out of his uniform. George might not even be Tim's "type," whatever that was, but with Nick out of town, Tim's type included much greater latitude.

Tim got dressed and walked down to 18th and Castro to pick up a prescription at Walgreens. The only other customer was sitting in the back across from the pharmacy windows with a backpack on the floor between his legs. He was yawning and Tim noticed that his legs were swirled with dark hair between his white shorts and blue sneakers, but his chest was smooth and well-defined. Tim hoped he didn't shave his chest. One pierced nipple poked out the side of his baggy tank top and he had a hooded gray sweatshirt draped over one muscular arm. He covered his yawn with his fist and then opened his eyes, caught Tim's glance and they both smiled. The pharmacist told Tim it would be just a couple of minutes so Tim sat down, leaving one chair between them, but just then the other guy's prescription was ready so he stood up and went to the window.

Tim was glad to see that the other customer he'd been cruising was still waiting outside on the corner of 18th and Castro. Tim couldn't remember later who spoke first, only the words, "my place" and "nearby." In the midst of all the folding of his clean clothes, Tim still hadn't made his bed, so he didn't want to bring the guy—he said his name was Rod— back to Hancock Street. Would they have used his bed? Was that another rule he and Nick should have talked about? It was Tim's bed, after all. Nick didn't live there, not full-time. He had his own bed up in Monte Rio. Tim tried not to let his thoughts go there. He didn't want to think about any other chores he'd left half-finished at home, the vacuuming—

at least the laundry was done—but he didn't need to think about any of that. They were headed toward Rod's place—in the middle of the afternoon—on a sunny San Francisco day in the Castro—to have sex, as simple as that, free and easy as any two single guys, as practical as getting a haircut, as matter-of-fact as buying a quart of milk.

Tim followed Rod when he turned left on the corner of 18th Street by the Edge. "You wanna smoke?" Tim pulled a joint and a lighter out of his own backpack.

"Sure." Tim lit up, handed the joint to Rod and realized they were heading toward Tim's old apartment. Aunt Ruth had talked about letting people stay there when she and Sam weren't using it. Wouldn't it be funny if Rod turned out to be some friend of a friend, one of her free tenants? Aunt Ruth was almost too generous, Tim thought, overly kind to strangers and especially welcoming to tourists from out-of-town. She wanted everyone to be happy and for tourists to love San Francisco as much as she did.

"I used to live up this way," Tim said.

"Oh yeah?"

"Yeah, on Collingwood…up in the next block."

Tim took another deep hit off the joint and thought it might even be fun to have sex in his old bedroom again. It was full of memories of hot times with Jason and Corey and Bob and Jimmy and…too many others to count. But what if he could smell Aunt Ruth's perfume? The last time he'd looked inside that room she had a lacy lavender dust-ruffle on the bed. It matched her drapes, a couple of shades darker than the lilac color she'd asked Arturo to paint the walls a long time ago. If Tim let his mind go any further, he would start to think about his Aunt Ruth and Sam having sex in that bed…

"I live on Seward," Rod said—to Tim's relief—as they crossed Collingwood on 19th and continued west past the Harvey Milk School, past Diamond and Eureka and Douglas.

"Do you live alone?"

"My partner's out of town."

"Mine too." Tim was getting stoned now and it only reminded him of how much he missed Nick. Still, this was only sex. It didn't mean anything. This had nothing to do with Nick. Tim and Rod didn't say much on their walk up to Seward Street. They exchanged lustful looks and nasty grins as they passed the joint back and forth a couple more times.

Rod's place was a small house, not an apartment. A garage was down the slope from the street below a bay window that turned out to be the master bedroom. A terraced garden bloomed in the rear behind a small deck off the kitchen. Walls must have been knocked out to open the little Victorian rooms and make it feel more spacious, but it still reeked of coziness in a masculine way. That was probably due to the framed male nude photography everywhere, a huge blow-up of a gymnast above the couch in the den. The athlete looked familiar to Tim, like someone he'd seen in the Summer Olympics in London...but nude? This Rod guy and his partner had pretty good taste, Tim thought. Then he wondered which of them had the money to buy this house. And what were *their* rules?

Now Tim's t-shirt was half-off, the blue cotton blinding his left eye while Rod's tongue lunged into his left armpit. Then they were both bare-chested and Rob was working at the buckle of Tim's leather belt. They were still in the hallway, retracing their steps from the kitchen where they'd grabbed a couple of beers. Tim tripped on his pants and shorts around his ankles, set the can on a bedside table, hopped over to sit down and untie his shoes. His cock bounced against his stomach with each hop.

They both laughed. Sex could be fun, after all. It didn't have to be heavy and serious. If he was only doing this to get his rocks off, Tim didn't need some unsmiling dude in full leather and attitude or a uniformed cop like George Tavares who couldn't even remember his face. Rod pulled off his sneakers and got naked first. They fell onto the bed and Rod became one giant tongue that made Tim's nipples tingle with tiny bites and soon enveloped his cock like a ravenous sea creature. Tim was stoned enough now that Rod's mouth became a sea snake that wrapped around his balls and started probing his ass.

Rod grabbed Tim's legs and lifted them over his head until Tim's feet touched the wall behind the bed. Tim didn't care about rules anymore. This felt too good. He could only moan and revel in the sensation of being touched, kissed and getting a rim-job that came straight from heaven. Any minute he would have to come back to earth far enough to say, "Hey, are you positive? I am. Shouldn't we...?" And then what would he say? Just wait and see what happened, see what Rod said and play it by ear? Maybe this guy—Tim had almost forgotten his name by now—would ask what Tim thought. Maybe he only wanted to eat his ass and they would both masturbate until they came. It didn't matter. That was fine. Tim could cum at any minute just like this.

Then the guy reached over toward the bedside table and brought out some kind of lube. Tim couldn't see it, but he felt it, slippery and cold. He was about to tell this Rod guy that he'd better have condoms when he heard, "Oh shit!"

"What happened? I'm not clean?" Tim asked.

"No, that's the garage door... He's home! Damn! You've gotta go *now*! Quick! Go out the back door and wait there until he's all the way inside. Hurry! There's no time to get dressed. Shit! Here, take your socks. Go out through the side door next to the garage, but wait 'til the coast is clear. Be sure you don't forget anything!"

Tim ran naked down the hallway collecting his clothes along the way. He felt a sliver of wood on the back stairs jab into the sole of his foot so sat down on the bottom step to pull it out and finished getting dressed. Blood soaked through his sock as he laced up his shoes. He waited downstairs in the back of the dark garage among the cobwebs until he heard two sets of footsteps overhead. Then he stepped out the side door into daylight and walked down the hill and all the way home, thinking this might be a good night to stay in and check out who else was logged onto dudesurfer.

Chapter 10

Ruth had just turned the last page on the latest Sue Grafton novel when the phone rang. She rarely brought her cell phone out to the pool—she wasn't one who felt the need to be available 24/7 like a dog on a leash—but today she'd had a funny feeling she might be getting a call. Maybe Tim wasn't the only one in the family who had inherited her mother's psychic gifts. "Hello!"

"Ruthie, it's Teresa. I hope I'm not disturbing you or anything. Are you busy?"

"No, dear me, I'm fighting off boredom these days. I'm turning into one of those old matronly types, just lounging by the pool, painting my toenails, reading fiction and fashion magazines. I hate to complain, since I was the one who insisted they take me off the schedule at Arts. What's up?"

"I'm worried about Birdie. She doesn't eat right lately and she can't get a decent night's sleep."

"I thought you told me Arturo was bringing over food from the restaurant for her. I know you're not much of a cook, but..."

"No, but you're right, Arturo is. He's been wonderful about it. They both are. Artie even stopped by and gave us half a Dutch Chocolate cake. That's just what I need. He said he had a weak moment at Costco and insisted we take half of it before he ate it all. He's so afraid of not fitting into his dresses, now that he's performing so much. Jan Wahl wants to interview him on Channel 4 on Saturday morning and you know how the television camera adds ten pounds."

"So I've heard…but what about Birdie?"

"She can't get those men out of her head…the ones who shot her, you know? Now she's started having nightmares too. If they could only catch them, maybe it would put her mind at ease."

"But Teresa, Birdie's *on* the police force. She must have the inside word. How is the investigation coming along?"

"It's going nowhere, according to Birdie. They've stuck her behind a desk since when she works at all and it's killing her that she can't be out there walking the beat with George, looking for those guys."

"Do they really think those robbers are still in San Francisco? They're probably long gone by now, Teresa, off to greener pastures."

"No, ma-am. They held up Rossi's Deli last night!"

"No!"

"Same two characters, same m.o., heads covered. One held the gun and the other one did all the talking, something about everybody keeping calm so nobody gets hurt. They were in and out in a flash with all the cash from the register."

"It's lucky no one *has* been hurt in these incidents… except for Birdie, of course."

"No, Ruth…this time someone else *was* hurt. When the robbers came running out of Rossi's, it wasn't the one with the money but the other one, the one with the gun. He collided with some guy on the sidewalk who was talking on his cell phone, oblivious to everything that was going on…"

"He shot the guy, just for talking on his cell phone?"

"No, but if it were me, I've been tempted a couple of times." Teresa laughed and Ruth was relieved to hear that her friend was able to laugh again.

"So he knocked the guy down?"

"What guy?"

"The one on his cell phone...you said someone got hurt, didn't you?"

"No, not him, but when they collided they knocked down some lady. She'd just come out of the MUNI underground and was waiting for the #35 bus to go home to Noe Valley."

"Is she all right?"

"I guess she will be. She's in the hospital now. She broke her ankle in two places and had a concussion.

"Well, this is interesting, but I don't know what you think I can do about it from here. Sometimes Hillsborough feels like a million miles away."

"Not you, but...I was wondering if you could talk to Tim, Ruth. Ask him if he knows anything, whether he's seen anything, you know?"

"When they were robbing Arts, Tim was in the kitchen and he stayed there. All he witnessed was what he could see through that tiny little porthole of a window in the swinging door."

"That's not what I mean, Ruthie...I hope this doesn't sound crazy, but...I wondered if he'd had any dreams about any of it...or if maybe you suggested it to him...whether he might..."

"Tim doesn't like to talk about his dreams much, you know. He doesn't like feeling that people are trying to psychoanalyze him and he gets very touchy about it sometimes."

"I know, but...couldn't you maybe find a subtle was to ask him?"

"Teresa, Tim almost never discusses that part of his life. He's not like my mother, even though he seems to have her powers. She didn't mind talking about it to anyone and everyone. It got to be so embarrassing to us when we were girls."

"Couldn't you just...mention it to him...casually?

"Oh, Teresa! The last time you had a bright idea was when you thought Artie and Arturo needed to sell the restaurant. I should have ignored you then or told you to talk to them yourself. I opened my big mouth and I think I hurt Arturo's feelings to even suggest such a thing."

"That was for your sake, Ruthie. I was only trying to help, since you said they were relying on you too much. Did they find a manager for the restaurant yet?"

"I don't know. All I know is that they haven't called me lately, so they must have taken me seriously when I said I couldn't do it anymore.

"Then my idea worked out just fine. And this time I'm only suggesting it for Birdie's sake. It's not as if I'm asking for something selfish for myself."

"Well, why can't you give Tim a call and you ask him about this if you think it's such a good idea?"

"I wouldn't dare…you're his family. You should be the one."

"I'll think about it, Teresa, but I'm not promising anything." When Ruth hung up the phone she knew she should have given her a flat-out NO. Agreeing to "think about it" meant it would be stuck in the back of her mind until she "did" it, so at this rate she might as well have promised that she would.

Tim took Buck for a run around the perimeter of Dolores Park a couple of times, stopping only to clean up the dog's deposits next to the sidewalk and drop them in the nearest trash can. The gay corner at the top of the park was hopping…if you liked them hairless and nellie. Obviously someone did; Tim remembered that some of these same guys had hair on their chests last season, but electrolysis must be big business these days. Tim liked men who looked like *men*, but he checked everyone out anyway; it was sheer habit. On a horniness scale of one to ten, he was at about a six or seven, which was low for him, but it was still early in the day.

When he and Buck got home to Hancock Street Tim took another shower and the phone started ringing as soon as turned off the knobs. "Hi, Aunt Ruth. How are you?"

"I'm fine, honey, whatcha' doin'?"

"Toweling my hair dry...I just got out of the shower."

"I waited until well past noon. I hope I didn't call you too early..."

She left that hanging and Tim could read all the questions behind it: *Did you go out last night? Are you alone? Have you been sleeping all morning? Are you depressed? Have you heard from Nick lately? Have you cheated on him? Have you been tempted?*

And those were only the obvious ones. Maybe he was paranoid, but he also heard: *Are you eating right. Are you getting enough sleep? Are you taking your pills? What's your HIV viral load these days? How much have you been drinking and smoking pot?* Sometimes she acted like he was still in High School and still living with her and her first husband, Tim's "Uncle" Dan in Edina after his parents threw him out. Aunt Ruth would never change.

Tim shook his head and wrapped the towel into a turban around it, plopping his wet naked butt down on the edge of his bed. Hs figured he might as well get comfortable. "No, you're not calling too early. I've been up for hours. This was my second shower today, actually. Buck and I just jogged around Dolores Park a couple of times and I got sweaty. What's up?"

"I'm calling because of Teresa, to tell the truth...she called me this morning and asked me to call you..."

"Teresa?" Tim always liked his old neighbor when he lived in the ground floor apartment on Collingwood Street and she was on the top floor across from Artie and Arturo's place with the Larsons in between. "Why didn't she call me herself? What did she want?"

"Now don't get angry with me Tim, but she's worried about Birdie."

"What does that have to do with me? What's wrong with Birdie? I thought her ankle was all healed and she was back at work."

"They've got her at a desk job and she hates it. Ever since she went back on the force, she's had trouble sleeping and she doesn't eat well. Teresa says she's lost weight. She wants to be back on the street with her partner, that guy named George—you remember him, don't you?"

Now Tim expected her to ask him *how well* he knew George, but George had moved on from Tim to his next seduction a long time ago, so his Aunt Ruth wasn't going to be able to go there, thank goodness!

"She wants *someone* to track down those guys who shot her in the robbery at Cliff's."

"They've probably skipped town by now," Tim said.

"That's what I thought, too, but they held up Rossi's yesterday."

"No shit. I didn't even hear about that and I'm right here in the neighborhood."

"It was on page two of the news section of the *Chronicle* this morning, but I missed it myself."

"I haven't read the paper, yet."

"First Cliff's, then Arts, then Rossi's…I'm surprised no one came into the restaurant last night to tell you all that the robbers were still at it."

"I was off last night."

"Oh, I see…did you go out?"

"No, I didn't." Tim wasn't about to tell her he'd spent hours looking for a play-date on-line, to no avail. The only one who had showed any interest in Tim was that guy with the user name Britlad, who had sent another cryptic message. "So what does Teresa want me to do about Birdie? I hardly know the woman. Artie knows her the best. They go back years to his big old North Beach drag queen headlining days at Finocchio's, or so I've heard."

"Teresa thought you might…*see* something…you know…in your dreams? She thought you might have a clue as to who those two characters are. Now, don't get angry."

"I'm not angry, Aunt Ruth!"

"Well, you sound a little angry."

"That was the second time you told me not to get angry." Tim hated to be told not to feel something. It was like someone asking again and again if he was depressed. No matter how good he felt, he could be talked into feeling depressed if someone dwelled on it. "It's just that I...I don't know...I've never had a dream about Birdie in my life, I don't think...or the armed robbers, either. I'm not on that Neutriva drug anymore, you know. I don't have many dreams at all these days, or at least I don't remember them very much."

Tim's toes tightened up when he told a lie. He started thinking about the vivid wet dream he'd had the other afternoon when he fell asleep on the couch and a couple of others since Nick was gone that came close to that intensity and realism. They weren't psychic dreams though, he was pretty sure, and his Aunt Ruth didn't need to know about them.

"You didn't tell me you'd stopped taking it. Does your doctor know? Is that a good idea, just to quit taking your medication like that? Should I be worried about you, dear?"

"I didn't just stop taking them. Jeez, I'm not that stupid. My doctor switched my HIV cocktail so I don't have those dreams anymore...well, hardly at all. Sometimes I think I'm still having Neutriva flashbacks."

"Well...Teresa thought maybe if I asked you, you could try to pay attention. Maybe if the seed got planted in your brain, you'd dream something helpful. It was just an idea. I know it's probably a silly one, but I promised her I'd mention it to you, at least, and I wanted to call you anyway and see how you were doing these days with Nick out of town for so long..."

Here it comes now, Tim thought to himself.

"...Isn't he due back pretty soon? Sam and I want you both to come down for a day by the pool or an evening when I can cook us all a nice dinner. You just let us know when he gets back from Europe and everything gets caught up for him at his nursery. You could invite his grandmother along, too. I haven't seen Amanda in ages and I'll bet she has some stories to tell about her book tour. And bring Buck too, of course. If Bartholomew fusses again I'll lock him up in the north wing of the house to go and sulk while Buck is here. That cat is so spoiled, having all my attention nowadays. Yes, I'm talking about you, Bart. Come over here, you big boy…"

Tim heard his Aunt Ruth's voice fade away and the loud meow of the cat, but then she came back. "Sorry, Tim. Where was I?"

"You were inviting us all down to Hillsborough, but I suspect that Nick and his grandmother might have had enough togetherness by now. Maybe you should call her and take her to lunch sometime, just the two of you. I'm sure she'd love for you to pick her up in Alameda and take her into the city someplace nice to eat. She doesn't drive at all anymore and she and Nick's mother get on each other's nerves, you know."

"What a good idea. It would give me something to do, too. You and Nick and the dog can come, though…anytime. Or you and Buck could come down for an afternoon by the pool anytime. You don't have to wait until Nick gets back. You know you're always welcome. Now about Teresa and Birdie…"

"I promise I'll let you know if I have any dreams about anything meaningful, okay?"

"Thanks so much, Tim. I won't keep you, then. Bye now."

Tim hung up the phone and touched the mouse on his computer to bring the screen to life. There was no new email since the last time he'd checked, but when he clicked on dudesurfer.com he found a brief reply to his last note to Britlad. <I'm in London and I want *you*.>

London was just what Tim had thought—still no name, but there was another picture attached. Tim clicked and a face appeared, but a face that was partly in shadow and he was wearing sunglasses. He looked young, but cute, from what little Tim could see—or was Tim just desperate? When he felt desperate his standards for cuteness plummeted. Desperation born out of horniness was even worse than the blur that comes from too many drinks in a dark bar as the hour nears closing time. Tim had made some poor choices that way too, but that had been a long time ago.

Maybe that was what was missing. He'd tried cruising the park, the Internet and he'd picked up someone at the pharmacy in the back of Walgreens—all to no avail—but he hadn't really put any effort into cruising the bars. That guy who'd followed him home from 440 didn't count. They met outside the bar. Did anyone go to bars looking for pick-ups these days? Or did they all find what they were looking for on-line? He'd already discounted meeting anyone at the gym because he feared he would run into them again…and again. There was plenty of action in the steam room, depending on the time of day, but that wasn't very satisfying and Tim didn't feel like putting on a show for everyone else.

That was part of the trouble with bars, too. He knew everybody or they knew him. Tim realized a long time ago that working on Castro Street, the bars were fine for socializing, but not for cruising. He'd picked up a few tourists over the years, but all too often they turned out to be staying with someone who ate at Arts. It was definitely a small world and San Francisco was a small town and Castro Street was a tiny little speck of an enclave within it. Tim supposed he could go South of Market sometime, but that seemed like too much work. He hated to leave the Thunderbird parked on the street. If he took the bus or streetcar it meant a lot of walking. His leather boots were perfect for standing around in a bar, but not for walking to one. Jason had always insisted that Tim wear big black biker boots back in the days when they went to the beer busts at the Eagle, even though it was afternoon and nobody could even see their feet in the crowd.

Maybe he should buy a motorcycle. Then he could drag out all his leather to go with it and he'd fit right in South of Market…in the 80s! Maybe leather was seeing some resurgence these days. They kept trying to get the Eagle re-opened. Tim pictured himself on a Harley and began to laugh. Sure, he could pull it off and look great doing it, but both Nick and his Aunt Ruth would have a fit of worry. Damn Nick! Why did he have to be away for so long? Nick was the only man Tim really wanted. Maybe he and Nick could both become bikers in his dreams.

Chapter 11

Nick's second morning back on board the ship for their return voyage, he could think of nothing that he wanted more than to be home with Tim. He'd thought about flying back from London to San Francisco alone after the book tour, but his grandmother wanted him to stay with her. It wasn't that she really needed him. She'd been a perfect traveler for her age, strong and healthy and in cheerful good spirits, especially when surrounded by her fans wherever they went. And his ship's passage back to New York was already paid for, after all.

Nick took his laptop and a cup of coffee onto the deck where the sunshine felt warm on his face but the misty air was cool. He hadn't even sat down when he heard a woman cough as she leaned her back into the railing a few feet away. She was smoking a cigarette, the collar of her mink coat wrapped around her neck while its hem revealed tiny feet in sequined high heels. "Lovely morning isn't it?" She had a thick British accent and she batted her false eyelashes through crusty mascara.

"Not very warm, but the fresh air feels good." Nick smiled and looked back down at his laptop. She reminded him of a homeless eccentric he might see in San Francisco's Tenderloin district. Both she and the mink had seen better days. Then he remembered where he was; no homeless people could afford to be aboard this ship. A stowaway wouldn't flash such jewelry—in the morning, yet—and her cigarette lighter was no cheap plastic throw-away. Maybe wearing an old fur, if she was determined to wear fur, kept the animal rights activists at bay. He imagined her defending herself against the PETA protesters in a British accent, "But these little brown rodents died of natural causes!" Nick knew he must be spending too much time with his writer grandmother. He was picturing characters everywhere.

Nick was downwind of her cigarette and he didn't want to interact with this woman any more than he had to. No one was at the swimming pool this early so he moved over there. The deck chair didn't give when he sat on it, like the ones around the pool at the r3 Resort in Guerneville. These had solid wooden slats on metal frames. The wood was weathered and faded to a dull shade of gray. When it was warmer, the ship's crew must put out padded cushions, Nick thought. If it grew warm enough later, Nick would take off his shirt and soak up some rays. He'd packed a swimsuit for this trip, but hadn't used it yet— teal green nylon, skimpy. He turned a lot of heads when he wore it at the r3. If he wore it here, he'd stick out like a sore thumb.

If it grew warmer Nick would go down to the clothing shop near the elevator and buy a new swim suit to wear on the ship, something in muted colors of plaid or pinstripes, maybe with pleats, maybe long-sleeved if he wanted to fit in with most of the other passengers. It was a stuffy crowd, to say the least.

Nick leaned back and closed his eyes against the orange ball of the sun. It got trapped against the back of his eyelids from looking at it too long. A spray of mist cooled his face and he turned his head. The golden ball just below his forehead reminded him of flowers. Then his greenhouses outside of Sebastopol lined up in a row in his thoughts. In a few hours, the same sun would make them sparkle, thousands of miles away. Nick pictured tulips and rubbed his eyes at a golden sunflower. Then there were roses, pink and yellow, bright red and crimson, almost black. His memory showed him a tender rosebud spreading open in the dewy light of dawn and he pictured Tim' sweet ass.

Nick sat up again and opened the laptop. He came out here to work, after all. He'd left his employee Jenny in charge of the nursery and she was doing such a good job that he'd forgotten to check in for longer and longer periods of time. His other senior employee Kent had set up this bookkeeping system in exchange for Nick paying for his computer night classes in Santa Rosa last year. Now Nick could keep track of every penny spent and every dollar earned from anywhere he traveled, as long as he had wireless access.

One page was a job schedule. Nick clicked on today's date to enlarge it and looked at the details; potted palms, ficus trees and scheffleras had to be picked up from a church in Napa. They'd been rented for a wedding and reception the day before. Nick wondered why his nursery didn't get the contract for the flowers too, but he only needed to click back a couple of days to find that order. It must have been a lavish wedding; dozens of roses, lilies, sweet peas, hydrangeas, orchids, poppies and ranunculus for all the bouquets, corsages, boutonnières and arrangements for the ceremony and centerpieces for the reception. That was also where most of the trees came in.

Another page spelled out finances. Outstanding bills turned from red to blue as the payments came in. Nick thought green might be more appropriate, but he wasn't about to mess with Kent's system on a minor point, especially with business going so well.

Nick dashed off a quick e-mail. <Jen—looks like you don't need me there. I'm heading back to the USA, on my second day at sea. Should be home in another week or so. Keep up the good work, all—Nick.>

He was about to close the computer when he thought of something else. It began with a tingling sensation in the pit of his stomach and a corresponding prickling at the back of his brain. He tried to remember the name of that gay web-site he'd heard about. What was it? He'd read about Grindr for the cell phone, but had never used it. With Tim in his life, Nick hadn't bothered to learn all the latest cell phone apps and internet dating sites. He wasn't sure what this one was called because he hadn't been paying close attention, but it had a silly name, he thought…manlust.org or manpig.net. Pig seemed likely, as he thought there was an animal in the name. Broncbusters. org? No, that wasn't right either. It was one of those sites where guys post their pictures and try to meet like-minded *dudes* into the same things they are. That was it. "Dude" was part of the name. Mostly they listed sexual proclivities, but sometimes others. Their wants and needs varied from "long walks on the beach" to "allergic to dogs." Some were looking for "champagne and candlelight" and others clearly stated, "Clean and sober—in recovery—no drugs!"

Nick had thought it had "men" or maybe "guys" in the name, but no, it was definitely "dudes." He finally found it, "dudesurfer.com," and clicked on the icon that would lead him to a free tour of the site. He could check out guys in any major city in the world, but he wasn't near any major city now. This was the open sea.

Nick clicked on San Francisco and scrolled through the list of guys who were logged in at this very moment. What time was it there? It was morning here at sea, although Nick hadn't worn his watch, he figured it must be late at night in California. Dozens of guys were on-line looking for hook-ups. A few of their faces looked familiar, if not their other body parts. Nick reached further into his memory for the meanings of the secret language of personal ads. SWM was "Single White Male," Nick was pretty sure of that. It couldn't mean "Straight While Male" on dudesurfer.com, could it? He'd heard of black guys on the down-low who might call themselves SBM and mean straight, but who would they be trying to fool on-line? NSA meant "No Strings Attached." LTR was for "Long-Term Relationship." Then there were the sexual proclivities like "BB," "WS," "FF," "Oral only," "S&M,"

"B&D," and some guys seemed to have just checked all the boxes. Nick figured either they were simply too lazy to decide or else they were open to anything and everything.

"Are you hard at work or do you mind some company?" Nick jumped at the voice and closed the laptop like a kid who's been caught with a comic book in class. The gentleman tugged at the knees of his trousers as he sat down on the next deck chair. He had a British accent too, so Nick assumed he was either a gentleman or a jewel thief. He seemed quite a bit older than Nick at first, but he couldn't be sure in the glare of the sun. Nick knew people twice his age who seemed young. His grandmother was a prime example. And he'd met kids in their twenties who were so serious and determined about their lives and careers that they'd missed out on enjoying their youth a long time ago.

"No, I don't mind," Nick said.

"You're American." This came more as a statement of fact than a question, so Nick wasn't sure if it required an answer.

"Just finished up with some work, actually, so you're welcome to join me." But the man already had. "How could you tell from three words that I'm American?"

"We noticed you at dinner last night—the wife did, truth be told. She's a big fan of the *who-done-it*. The author lady's your grandmother, I take it?" This was clearly a question.

"Yes, my grandmother is Amanda—"

"…Musgrove," the man finished for him. "We knew who she was; it was the grandmother part we weren't so sure about, but you treated her so gently, pushing in her chair and the way she touched your arm when you talked, it was more familiar than a hired companion would have been."

"Very astute…are you a private detective?" Nick asked.

"No," the man laughed and moved his hands to his lap. Nick could swear he was adjusting a growing bulge there. "Finance. The wife's the one who figured it out. She said you had an independent look, besides…looked like someone who didn't have to bow and scrape to the old gal, like someone who knew she couldn't give him the axe, no matter what."

"No, she'd better not fire me, not in the middle of the Atlantic, anyway," now it was Nick's turn to laugh. "Your wife sounds very perceptive, then. Is she a private eye?"

"No, but she reads the damned horoscopes every morning in the Sun and she follows the phases of the moon like a gardener."

"You're on vacation?"

"Business, mostly, but the wife came along, so we sailed. She refuses to fly ever since that 9/11 nastiness of yours. She never cared much for air travel before then, either. I fly all the time, do a lot of business in New York, Tokyo…"

This time Nick was sure the man rubbed his crotch, but why, when he was talking about his wife? It was almost imperceptible at first, but Nick could almost smell the sexual tension in the air. Maybe he'd picked up some of Tim's psychic powers. "Where's the wife now?" Nick was only curious, but the words came out of his mouth like someone who was playing along. The moon must be full and the man wasn't bad looking. It was hard to ignore such blatant sexual cues.

"She's in the casino. She'll often stay in there all day. She'd stay all night if I didn't interrupt her for dinner."

"I hope she's lucky."

"It doesn't matter. Seems a waste, though, taking the time to sail the Atlantic and spending it all in a dark room with flashing lights. Still, it keeps her out of my hair, if you know what I mean." This time he winked as he shifted positions, lifting one leg for a moment as he adjusted his swelling pride. Nick couldn't believe he had the audacity to wink at him right after bringing up his wife's gambling addiction. "Getting a bit brisk out here, I dare say. Need to warm up. A spot of brandy in my stateroom might do the job nicely. Care to join me?"

Nick was more than curious, now. "Sure, why not?" What could be more NSA than a shipboard liaison and who could be less likely to be looking for an LTR than a married man who was traveling with his wife?

Twenty minutes later, Nick peeled off the sticky condom and the Brit rolled over onto his back. "Thanks, chum. That was first rate! Hello there, dear, did you have any luck at cards today, then?" The smoking woman in the ratty mink stepped forward and smiled. Nick jumped. He hadn't heard her come in and now he made quick work of getting dressed. "Oh, my good man, please don't be startled. She enjoys watching me getting buggered now and again."

"It was a lovely show, thanks. Perhaps we'll see you at dinner," the woman said. "If you'd be good enough to introduce me to your grandmother, I'd love an autograph..." But Nick was already running down the passageway trying to zip up his pants with his laptop tucked under one arm and his shoes in the other hand.

Chapter 12

On Saturday morning at San Francisco's KRON television studios on Van Ness Avenue, Artie did a slow turn in front of a full-length mirror. "Arturo, does this dress look tight on me?"

"You look fine, Artie. Please, just try to relax."

"That doesn't answer my question and you know it. I've been absolutely starving myself lately, salads for lunch every day, no carbs at dinner, no bread, no potatoes, no candy..."

'What does the scale say?"

"Scales lie! I won't step on a scale unless I'm at the doctor's office and then I refuse to look! Let the girl write it down. I don't want to know. I'm always puffy in the morning, that's all. And here I am, up at the crack of dawn just to be on some local television show. Who's awake at this hour on a Saturday morning but kids watching cartoons cross-legged on the floor in front of the TV set with bowls of cereal in their laps? They're not watching channel 4. They're not my audience. I never met Jan Wahl in person before we showed up here at the studio a few minutes ago. She does seem kind of nice, though, doesn't she?"

"She seems very nice, Artie. I'm sure your interview will go fine...and she remembered you from Finocchio's."

"Oh, people always say that when they want to butter me up. I've done some interviews lately with *kids* who claim to remember. Maybe their grandparents went to Finocchio's as part of a package deal when they stayed at the St. Francis on their wedding anniversary back in the 70s!"

"You were still performing there when they closed in 1999, Artie. That's hardly ancient history!"

"It was another century, Arturo, especially to these kids today..."

Anyone younger than middle-aged was a "kid" to Artie. He didn't mean it to sound derisive, but affectionate, much better than some of the expressions he heard young people yell out at one another in public these days. *Oh you kid* was a Johnny Mercer song from *The Harvey Boys*, which was slightly before Artie's time, but he longed for those days before the world had gotten so old. It had to be the world that was changing; it couldn't be him.

"I would never have agreed to this at all if the kids at the restaurant hadn't talked me into it. Jake says he's a big Jan Wahl fan and James and Tim both said they'd watch this morning and tell all their friends to watch, too. I can't imagine any of those boys getting up this early, either."

"Maybe they'll tape it, Artie," Arturo said. "Or they'll all use those TIVO machines everyone uses nowadays. I asked Ruth to tape it and she promised she would."

"Don't you know how to program a VCR, Arturo? Couldn't you have programmed it to tape the show when we're not home?"

"I suppose if I could find the manual and follow the directions I could, but Ruth is going to do it right from then and there in front of the machine so all she has to do is hit one button. Don't fret about it. I don't know if we had any blank videotapes at home, anyway. Ruth said she did."

"Do they still make tapes for those old machines? Doesn't everyone just use DVDs these days?"

"I don't know, Artie."

"It doesn't matter, Arturo. I'm not even gonna be singing. It's just an interview…"

"Phil couldn't make it this morning, Artie. You wouldn't want to sing without your musicians, would you?"

"No, I suppose not, and they're only giving me a tiny little time slot. Well, if Jan Wahl asks me any questions about the old days, I'll know right away whether or not she was *really* at Finocchio's. I'll bet you none of that old crowd would get up at the crack of dawn after a night on the town just to see me do a television interview."

"We sure never did in those days, did we Artie?"

"Who am I kidding? If any of my old fans from the North Beach days are still alive, they're in nursing homes by now. Maybe they prop them up in front of the television set on Saturday mornings with their gruel and pills to watch the Channel 4 news and weather report before they wheel them down the hall to play bingo, but none of them are going to buy my album or come into Arts to spend any money."

There was a knock at the door, a pause, and then it opened a crack. "Five minutes, Miss Glamóur."

"I'm as ready as I'll ever be!"

Saturday morning on Hancock Street in the Castro, Tim was dreaming about the house where he grew up in south Minneapolis. The house was gone now, along with his mother—nothing left but a pile of ashes on a vacant lot with a singed tree. The lot had probably been redeveloped by now, the tree gone or regrown so it didn't even show a scar from the conflagration, but in Tim's dream the house was still all in one piece. It even seemed to get bigger right before his eyes. In his dream the house was growing like a plant from a fairy tale, a giant beanstalk with slick green leaves the size of wheelbarrows filling all the rooms and bursting out the windows. The house was growing on its stalk now too, going up—up—up into the sky as the trunk grew fatter, underground veins bursting through soil, breaking through lawn grass, knocking Tim's feet out from under him. He fell back and rolled down the embankment into the street. Brakes squealed and Tim looked up to see Metro Transit painted on the side of a Minneapolis city bus from his childhood. The driver wore black pants and a short-sleeved white shirt with a thin black stripe. He opened the door and looked down at Tim from behind the steering wheel. "Are you all right, then?"

Tim's Minnesota accent came right back. "Yah, you betcha! I'm just fine, thanks." And he stood up to brush himself off. He had grass stains on the seat of his blue jeans, but he did feel fine and now the stem of the plant had grown so tall that the house was beyond the clouds, clear out of sight. There was nothing in the yard but the base of what looked like a century old cartoon cottonwood tree.

Tim rolled over in bed and opened his eyes. That stupid dream wouldn't help him solve anything. Tim doubted if he would ever have a dream about Birdie Fuller and the masked robbers. Sometimes dreams didn't point out things as specific as all that. Masked robbers, he thought to himself. No, that was wrong. They wore stockings over their faces; that's what someone had said. Should he call them stockinged-robbers? Nyloned-robbers? Pantyhosed-robbers? Whatever...Tim got up to start the coffee, turned the TV in the kitchen to the morning news and let Buck out the back door.

If it were up to Tim he would dream about Nick every night until they were together again. Wet dreams, kinky ones, dreams where he might even learn something new they could try in real life, not that their sex life needed spicing up. Sex was always fun with Nick. Sex was supposed to be fun, wasn't it? It was fun and loving and reassuring and when it was over, relaxing, every bit as satisfying as a great meal. Sex was supposed to be fun—PERIOD. What else was the point of it? They weren't trying to make babies!

Tim popped a muffin into the toaster while his head spun with more deep and fleshy thoughts. If he couldn't have sex with the man he loved, why couldn't he at least have some innocent fun with someone else until that day came along?

Or that night...or that afternoon...or morning? He craved human contact.

Tim lit a joint and sat down at the computer to check his email. Sometimes a hit of strong pot was the best way to wake up and come back from a strange dream. Then he heard an announcement from the television set in the kitchen: "Coming up after the break, Jan Wahl will interview Artie Glamóur, who is live with us here in the studio today, plus Henry Tannenbaum will have a segment on transplanting your day lilies and we'll have a check on the overnight fire in the Richmond district."

Tim had forgotten all about Artie. He jumped up and turned on the television set at the foot of his bed. The power ON switch made the DVD player slide open and he put away the porn video he'd fallen asleep to last night. He'd promised to watch Artie's segment, but it was only luck that he happened to be awake this early and have the TV turned on. He went back to the computer. Somewhere...if he could only find where he'd saved them...he had some fairly decent pictures of himself from a party. They were more recent than the ones he had posted on dudesurfer.com; that was for sure. They weren't nudes and they weren't even very sexy, but at least they were current. Tim thought he would leave up the old ones that showed off his assets and replace a couple of the face shots of the way he looked now. He couldn't be accused of false advertising if the pictures showed him with the soul patch he'd been growing—an *Imperial*, Artie had called it— without the moustache and with his hair a little shorter. He hated to admit that his hair was a little thinner these days too.

Just the other day at work, Tim's co-worker Jake was complaining about meeting guys on-line. "I hate it when a guy looks great in his pics and then ages twenty years and gains twenty pounds in the time it takes him to drive across town to my house. It's even worse if he lives in my neighborhood and I might run into him again." Jake lived in the Mission District on Folsom Street near Army and he had quite the set-up. Tim knew because he'd helped Jake install his sling.

Then Tim had another thought. What if he did hook up with someone on-line—or anyplace else, for that matter—and then he ran into the guy again somewhere when Nick got back to town and they were out together...and the guy said hello to him? That wasn't covered in any rule book, was it? Maybe it was an unwritten rule in gay life that you didn't say hello to someone you'd tricked with if you saw him out with another guy. It might just be a friend or a roommate, but it could be a jealous husband. Most guys would know enough not to do that, wouldn't they? Tim was sure *he* would. Then again, there was no sense in worrying about that scenario right now, considering the way things had been going.

Tim clicked on a photo to download to the dudesurfer site. It was just okay. He wasn't really smiling in it. He had on a tight blue t-shirt that showed the outlines of his nipples. His biceps looked pretty good. At least he didn't look too goofy.

Jan Wahl was holding up the CD Case of Artie's new album when the camera went to the two of them. "Artie Glamóur, I'm thrilled to finally have you on the show! Thank you so much for coming!"

"Thank you, Jan. It wasn't easy getting it together so early in the morning."

"Tell me about it...I tried to catch your act on Castro Street a while back, but there were a couple of other entertainers there in your place..."

"You must have seen Rochelle and Roxeanne," Artie said. "We fill in with other acts when I have an engagement out of town." Artie was already tensing up. He was here to plug his album, not his replacements.

Now Jan Wahl set the CD case down where it was no longer in camera range. Artie hoped this wasn't going to be difficult. He was used to giving interviews, but this one was live and in his home town. There *might* be friends and regulars and local fans watching this, not just "the cameras and those wonderful people out there in the dark." He tried to channel

Norma Desmond in *Sunset Boulevard*. Strangers were always an easier audience than people he knew, somehow.

"Yes, Rochelle and Roxeanne were a delightful pair and our brunch was delicious. You know, Artie, my good friend Donna Sachet is a wonderful performer, too. You might consider her the next time you're out of town and you need a replacement..."

"Donna Sachet is already doing her Sunday brunch show at Harry Denton's. Now you're plugging my competition, Jan..."

"So I am..." she laughed and gave Artie a playful slap on the arm.

In their bedroom in Hillsborough, Ruth crouched in front of the television. "Are you sure it's recording, Sam? Shouldn't there be a green light on? I don't see the word RECORD lit up anywhere."

"Don't worry, Ruth. It's TIVO. It's working just fine. We tested it, remember?"

"I promised Arty I'd record it for him. I don't know why he even wants it if he's not going to sing."

"Now Ruth, let's just listen..."

Jan Wahl went on, "Well, I will definitely come back to Arts again to see you perform, but today we're here to talk about your new album, Artie. I've listened to it at least five times and I simply love it. You've covered everyone from Peggy Lee to Keely Smith to Billie Holiday. Who were some of your influences when you started...?

Tim was half listening to Artie and Jan Wahl while he deleted the junk in his email. He was about to log off the computer when he noticed an instant message pop up from Britlad on dudesurfer.com. <Hey Tim! Do you have a boyfriend?

Tim wrote back. <Yes, but he's in Europe right now.>
<Are you positive?>

Tim was tempted to write: <Of course I'm positive I have a boyfriend and he's in Europe. Where else would he be?> Did this Britlad in London know something about Nick that Tim didn't? Tim was just being paranoid again, that was all. Sometimes grass helped him get past a dream, but other times it made him paranoid. Now it was also giving him the munchies and he didn't want breakfast; he wanted vanilla bean ice cream with hot fudge, chopped nuts, whipped cream and two cherries.

Positive? Tim finally got it. The guy was asking if Tim was HIV positive. Tim typed: <Yes.> and left it at that. He wanted to say <Take me as I am!> He was so sick of those guys that proclaimed themselves to be free of any STDs and added <UB2!> How could guys who regularly hooked up on-line be so sure that they were negative unless they got checked after every single date or absolutely *never* had an accident with a condom?

Tim started typing again: <Are you negative? What difference does it make? You're in London and I'm in SF. We can't spread anything from that far away except a computer virus and that's waaaaay different.> Tim laughed at his own little joke.

< I'm flying to SF 4 my birthday & I want you.>

<Right.> Tim typed back. <I'd need to see more than one butt cheek & shadowy face in sunglasses before I make plans with anyone.>

<Send me your email? I'll send pics.>

Tim typed it in. He could always block him later if anything got weird enough to make him regret this.

<Use rubbers?> Britlad asked.

<Yes, with anyone I don't know. There's all sorts of other STDs out there.>

Tim remembered Nick's voice on the phone the other night reminding him to play safe. He tried to think how long it had been since he'd had sex with anyone besides Nick. He wasn't counting those few seconds' worth of a rim job on Seward Street from the guy he met at Walgreens before his lover came home unexpectedly. And how could you put a condom on a tongue, anyway? Dental dams? Only in theory.

Tim typed: <I don't use them with my boyfriend. We're both poz.>

<Send me his picture?>

<Hell no! How old are you?>

<18.>

"No way," Tim muttered and saw that Britlad had logged off. He was not into chicken and he didn't believe anything from this guy half way around the world. He was about to log off the site completely when he saw a flashing light on his computer screen which made him forget all about Britlad for the moment. Someone with the screen name HungJockonDuboce was trying to send him an instant message. At least this guy was here in town. Artie's television appearance with Jan Wahl was wrapping up now too.

Chapter 13

Ruth had endured one hell of a morning in Hillsborough, so it was with an audible sigh of relief that she sat down in Rene's hair salon near Union Square.

"Well, Miss Ruth, I was delighted when I noticed that Mai Ling wrote you in on the schedule for this afternoon. I haven't seen you in so long I figured you must have found some other fancy place down there in the suburbs to go and have your hair done by now."

"No I haven't, Rene, and I don't intend to as long as you're here. Can you believe I haven't had a thing done to my hair since the last time I saw you…well, not professionally, anyway."

"Yes, ma-am, I can believe it all right; just look at these split ends!"

Ruth tensed at the insult and then started to laugh. They both laughed. Rene had only been teasing her. "You seem a might bit on edge today, Miss Ruth."

"I had a trying morning, Rene. The pool filter was clogged with leaves from that wind last night. Then I dropped the coffeepot on the kitchen counter and it broke into a million pieces and to top it all off, when I was on my way into the city

I had a flat tire. Thank goodness I'd allowed myself plenty of time!"

"You just settle back and relax, now, you hear? You're in my hands. Did Mai Ling give you some coffee in the waiting room?"

"No, I don't care for any coffee, thank you."

"I wasn't offering; I was asking. I think you might need a glass of wine instead. Or vodka. I have to keep a bottle of chilled Grey Goose on hand for Miss…oops, I almost slipped and told you her name. If I started telling tales out of school nobody would trust me with their secrets. You wouldn't believe some of the tales I could tell you, anyway… Gin? Brandy?"

"Maybe a glass of white wine would be nice, but just one. I still have to drive back when I'm done here and I should stop at the grocery store."

Rene slipped away for just long enough to pour them both a glass. "Don't mind if I do… Cheers, Miss Ruth! Now tell me how is that sexy nephew of yours? I haven't seen Timmy since I was in the restaurant that day at brunch. Is he still happily married?"

"No, he and Nick never had a ceremony."

"Married is married in my book, Miss Ruth. You don't need any fancy words or a piece of paper to make a promise any stronger. Either your word is good or it isn't. All married people should know that."

"I suppose so." Ruth smiled and thought of Sam. Then she thought of Dan, her first husband, and the smile went away, so she thought of Sam again as she lay back in the sink and let Rene's long fingers guide the warm water through her hair and massage deep into her scalp. "Nick is traveling in Europe with his grandmother…ooh, that feels absolutely wonderful…"

Tim had the entire day off and it was sunny, so after Buck's morning run he headed back to Dolores Park by himself. He tried to relax on the "gay beach" section near the top corner of Church and 20th Streets, but so many buffed male bodies were too distracting.

As each one arrived he went through the ritual of settling in. Tim was no exception. Getting undressed in front of the rest of the guys at the park could be as sexy as any strip tease and it was somehow even more exotic by daylight. Tim spread out his big yellow beach towel. Some days he brought a blanket, sometimes a sheet. Some days he even took the time to pick out something to lie on that would compliment what he was wearing, but not always. No one would ever admit to that, would they?

Today he didn't. He wore black and white striped shorts, spandex, but not quite as short as a standard Speedo. The yellow beach towel had a floral print, Hawaiian. Tim couldn't remember where it came from; he'd never been to Hawaii.

Next came the arranging of the clothes, shoes, water bottle, reading materials—everything had to be placed precisely according to its purpose. Shoes held down the bottom corners of the towel. Shirt and pants were rolled up for a makeshift pillow and the rest had to be near at hand.

Tim hadn't had sex in so long he was afraid that his dick might just shrivel up and fall off. Or wear out from self-abuse and fall off. He had that down to about a seven minute routine these days. *HungJockonDuboce* had left him hanging and Britlad had ended their instant messaging soon after Tim refused to send him a picture of Nick. Eighteen? Who was he kidding? No one was eighteen!

Tim watched a pair of guys he recognized from waiting on them in the restaurant. They arrived together, waved at him and made their joint ritual of settling in look like a strip tease for two. Tim had always heard that straight men got off on watching lesbian porn. He wondered if straight women enjoyed watching two gay men together. Sometimes he did. Other times it was just frustrating. These two rubbed suntan oil on each other's backs like a pair of perfectly matched porn stars getting warmed up. Tim couldn't stand it. He had to go home and try that stupid website one more time.

He stood up slowly, unfurled his red T-shirt like a flag or a picnic tablecloth, snapped it open and slid it over his shoulders, popped his head through and then one arm at a time, then used his fingertips to pull it down over his pecs. Tim knew if he worked it right, getting dressed to leave could be just as sexy as the arrival routine.

"Did your cousin Antoine go back to New Orleans, Rene?"

"Yes ma-am."

"I hope he enjoyed his visit…"

"I'm sure he did. He always has a good time no matter where he goes, but he never likes to leave San Francisco. Say, I heard you've had some excitement over on Castro Street lately what with the hold-ups and all…"

"The robberies? Oh yes. I was at Arts the day they hit there."

"You were behind the bar?"

"No, I try not to work any more bar shifts, Rene. Thank goodness I wasn't behind the bar. I would have been scared to death. They'd asked me to come in that day to seat people for Artie's show, but that was all over and done by the time of the robbery."

"But you got a good look at them, didn't you?"

"Not really…it all happened so fast. They wore gloves and hooded sweatshirts and they had stockings over their faces. There was no way of even telling what race they might have been."

"I hadn't heard anything about them being brothers."

"Oh, I don't know that the police have any reason to suspect whether they're related or not, Rene."

He stepped back as if to get another angle on his work, but he had to shake his head at Ruth's last comment and she caught his expression in the mirror. "Oh…Rene…I get it… you meant African-American, didn't you?"

"Yes ma-am," he smiled at her in the mirror. "So that was why you wondered if Antoine was still in town? You were thinking maybe my cousin and I were moonlighting as masked bandits?"

"No, of course not! Nothing could be further from my thoughts!" Ruth was mortified. Had she ever suggested such a thing?

"You know I do just fine here in the beauty business, Miss Ruth. I don't need to be holding up no bars nor hardware stores. And besides, if the Universe is holding onto anything I want, I know that all I have to do is open up my mind and ask for it."

"That's so true, Rene, and what a nice way of putting it." Ruth relaxed again.

Tim had left his computer open to the dudesurfer.com page. At least a dozen guys had checked out his profile since he posted his new face pics. Nine of them had stars besides their names. He knew that was a signal that they liked what they saw and wanted to acknowledge their interest. It was like giving someone a wink or a nod while cruising on the street. It might not mean you were headed directly to bed with that person. Maybe nothing would ever come of it, but it was flattering to be noticed. As Tim began reading the profiles of those who had expressed an interest, a box popped up in the corner of the screen. CASTROSTUD wanted to chat. <Woof! nice profile! where r u?>

Tim still hadn't grown accustomed to all the abbreviations people used on their smart phones. Since he was at home on his computer, it seemed like typing out whole words took less time than trying to decipher some of their shortened versions. Tim wrote back: <Hancock. You?>

<noe & ford.>

<So we're neighbors, huh? Looking for now?>

<i'm new to this. can we meet in public?>

Tim scratched his head. Did that mean this guy was new to the menu of sexual interests he'd checked off on his profile or was he new to meeting guys on this web-site? Maybe his innocence would be refreshing. On the other hand, maybe not. Tim was trying to quickly re-read everything in *CASTROSTUD*'s profile before he replied. Judging from the wicked grin in the main photograph, it would be hard to call this guy innocent. Tim typed:

<Where?>

<i'm new in town. a bar? you pick.>

Tim glanced at the clock. Some bars opened at noon, others at four. He wasn't sure. Last Call on 18th and Noe was one of those places he'd walked by so often that it almost became invisible. He couldn't remember the last time he'd been inside and Tim didn't think he would run into anyone he knew there. The place had been a gay bar forever, just holding up its little spot in the world of flashier Castro bars that came and went over the years. It used to be called the Men's Room and now that new owners had changed the name, they still didn't try to compete with anyone else. It just was. Tim liked that—good drinks, friendly bartenders, no attitude.

<Last call? 18th and Noe in half an hour? How's that sound?>

<great! cu then!>

"Miss Ruth, you are much too sensitive. I knew you meant no offence. I just like to tease you a little. More wine?"

Ruth let her shoulders relax even more. It had been a hell of a morning, but the afternoon was going much better, now that she was in Rene's chair. "I would never be so foolish as to risk alienating the good-will of my hairdresser, Rene. Perhaps a touch more wine would be nice. It's delicious."

"Mai Ling, when you finish with Miss Ruth's big toe there, would you run and get a fresh bottle out of the big cooler in the back please? I'm about to kill this one. "Once Mai Ling had left, Rene poured the last of the first bottle of wine into Ruth's glass and it almost spilled over. "Whoopsie! So, Miss Ruth, we've established so far that the robbers could have been of any race. What else do we have to go on?"

Ruth reached for her refilled wine glass and took a dainty sip off the top. "Not much, I'm afraid. They wore long sleeves and gloves and they had everything covered, at least they did when they robbed Arts. I couldn't see enough of them to swear to anything."

"And they were quite tall? You know, Antoine and myself are both over six feet. Now I'm not saying you're accusing anybody, but were the robbers as tall as us?"

"They might have been. I don't know, Rene. I was clear across the room from them, but yes, I think the police did say they were about six feet…same as the first ones at Cliff's and later at Rossi's"

"My, my, my, and in the immortal words of Margaret Hamilton, 'What a world, what a world, what a world!'

"Who?"

"Margaret Hamilton was the Wicked Witch of the West. That was what she cried out when she was melting, right after Dorothy threw the water on her."

"The Wizard of Oz," Ruth said, "with Judy Garland! I've seen that one." Ruth was very proud of herself that she knew right away what he was talking about this time. "What a world, indeed."

Chapter 14

Artie made coffee in the kitchen on Collingwood Street and took his mug out to the deck. It had just enough room for a small bench, two comfortable chairs and a glass-topped table which held a stack of all the latest gay magazines. Arturo and Artie had never been big on plants, even though they had eastern exposure. Teresa's deck was only inches away. She had plants. She always said she had a brown thumb, but she stuck to the basics—petunias, geraniums and a hanging basket spider plant that thrived outdoors. Since Birdie moved in they'd added dahlias and a bird-of-paradise that looked healthy but had yet to bloom.

Artie glanced across at the explosion of colors next door and let his eyes glaze over. The petals lost their shapes and the colors ran together like a kaleidoscope in the sunshine. He didn't even notice when Teresa stepped outside to shake out a throw-rug.

Snap! "Hello! Earth to Artie!" *Snap!* A cloud of dust flew in the air, but not in Artie's direction.

"Oh...Hi, Teresa. I was just admiring your flowers."

"You were sitting so still I thought you might have had a stroke or something. How are ya'?"

"Fine now, I guess. I didn't sleep well, though, just tossed and turned."

"Sleep! It's the middle of the afternoon. I just got home from school a half hour ago and now I've got housework and chores to catch up on. What are you talking about...sleep? You night people!"

"How are the little darlings in your class?"

"They were all pumped up today like they'd each swallowed a gallon of sugar-water! Must be the full moon."

"Maybe that's what it is...how's Birdie?"

"A little better, I think. The doctor gave her the okay to go back on the beat. Her foot's all healed up from the bullet. She'll be happy to get out there again and try to catch those guys that shot at her if they're still around town."

"I doubt it."

"Me too. I'll bet they split after they knocked off Rossi's and that other woman got hurt, but I don't say anything to Birdie. Let her think what she wants if it makes her happy. At least she'll be back on her feet and be able to get outdoors in the fresh air again."

"Will she be back with the same partner again? What was that gorgeous man's name...the one who was at your party?

"George..." Teresa scowled. "George the twit. George Tavares. I don't know if she'll be assigned to him again. I don't know how the police department works those things out. I haven't bothered to ask Birdie about all that. I'm just glad she's getting out from behind the desk again, although I always felt she was a lot safer when she was back there. I guess I have a choice between listening to her gripe or worrying about her."

"George...that's right. He was a real beauty. Too bad the prettiest ones can be so dumb. What was that old song...*I like 'em big and stupid*...that was it. Julie Brown did it back in the 80s. Maybe I should work that one up and put it into my act for a little novelty...'Superman with a lobotomy'...nah, I don't know. It was cute song with some clever lyrics, but it was no classic...'I like a moron with talented hands'...what do you think, Teresa?"

Teresa just shook her head. "I'm not the one to ask about music. All I know is that I'm heading back downstairs. I've got three more loads of laundry to run through while there's no one in the utility room. Say, is someone staying in Ruth's place these days? One dryer was full of T-shirts advertising different places all over the country."

"What kind of places?"

"Judging from the pictures, they look like gay bars."

"That must be Tony's cousin Eddie from Phoenix. I didn't think they were going to stay, but I heard Ruth offer her place. Just leave the T-shirts on the table."

"I already did. They were cold, so I think they'd been left there quite a while. Say hello to Arturo for me."

"And you give my best to Birdie, darlin'"

Artie turned back to his coffee, but it was cold by now. He wasn't sure what time it was, maybe mid-afternoon. There was nothing at all that he had to do today. He went back to paging through the stack of magazines. There was supposed to be an advertisement for his new album in one of them. Arturo had told him about it, but which one? That detail had gone in one ear and out the other. Where was Arturo, anyway? Artie picked up The Advocate and leafed through it for a few minutes until he heard Arturo's key in the front door. "Artie, where are you?"

"I'm out here on the deck. Where have you been?"

"Costco. I told you."

"I forgot."

"Whatcha doin'?"

"Trying to wake up. I tossed and turned all night. Didn't you hear me?"

"Nah, you know I can sleep through anything."

"I ought to know by now, I guess. Say…Arturo, which magazine did you say that ad was in?"

"What ad?"

"For my record…or cd…whatever you call it. I picked up every gay magazine they had at that newsstand by the Castro Theatre. Do you know what they charge for these things nowadays? And for what? If I want to look at naked men, I can just walk out to Castro and Market on a sunny day. These ones in the magazines are a lot better looking, I'll give 'em that, but..."

"They passed a law against those naked guys at Jane Warner Plaza. Didn't you hear? And your ad isn't due out until next month. I told you."

"I suppose you did. Look at this one. Look at this boy's eyelashes. He has the face of an angel, but he looks so sad. I suppose it's from having to carry around all that extra weight between his legs, swinging away like a pendulum, day in and day out..."

"What magazine is that?" Arturo took Artie's hand and pushed the magazine shut so that he could see the cover. "I wouldn't have bought an ad for your new album in a magazine called *Inches*, Artie!"

"He reminds me of you when you were his age. Same cheek-bones, too. He's gonna be a handsome man when he gets a little older. Too bad he doesn't smile more."

"People don't buy *Inches* to see cheek-bones, Artie... or eyelashes...or smiles, either." Arturo stepped inside the kitchen to unpack his Costco purchases.

"I suppose not...anyway...I was reading this article earlier. Where did it go? It was in one of these rags. It was all about rules."

"Rules for what? Card games? Sports?"

"No, Arturo, rules about love. It was written by a gay psychologist. He does couples counseling and he seems to write from experience. He says it's important for gay couples to firmly establish the rules of their relationships, especially with so much temptation everywhere. That way the lines of communication are open and clear and nobody gets hurt."

"The only rules we ever needed was whoever got up first put the coffee on and the last one to get into bed at night turned out the light."

"Until we got the clapper!"

"What kind of rules does he write about?" Arturo stepped outside and looked over Artie's shoulder at the pile of magazines.

"About sex outside the relationship, mostly. One couple has a rule that they never bring anyone home to the bed they share unless it's a three-way and they both agree on the person in advance."

"We never had a three-way, did we Artie? Not in all these years."

"Did you want to, Arturo?"

"No, not much. You've always been all I could handle, Artie."

"I've lost nearly thirty pounds in the last year!"

"That's not what I meant and you know it. What else does he say in that article?"

"He says that some couples have rules about exactly what they're going to do and not do when they plan on having a night apart."

"Why would they plan a night apart?"

"To fool around, silly! This one couple he talks about, they set aside the first Saturday of every month, whether they think they need it or not. They go out separately and if either one of them picks someone else up, they take them to a hotel ONLY. No going home with someone to their place. And they have to have safe sex, of course...condoms if they're doing that. Some couples have rules that they only do blow-jobs when they go off with other people."

"Aren't we lucky we never had to worry about those things, Artie?"

"Which things?"

"Rubbers...you know...and diseases."

"You gave me the clap once, Arturo. Remember before we were living together when you came up from L.A. that weekend over Labor Day?"

"That was before I even lived in San Francisco, Artie. I can't believe you still remember that!"

"An elephant never forgets."

"I wasn't talking about the clap, anyway. I was talking about AIDS. At least you and I never had to worry about that."

"Never had to worry? What are you talking about? How many friends have we buried over the years? How many employees?"

"You know what I meant, Artie. Now don't start that old stroll down memory lane through the graveyard again. You'll only upset yourself. How would you like to do some traveling next summer, Artie?"

"Where to? Hawaii?"

"I was thinking New York, Provincetown, Key West, Atlanta. Instead of going on all these little weekend trips to perform, I could book Artie Glamóur on a tour of all the gay hot spots. Cruise ships would hire you too."

"You mean work. I thought you meant a vacation."

"It'd be both. I'll come along and we'll book plenty of time to see the sights, look up old friends, go out to dinner, do a few interviews, appear on some of the local TV stations plugging the album…"

"Work!"

"Is there any more coffee?"

"I think I drank it all." Artie turned back to the Inches magazine and opened it to the young model with the long eyelashes. "I'll think about it, Arturo…this touring idea, I mean."

"If I make a fresh pot, will you have some more?"

"No, I've had enough coffee. It must be past four o'clock by now, isn't it? If you want to talk me into work, maybe it's time for something a little stronger than coffee, Arturo. *The bigger they come…the harder they fall…*" Artie sang.

"What's that, Artie?"

"Just an old Julie Brown song I was thinking about earlier when Teresa was… by the way…she said we have strangers staying in Ruth's apartment now."

"It's Tony's cousin Eddie and his lover from Phoenix. I thought I told you about them. It's only for one night."

"Nevermind that right now," Artie held open the Inches magazine again. "This one reminds me of you a lot and I don't mean the eyelashes. How about making us a couple of nice gin and tonics and joining me out here on the deck, Arturo? Maybe I can talk *you* into something…"

Chapter 15

Tim figured if he allowed himself five minutes to walk from his house on Hancock to the Last Call on 18th and Noe, he'd still have at least two minutes left over. There was no hurry. CASTROSTUD lived even closer at Noe and Ford. Tim stared at the face shot of his potential playmate on the computer screen long enough to be sure he had it memorized. He hoped it was a current picture. Neither of them had thought to suggest anything like "I'll be the one in the green cowboy hat with the pink feather boa." How crowded could the Last Call be at this time of day?

Tim glanced at the clock. It was getting on toward Happy Hour, but even if the bar had a good after-work crowd, Tim was sure he could find this guy. And then what? Would they have a beer and talk? He could use a beer, he supposed, or a stiff drink. He reached for a freshly rolled joint and took one deep hit, then put it out. It was killer grass that Nick had brought down from one of his clients who grew it near Cape Mendocino in Humboldt County. Tim would share the rest of the joint with his new neighbor if it seemed appropriate. They could light it up again on their way back to Tim's house or on their way to Ford Street, whichever.

Tim opened his dresser drawer and reached for a clean T-shirt. The one he had on was clean this morning, but he felt sweaty again. Did he have time for one more shower? He'd gotten all cleaned up when he came home from the park with the dog not twenty minutes ago. He hated to think of his water bill this month. Tim glanced back at the photographs of HungJockonDuboce and hoped he'd made the right decision in picking CASTROSTUD instead. Too late to back out now, he headed down his front stairs to the sidewalk.

Tim spotted two empty bar stools at the back of the bar near the toilets. When he got there he noticed a coat on one and a half-full drink in front of it. Tim was nervous and excited about the prospect of finally getting laid, enough so that the glass looked half-full, not half-empty. He was also stoned enough to be aware of something as inconsequential as a total stranger's partial cocktail. Tim pulled a twenty out of his tight blue jeans before he even tried to sit down in them.

Most of the customers looked like they might be regulars. Tim thought he might be the only one here who didn't know anybody, but he didn't mind. The bartender looked vaguely familiar and flashed him a big smile that seemed to say, "I'll get to you in a minute" while he finished someone else's order. The only mystery was the person who belonged to the half-full drink. More important, where was CASTROSTUD from Ford Street? Tim tried to look closely at the face of each person in the room. He simply hadn't arrived yet, that was all.

Tim hadn't been in this bar in so long he couldn't remember; back when it was called The Men's Room. He must have come here with Jason years ago, or was it some other boyfriend? He liked it here. It was a nice little neighborhood bar that might be anywhere on earth, but by virtue of the fact that it was a short walk east from Moby Dick or the Midnight Sun or the Mix and on the far side of Noe Street, it seemed to have been left off the gay guidebook listings of "Must See" places in the Castro. It was almost as if there was an invisible barrier this side of Hartford Street. Tim had heard that the corner where the Edge is had been the same way for years, almost jinxed when it had been a lesbian bar called Francine's, but now it had been thriving as the Edge for a couple of decades.

Tim looked around at the fans in the arched wooden ceiling and the old framed poster of Queen Victoria over the caption: *Even a queen can get the clap*. Boy, that must date back to the 70s, Tim thought. Nobody talked much about the clap anymore these days. Syphilis was a bigger problem, not to mention AIDS and Hepatitis C, of course.

The Last Call seemed to be shut off in a time warp from the rest of the neighborhood, but Tim thought that might be part of its charm. You never knew who might walk in the door and right now he was waiting for CASTROSTUD. He ordered a drink and the next thing he heard was the friendly bartender's voice, "You must have been thirsty...same?"

Tim looked down at the empty glass in his hand. "Gee, I guess I inhaled that one. Man, I'd better slow down! Sure, I'll have another, but I'll try to sip on it this time." He'd only had one toke off that joint, but it had hit him hard.

"Not a problem as long as you stay vertical. Coming right up!"

Tim sensed someone behind him and glanced in the mirror behind the bar at the reflection of a face he knew but couldn't place right away. The guy must have been in the john all this time and now he was sitting down on the empty stool, picking up the drink that had been melting since before Tim arrived. Tim turned around to lean his back against the bar, getting a better look. Bad idea. There was nothing much to see in this direction—the woodstove, a beer sign and a couple of guys necking on the meat rack beside the video game, but at least now he recognized the man on the next bar stool. George Tavares, the hot gay cop, Birdie Fuller's partner. Out of uniform, he was just as sexy, maybe even more so, dressed in a gray muscle shirt, boots and Dockers.

"Hello," they both said at the same time. "How's it going?"

"Good..."

"Okay…"

Tim smiled, nodded and turned back toward his drink, his knees brushing George's beefy thigh this time. "You're looking really good!"

"Thanks, you too," the words came out of Tim's mouth without thought. Then he realized that George didn't recognize him; he was just saying lines like an actor who's grown bored with the play. It was all out of habit. It made Tim angry and it hurt a little, after that big come-on George had given him on the deck at Birdie's party. Tim was almost ready to forgive him for not remembering him at the restaurant the next time they saw each other, but now he wasn't sure. This time they were face to face and George looked at Tim as if he were just anybody. George Tavares either had a terrible memory or a total lack of discretion or maybe it was one other thing…he was drunk.

"You live in the neigh—rhood?" George was even slurring.

"Yeah, and your name is George, right?"

"How'd you know?" He jumped back a little.

"Everyone knows you, George, but you and I met at a party a while back, too…at Teresa and Birdie's place…your partner on the force, remember? The one who got shot in the hold-up at Cliff's?"

"Birdie, sure! Sure, I remember. I mean…I remember you…Gene, right? Glen? Gaylen?"

"Tim Snow."

"I was close."

"This must be your day off, huh?"

"Yeah…no…I'm on vacation. Birdie's coming back on the beat next week. Her foot's all healed now. They gave me some time off before we start up again. You're pretty hot. You work out a lot? Hey, you never answered my question, Tom. Where do you live?"

"It's Tim, George. Not too far…on Hancock."

"Very con…hic…convenient. Two more here, bartender."

Tim took another sip of his drink and scanned the bar again, looking for CASTROSTUD. No luck. He looked down at his watch. It was two minutes past the appointed time. Tim would give him ten more minutes and then…he wasn't sure what he'd do, but it pissed him off when people kept him waiting, especially in a nervous-making situation like this one. Ford Street was only half a block away!

George Tavares threw some more money on the bar for both their drinks and then put his hands below the ledge. Tim glanced down and to his right and saw that George was unzipping his pants. Now he was hard and stroking himself and smiling. "Check this out, Tom."

"The name's Tim, not Tom. Tim!" George did have a very nice cock, Tim had to admit, and it was still growing. Without conscious thought, Tim's hand came unwrapped from the cold glass of his drink. He'd planned to lift his drink to George's glass and thank him, but George's hands were too busy for a toast at the moment. Tim's fingers held their curved formation and moved down to his own knee where he rubbed the droplets of condensation into his jeans and then rubbed them up and down against the fabric to warm them.

Then Tim's hand reached across to George Tavares' knee and slid up his thigh until Tim's fingers replaced George's hand and continued the same stroking motion as George continued to grow bigger and harder. Tim could hardly believe what he was doing! He wanted to tell someone about it, but who could he tell? Not Artie or Arturo, not his Aunt Ruth or Sam, certainly not Sam! Sam was straight. What was he thinking? Jake, Tim's co-worker, was the only person he could think of right now that he could possible tell. Maybe someday, if he and Nick ever got all their rules ironed out and they agreed to tell each other about their sexual escapades, maybe then he could tell Nick about it and they could have a good laugh, but right now he was too excited. If the boys who stood in line outside the Badlands on a Saturday night knew about this, they'd be so jealous! All the guys on Castro Street who swooned every time George Tavares walked by in his uniform…if they could be in Tim's place right now, they'd just…

"You like that?"

"That's a really nice cock you've got there, George, but don't you think you could get in trouble, flashing it around like that? There must be some kind of rules…I mean *laws* against that. You're supposed to be enforcing the law, right?"

"I'm off today. Damn, that feels good. You wanna head over to your place?"

"Um…I'm supposed to meet someone here…" Tim glanced around the room and saw him walking in the front door, CASTROSTUD. He looked even better than his pictures. He was kind of handsome, actually. He was a little taller than Tim expected, but maybe he was wearing boots. He ordered a beer and handed the bartender some money. Then he looked around the room while he waited for his change. Tim caught his eye and they both smiled and Tim lifted his free hand to wave, but that was when the front door opened again. It flew open this time. Two tall men in black hooded sweatshirts burst through the door and one of them yelled, "Everybody be quiet and do what you're told and nobody gets hurt!"

They had stockings over their faces that distorted their features into cartoon creatures or faces from long ago deep-sea dreams or something Tim had once seen under a microscope. They wore gloves again, too. There was no telling their race. The gloves reminded Tim of his own hand, which he now removed from George Tavares' huge cock. The excitement hadn't made George lose his erection at all, while Tim went totally limp in his own pants. If anything, George got a jolt of energy all of a sudden.

"All the money goes in the bag!" One of them held the gun and did the talking, just like when they robbed Arts and Cliff's and Rossi's Deli. The other one came around behind the bar and held the canvas sack open for the bartender to empty the register into it. "Everybody sit still and keep your hands where I can see them!"

Tim instinctively reached for the change from his drinks, but kept his hands flat on the countertop. The bartender had already picked up his tip. As someone who worked for tips, Tim wondered whether the robbers would take them, too, but they didn't. Tim somehow respected them for that...armed robbers with integrity and a feel for the working man. "Don't anybody think about trying anything..."

The one with the canvas bag was only inches away but Tim wasn't really frightened. Maybe he was too stoned to be frightened. He sensed that they weren't there to hurt anyone. There was something almost familiar about their movements. They were both at the front door again and George was standing up, reaching for his coat. His pants were zipped up now, but Tim could still see the bulge there.

"Stop right there and drop the—hic!—bag or I'll shoot!" George Tavares had a gun and he was drunkenly waving it over Tim's shoulder, inches from his ear.

But nobody stopped. The robbers flung the door open and were outside running toward Castro Street by the time George pulled the trigger. Tim watched, as if in slow motion, as a single bullet crossed the room from one end of the bar to the other. It caught CASTROSTUD in the left shoulder and Tim watched his prospective date slump to the floor before they could even say hello.

Chapter 16

"Hello!"

"Hey, Snowman! I was afraid I'd have to leave a message."

"Nick! Where are you?"

"Still somewhere in the middle of the Atlantic Ocean. It all looks the same after a while, especially in the dark. We just finished a late dinner and I was about to hit the hay. Remind me not to get on another ship for a long time, will you?"

"Damn! I was counting on us going on one of those gay cruises just as soon as you got home."

"You can go without me...please!"

Tim had been pulling off his shoes while he talked on the phone. Now he switched ears to take off his jacket. "What'd you say Nick?"

"I don't want to go on any more ships for a while."

"No...what you said after that."

"I said...I don't remember now..."

"I thought it sounded like you said, 'Go without me.'"

"Maybe I did."

"Nick, I can't believe you'd say a thing like that. You've been gone all this time! When you get back I thought you'd at least want us to be together."

"I do, babe. I was just making a comment. I didn't mean anything by it, not about us. What's gotten into you? Are you okay?"

"I just miss you so much, Nick..."

Tim caught his reflection in the mirror and noticed how scrunched up his face was, as if he'd just gotten out of bed. And the whininess in his voice was disgusting! How could Nick stand to listen to him when he sounded like this? How had Nick put up with him for all these months? Years? How long had they known each other now? It seemed like always, but lately they'd been apart more than they were together. Tim could hardly believe he hadn't driven Nick away with his neediness ages ago. How had Tim ever found such a hot guy as Nick in the first place? And how come Nick stuck around when Tim was such a neurotic mess sometimes? Nick wasn't around now though, was he? He was thousands of miles away and he'd been gone so long Tim was losing his mind. No, it was just that he missed him so much, that was all.

Tim hadn't had sex the entire time Nick was away. The only relief he'd had all this time was at his own hand...mano a mano? No, that involved two people's hands, didn't it? Tim wondered if masturbation sounded better in French or Italian. Nick had him so spoiled, giving Tim all the great sex he wanted, but not lately. These days Tim felt lost, as needy as a flightless baby bird, just waiting for that big long juicy worm to come sliding down his throat.

This wasn't like the old Tim, the Tim Snow who used to have a different hot man in his bed every night, the Tim Snow who rented a little apartment on Collingwood and worked as a waiter and always wanted a man like Nick in his life, but didn't have a care in the world while waiting for the right one to come along. Now he had a man, this man on the phone, still thousands of miles away instead of here in his bed where he needed him. Now he had this wonderful man in his life and Tim was whining about an innocent remark, something about "Go without me..." when all Nick had meant was...nothing!

Hearing Nick's voice on the phone only made Tim more miserable, knowing that he had to wait for it. Horny… lonely…needy…weren't they all the same thing? Weren't they all coming from the same dark part of the soul? Wouldn't solving one solve the others? Wasn't that why gay men made sex so easy? Meet the most basic need in life and all your other problems fall into place. Or were horniness, loneliness, neediness each in its own category—akin to each other, but distant cousins, shirttail relations. Or did they act as parts of the same physical, psychological body, like having a toothache and then stubbing your toe so hard it made you forget all about your tooth.

"Hey…Tim? Snowman? Are you still there?"

"I'm sorry, Nick. Yeah, I'm here. I guess I'm a little upset, that's all. I just witnessed someone getting shot."

"What? Who? Where? On Castro Street?"

"In the Men's Room."

"Which men's room…at Arts?"

"No, not in the john and it's not even the Men's Room anymore, I forgot. They changed the name of the place to Last Call. You know…that little bar next to the 7-11 on the corner of 18th and Noe."

"What were you doing in there?"

"It's a nice little bar, Nick. Have you ever been in there?"

"Sure, I guess I must have been. I just didn't think it was someplace you hung out, that's all…maybe if the Edge got too crowded, but you like the Mix and Moby's too, when you're on your way home from work, don't you? Who got shot? Was it someone you know?"

"No, not really… It was some guy… I was in the back and he had just come in the front door a minute before. The place was kinda crowded. I was sitting near the back, next to George Tavares…the policeman, you know…Birdie's partner? Then those two guys with their faces covered up came in and robbed the place and George pulled a gun on them."

"Did he kill them? I thought you said some guy got shot, not some guys. How many people got shot? How many robbers were there?"

"No, there were just the two robbers, but they didn't get shot. They got off scot-free, the same ones that robbed Arts and Cliff's and Rossi's, I imagine. They looked the same to me, but I didn't really get a good look at them at Arts because I stayed in the kitchen. Only one guy got shot, but it was George the cop that shot him. The robbers were already gone when George pulled the trigger. He was off-duty. And he was drunk."

"He was carrying a gun, out of uniform, off-duty and getting shit-faced? Aren't there regulations about that sort of thing?"

"Oh yeah…I'm sure he's in deep shit by now. I didn't stick around for very long to find out. The ambulance must have been right outside because they arrived in no time. Then the police cars. I got out of there as soon as I could. They had plenty of other witnesses who were closer to the front of the bar if they needed anyone to make statements."

"They might have wanted to ask you how drunk George was."

"They can ask the bartender. They don't need my word for it. He'll be in enough trouble already." Tim looked down at his right hand where George's stiff cock had been less than twenty minutes earlier and shook his head. "And he and Birdie were supposed to start back on their old beat next week. I'll bet that won't happen now."

"So you didn't know the guy that George shot…"

"Not really…"

"What does that mean?"

"He looked familiar like I'd seen him around…or maybe like I'd seen his picture someplace…"

"His picture?"

Damn, Tim hated to lie. He wasn't very good at it and he especially hated to lie to Nick. He hadn't quite told a lie yet, but this was getting too close for comfort. One of these days they would have to sit down and have a long talk. And it had to be before their next separation. Better yet, maybe they wouldn't have to have another separation...not for a long time, anyway. Not if Tim had his way about things.

When Nick got home they would settle back into their old comfortable habits with Nick in the city most weekends and Tim driving up to the Russian River for at least a couple of nights during the week. Tim always thought he wanted more, but maybe it worked so well because this was the way it was. When they had more than three nights in a row together, they wore each other out! Sometimes one night could do that. Tim didn't even think about having sex with other guys when he was getting that much from the man of his dreams...well... hardly ever.

"How are your extraterrestrial powers these days? Have you been dreaming about me, Snowman?"

Nick was almost frightening when he did that. Tim's thoughts from the time Nick asked who got shot ended up with that phrase about *the man of his dreams*. All those thoughts had taken place in the time of a blink of an eye the way things sometimes happen in dreams. And now Nick asked about Tim's dreams. It was as if Nick was the psychic one.

"My dreams are different now, Nick. Ever since I stopped taking Neutriva I hardly notice my dreams. My Aunt Ruth called and wanted to know if I could help the police with the robberies in the Castro. I guess it was Teresa's idea to ask me. She wanted to help Birdie, but I'm no help at all. You'd think my dreams would at least go back to the way they were before I ever took that drug in the first place, the way they always were."

"Maybe they will, babe. Be patient."

"Oh, I don't care if those dreams ever come back. I never wanted them in the first place. But it's funny...you telling me to be patient. Here I've been, patiently waiting for you to come home all this time. No, that's a lie, Nick. I'm not patient at all. I'm going crazy!"

"It sounds like you just need to get laid, Tim! You've got the whole city of San Francisco out there waiting for you. I'll bet you're dragging home a different hot guy every night. This is the perfect time for you to get it out of your system, while I'm out of town. Just play safe. And make sure to wash all your sheets and towels before I get back!" Nick laughed.

"Nick, I thought we agreed not to talk about this over the phone! I need to be in the same room with you when we establish our rules, not thousands of miles apart. Jeez! I'm losing my mind with missing you!"

"I'm just teasing with you, Snowman. I miss you too, you know. I'm getting hard right now just hearing the sound of your voice."

"Ooooooh...me too, Nick!"

"How's Buck?"

"He's fine. I opened the back door when I came in just now and he ran downstairs already."

"Don't let him leave the yard again."

"I'll take the phone out onto the deck. Wait. No, he's okay. Sarah's down there playing with him."

"Tell her hi."

"Sarah, Uncle Nick is on the phone. He says to tell you hello, Sweetie. Buck, don't jump up on her like that. Sarah, don't let him do that. Buck! Settle down! Jeez, he ran all over Dolores Park this morning. I thought he'd be worn out by now. Sarah wants to know when you're coming home, Nick. So do I."

"We get to New York in a couple of days and then my grandmother has a few more appearances to make. Two are in New York, one in Chicago, one in Milwaukee on the way home."

"You have to go along for all of those? Why can't you just fly back from New York?"

"She likes me to be there. We've worked out sort of a routine where I help keep the line moving. I've stuck it out this long; I might as well finish up the tour with her. We should be back in San Francisco on the 19th. I think that's a week from

tomorrow…or today…I don't even know what time it is. I left
my watch on the drawer when I got undressed for bed."

"It's still daylight here."

"I'll be there soon, babe. I'll make it worth the wait,
okay? I promise. Goodnight, Snowman."

Chapter 17

Tim had more dreams that night. He had dreams inside of dreams. He went to lie down on top of the blue comforter on top of his bed and he rolled himself into a ball and fell fast asleep and dreamed he was flying. Flying dreams were the best! To hell with trying to find the armed robbers in the Castro. To hell with trying to get laid. Flying was better than anything. He could go anywhere and do whatever he wanted as long as he stayed in control. Flying dreams were the only kind of dreams he had when Tim knew that he was dreaming and didn't want to wake up.

Tim tried not to analyze flying dreams too much because that would make them stop. He felt like a bird on the perfect updraft of wind. Then he was a surfer on the crest of a wave so magnificent that he thinks he's only dreaming. If Tim could stay in this dream it would be better than any pot or alcohol, way better than the best high. Tim flew around the block at first, Hancock Street to Dolores Park at Church Street, down to 18th and west to Noe. He glanced down at rooftops and chimneys. Then he made another loop and skimmed the tops of the magnolia trees that lined the south edge of Dolores Park above the playground and the gay beach. He flew back over Castro Street and Collingwood and Diamond where people in cars drove around and around looking for parking spaces that Tim could spot easily. Their impatience was as visible to Tim as their noxious waves of exhaust fumes. If only Tim could tell them where to park he could save the planet.

Tim flew high over Twin Peaks and down over the treetops in Golden Gate Park and all the way out to the ocean. In the windows of the Cliff House an elderly couple raised glasses of champagne to toast their anniversary. Tim smiled and watched them for a moment before he soared across the towers of the Golden Gate Bridge and flew clear past Sausalito. He soared high over Mt. Tamalpais and low over Stinson Beach. Sand sparkled pink and lavender in the sunset. He soared over Bodega Bay and Jenner-by-the-sea at the mouth of the Russian River.

Tim was flying toward Monte Rio. That must have been where he was headed all along, but he hadn't been conscious of his destination. He could see the roof of Nick's house above the Russian River through the redwood trees and then SNAP! It felt like a kite string broke and Tim went into a free-fall. Then he heard a ZING and he was reeled in, quick as a tape measure and he landed back in his own bed. He groaned and reached for Nick, but no one was there.

Tim rolled onto his stomach and he was back in high school now. He was living in Edina with his Uncle Dan and Aunt Ruth after his parents threw him out. Tim came in through the back door, still drenched in sweat. He'd stayed after practice in order to shower and have sex with Dave, his track coach. That day Dave couldn't give him a ride home like he usually did, so Tim ran all the way and got sweaty again. Dave had said something about having to pick up his wife, but Tim wasn't listening. Tim didn't want to hear about Dave's wife. He didn't want to acknowledge any reality outside his fantasies. He felt great after sex on the bench behind the last row of lockers. They usually did it in the coach's office with the door locked, but Dave was getting more daring and Tim just followed along. Why not? They'd never been caught.

But they *had* been caught! That was why Tim's parents threw him out and Dave moved away to coach and to teach at another school. That all happened before! That was when he still lived in South Minneapolis with his parents. So he knew this must be a dream too, even though he wasn't flying.

Now he dreamed that his Aunt Ruth was fussing over something in the kitchen. "What are you doing?"

"I'm baking cookies."

"But you never bake cookies. I've never seen you bake anything except bread and only at Christmas time."

"I'm baking cookies for your graduation next week, to prove that I love you."

"That isn't necessary."

"But we're having a party for you here and I have to serve cookies. It's a tradition."

"Did you bake cookies for Dianne when she graduated from high school?"

"I tried, but they didn't turn out. That only shows that I love you more."

"I think my cookies are burning."

Now it was graduation night and Tim waited for Dave outside the gym, even though it had been two years since they'd seen each other. Tim didn't even know where Dave Anderson lived anymore and Dave wouldn't have known that this was Tim's graduation night. As far as Tim knew, Dave had never set foot in Tim's new high school in Edina, but Tim waited for him just the same. Tim still had on his graduation gown, but he held the mortarboard in both hands at his chest. He swung the tassel back and forth, up and down, and then in circles like a stripper he'd seen in a movie.

A car pulled up and honked, but it wasn't Dave. "Get in!" It was his Uncle Dan.

"Where's Aunt Ruth?"

"She took her own car. She wanted to be home before the guests arrived and she didn't know how long you'd have to stay afterward. Are your friends all finished taking pictures?"

"I guess."

There were mounds of cookies on every flat surface as far as Tim could see from the front door into the living room and down the hallway—sugar cookies, mostly, but decorated in different colored frosting and patterns so they might have been different kinds. There were brownies too, and toffee bars. Then he found oatmeal raisin cookies and chocolate chip with black walnuts, Tim's favorite. Tim went up to his room and his bed was piled high with gift-wrapped packages. Who were these people who had brought him gifts? Tim's high school friends were at their own commencement parties, not that he had many friends. Beth had given him a new roach clip for graduation earlier. He gave her an autographed copy of *The Stranger* by Albert Camus. Tim autographed it himself:

For Beth –
Don't be a stranger after graduation.
Love,
Al Camus
p.s. Tim says Hi.

Tim figured if he was giving her a gift, she would like something silly and it was the best he could do on a limited budget.

"There you are, dear!" Aunt Ruth swept into his bedroom like a movie star. Tim had never seen her wearing so much jewelry, diamond earrings and a huge sparkling necklace that must have been real. "What on earth...what are you doing up here locked in your bedroom? The guests are all downstairs waiting to congratulate you."

"I'm not locked in. The door wasn't locked. You walked right in, didn't you?"

"Well..."

"I just wanted to change clothes...at least ditch the mortar board and the choir robe, you know."

"Well, come right downstairs this very minute. There are some people who are dying to see you again. We're all so proud!"

Aunt Ruth couldn't have loved him as much as she said she did or she wouldn't have let this happen. Tim's parents were here! His father held his enormous silver belt buckle in one hand and a can of beer in the other. His mother's tears dripped into her glass of bourbon. He could smell both of them from the top of the stairs. They were drunk and Tim's Aunt Ruth was long gone. The cookies were gone. Everything was gone. Now the three of them stood outside his parents' house on the sidewalk. "Faggot!" his father yelled while his mother whimpered. "I won't have a cocksucker living under my roof!"

Then Tim was home on Hancock Street in his own bed with his parents' words burning in his ears. Tim wondered if "no cocksucker under this roof" meant that his mother never gave his father head. She probably wouldn't, as holy-roller as she always was, at least when she was sober. Tim didn't want to picture his parents having any kind of sex, but he couldn't help being curious. People did a lot of things when they were drunk that they wouldn't do sober, at least for the first time. Tim knew that from his own experience…some of his favorite things. He didn't need to be drunk to do them after a while, although poppers helped.

Now in his dream it was only a couple of weeks until Christmas and Tim was already sick of it. Or was it nearly Easter? He couldn't tell. Every holiday was a gay holiday, any excuse to decorate the bars in the Castro and run a drink special, any theme for the drag queens to plan a costume around, but the big holidays got on his nerves. The big holidays overwhelmed him. He was turning on the morning news on the kitchen TV while the coffee brewed. Each time a commercial showed a happy couple he had to hold back from throwing something at the screen. It didn't matter if they were a straight couple surrounded by bright-eyed children. Tim was irritated by romantic ads with parakeets or dogs or cats or a male and female turtle bickering back and forth in an ad for Internet service. Buck rubbed his nose against Tim's leg and demanded a pat on the head. "Come on boy…I'll let you out the back door, but don't go running off, okay? We'll go for a walk later."

Nick and his grandmother should be back in New York by now. It must be nice taking a trip like that with his grandmother, Amanda Musgrove, paying for everything, or at least her publisher was. As long as she made appearances in bookstores and signed autographs, they could write off the cost of the trip. She didn't even have to speak or read at most of the signings; her mystery books had been translated into at least a dozen languages now. She and Nick didn't need to know any of the languages.

Tim poured his first coffee from the full pot into a 49ers mug. One cup was never enough and neither were two on most days. This felt like it was going to one of those days, with Nick still miles away. At least he should be off the ship by now. Those cruise ships were probably full of gay stewards and rich old closeted Republicans, so Nick could get all the sex he wanted. Tim didn't want to think about it.

Tim opened his eyes and looked around but he didn't recognize the room. He wasn't flying, so he wasn't sure if he was still dreaming. He saw the first dim ray of dawn at the windowsill and he heard someone snoring. It was Artie in the next bed. They were in a hotel room. Tim remembered now that they'd been in L.A. the night before and Artie performed somewhere, but Tim couldn't remember what happened last night…only that it hadn't gone well. Tim couldn't remember how he got roped into going along on this gig with Artie instead of Arturo. Maybe Arturo was sick. Artie wanted to get drunk after the show and Tim had nothing better to do than join him. Now all Tim wanted was to go home.

Last night came back to Tim slowly, but he still didn't know it was all a dream or whether he was still dreaming now. Artie was onstage in an L.A. nightclub. The audience was cheering for him the same way they do at Arts sometimes on Sundays when he's really on fire. Artie feeds on all the energy in the room and then he pours it all right back at them, whether he's laying into a poignant ballad or telling a raunchy story. There's such an electric feel in the air you can almost see it, taste it, touch it—a gay revival meeting with Artie carrying on like the Aimee Semple McPherson of Castro Street.

Then they *were* on Castro Street. Last night's L.A. hot spot turned into Arts with an enormous stage. The platform at the real Arts was just big enough for Phil's baby grand piano and a few bar stools with the bass and drums one step down on the floor, but in this dream the stage had a proscenium arch with traveling lights around it. If you squinted, it looked like an old-fashioned Wurlitzer juke-box with Artie trapped inside.

Layers of curtains began to open and the stage grew big enough for two back-up singers, then four, then eight. Then Artie was fronting the Radio City Music Hall Rockettes except that all of them were drags queens in pairs, two red, two yellow, two green but there were more colors than any rainbow Tim could imagine. Then the pairs were dressed in the clothes of another era with flappers, showgirls, ballet dancers from a Monet painting and a pair of go-go dancers in a suspended cage. Tim noticed two of them dressed in black, their faces covered with stockings and shaded by hooded sweatshirts...one of them held a gun. Now all the dancers turned away from the audience and Artie was nowhere to be seen. When they turned back to face the front they were all dressed in black with their faces covered, neither male nor female, neither black nor Caucasian. One of each pair held a gun and the other had a canvas bag for the cash and the ones with the guns spoke in unison:

"Everybody be quiet and do what you're told and nobody gets hurt!"

But people did get hurt. The guns went off. Bullets flew everywhere until the entire audience at Arts was dead on the floor. Tim held up his cocktail tray to deflect the bullets. He was safe. He watched the scene unfold as if he wasn't there. Then he watched from above, looking down from the ceiling at all the bloodshed. And then he was flying again. He flew out the door and over Castro Street, over Buena Vista Park, over the Golden Gate Bridge. He was flying again, so he knew that he was dreaming and once again he was headed toward Nick's house at the Russian River.

This time he made it all the way. This time Nick was actually there. Nick was naked in bed like he'd been waiting for him, but Nick was fast asleep. And as crazed for sex as Tim thought he had been all this time that Nick was away, as tooth-ache crazed, as toe-stubbing blind with lust as he'd been for weeks, Tim was content to get undressed and curl up under the covers beside Nick's naked body, to hear his gentle breathing and to hold the man of his dreams in his arms.

Chapter 18

It was late Saturday afternoon when Ruth and Sam stopped for cocktails at Arts before going to Postrio for dinner on their way to the symphony. Ruth wanted to check up on her nephew without Tim suspecting that she was checking up on him. In Ruth's mind, she and Nick were the only stabilizing forces in Tim's crazy life and Nick had been away far too long. Ruth too had dreams sometimes and in them Tim was balanced on a tightrope with her and Nick holding up the ends. When Nick was around she didn't worry so much, but Ruth's dreams grew more frightening with each week that passed while Nick was in Europe. Tim sounded all right on the phone when she called, but she needed to see him in the flesh to make sure.

Ruth, Sam and Tim nearly collided in the doorway when they arrived. Tim was embarrassed by his clumsiness. He moved the empty cocktail tray he'd been twirling on his fingers and tucked it under one arm so that he could shake Sam's hand, but Sam's right hand was holding the door for Ruth, who had stopped and knelt down to admire a tiny dachshund puppy on the sidewalk and chat with the puppy's proud parents, a gay couple from Noe Valley.

Tim had grown unfamiliar with the formality of shaking hands lately, especially on Castro Street. People might wave, clasp a shoulder, give a hearty pat on the back or that clumsy tradition known as the "high-five." Tim didn't like that one and usually ignored anyone who lifted one hand to slap his. What were they trying to prove, how cool they were? Was slapping someone's hand more macho than the firm grip of an old-fashioned handshake?

It turned out that Sam wasn't planning to shake Tim's hand anyway, but intended to give him a manly embrace. Tim checked himself from also giving Sam a peck on the cheek, but the habit was so ingrained that Tim had to force himself not to pucker his lips at all. Then he set the tray down on a table and his Aunt Ruth melted into his arms. All was well with both of them now.

When Ruth looked up again she was startled to see who was behind the bar. "Artie! What are you doing back there?"

"I'm working. What does it look like?"

"I thought your bartending days were in the past, now that your singing career is going so well."

"The real reason I'm here is because I'm supposed to be training a new bartender tonight and he's late! That's not a good sign on his first day at a new job, but at least he called. He said he was stuck in heavy traffic on the Bay Bridge."

"I heard on the news that there was a crash."

"Well, he should have taken BART, but he was worried about how he'd get home later. By the time he finds parking in the Castro it'll be last call. Jake is late too and he didn't even bother to call. He walks to work and I know where he lives, so he'd better have a good excuse when he shows up."

"Where's Scott?"

"We gave him some time off to go visit his family before he starts his new job."

"Scott's leaving? Oh no! I'm so sorry to hear that."

"No, he's not leaving, Ruth. He's going to be the new manager. It was your idea."

"It was?"

"It was your idea to hire a manager and Scott was the logical choice. He knows everyone. He's responsible, reliable, has a good head on his shoulders. He'll still work some shifts behind the bar and when Arturo and I are out of town with my performing appearances, he can be in charge of things. I'll never have to bother you again."

"Oh, Artie...you know I didn't mind that much. And if there's ever an emergency I'm always glad to help you fellows out. It was just that I didn't want you to rely on me so much. It was getting to the point where Sam and I never had a weekend together at home and my little apartment on Collingwood gets to feel awfully cramped with the two of us, especially when we're used to Sam's big estate in Hillsborough..."

Ruth prattled on without thinking of what words came out of her mouth. She knew she ought to be careful about doing that. It had gotten her into trouble in the past. What was going through her mind was the news that Scott was being promoted to manager and Tim wasn't. What had Artie called him? *Reliable?* Wasn't Tim? Well...sometimes. *Responsible?* Tim was more responsible now than he used to be. Owning Jason's old house on Hancock Street had grounded him a lot. Having Nick in his life grounded him even more. Oh, where *was* Nick? He must be due back from Europe any day now. And where was Tim? In the kitchen, no doubt.

"...and the boys upstairs have a set of keys to my apartment if they ever want to use it. I told them they were more than welcome, since Sam and I are rarely there. Tonight we're just in town for dinner and the symphony and then we're driving back to Hillsborough afterward—"

This time her words were cut off when Teresa stormed into the restaurant with gale force. "Artie! Where the hell is Arturo? I need to speak to both of you right now! I have just about had it!"

"He's in the kitchen like always. What's the matter? What happened?"

"I am trying to do laundry, but the washers and the one dryer that still works have been tied up all afternoon by someone who doesn't even live in the building! Birdie's going back on the beat next week and I've got a ton of laundry to do for both of us. She's been a real pain in the ass to live with ever since she took that bullet at Cliff's and I'm fed up, I tell you! *Fed up!*"

Ruth stepped forward to confess to giving a set of keys to her apartment to Jeff and Tony. "I hope you don't mind, Artie. It's just that I hate to see that apartment go to waste when we use it so seldom and someone has guests in town. The t-shirts sound like Tony's cousin Eddie must be staying there again."

"Well, it wouldn't be so bad if all the washers were working and both of the dryers, but now it's down to one of each and the dryer is questionable. It's time you and Arturo bought some new ones, but until you do, you might at least call out a repairman and get them all working again for a—"

Teresa was cut off when Jake came running in the door, so she headed back toward the kitchen with a "Harrumph!" and went in search of Arturo.

"Hi everyone. Sorry I'm late! Oh…hey Ruth. Are you coming back to work?"

"Where have you been, Jake?" Artie demanded.

"I would have been on time, but I was walking through Dolores Park and I looked up and there was a hummingbird so close to me I could almost reach out and touch it. It just hovered there with the sun reflecting off its body, so I stopped and held out my hand. I really thought it might perch on my finger for a minute."

Ruth said, "How lovely!"

"Are you stoned?" Artie asked. "Then what happened?"

Jake broke the spell, "It took a shit in mid-air all over my fingers!"

"Jake!" Artie scolded him. "There's a lady present! Couldn't you have said it went to the bathroom?"

"No I couldn't, Artie. Hummingbirds don't have bathrooms. Besides, I've heard you use lots worse language on stage in your act while there are plenty of ladies in the room."

"You've never heard me talk like that. You've heard my evil twin, Artie Glamóur. But that still doesn't explain why you're late for work. You could have washed your hands when you got here."

"It got hummingbird shit all over my shirtsleeve too. I had to go all the way back home and change."

Ruth couldn't help herself and burst out laughing, while Artie glared.

When Tim caught Jake alone at the waiters' station he asked him, "What really happened? I didn't buy a word of that story."

"I know, but Artie loves hummingbirds."

"But you're hardly ever late."

"Sorry, Tim. Thanks for setting up for me. My new boyfriend Ron was over. He's moving in with me on the first of the month, you know."

"Congratulations."

"Yeah, it'll be nice, I think."

"But why were you so late for work?"

"I was on my way out the door when the doorbell rang. Someone else in the building had a package from UPS and the driver pressed the wrong button. Ron buzzed him in, which would normally piss me off. There used to be some dealers that lived downstairs and people rang the doorbells at all hours of the day and night looking to buy crystal meth. I told Ron not to buzz anyone in without looking out the window to make sure it was someone we expected, but I wasn't going to let that be our first fight."

"So what happened?"

"You should have seen the UPS guy! Hot! He may have rung the wrong bell, but he had a package that worked out just fine in my apartment...or should I say *our* apartment?"

"You and Ron? The two of you...both?"

"You bet. We got it *on*! All three of us...it was fun!"

"But with Ron moving in and all, I mean...had you done three-ways together before?"

"Nope."

"Didn't you stop and think about what it all might mean?"

"What *what* might mean? It was all safe-sex. I mean, Ron and I are both negative and the UPS man must get around a lot, as hot as he is. Once we got down to business we brought out the condoms. We're not stupid."

"But besides that, didn't you and Ron ever talk about the possibility of doing three-ways before?"

"What's to talk about? It's not like we were virgins when we met. There wasn't a lot to talk about when we were too busy helping that UPS driver out of his brown uniform and you should have seen what he had underneath it! He was gorgeous and totally versatile too—hung like a horse and with a great ass! You've got to seize the moment. Sometimes you think too much, Tim."

Jake grabbed a stack of menus and seated the customers who were coming in the front door, a straight couple who lived in the neighborhood and had patronized the restaurant for years. They liked to get in early before it got too busy. They sometimes felt out of place when they were surrounded by the gay crowd.

Tim stood in the center of the dining room with his empty cocktail tray balanced on three fingers and then two and then he gave it a twirl, the old plate-spinning trick from some ancient circus blood in his veins. He used to have a recurring dream that his psychic grandmother was descended from carnival people. Tim spun the tray and thought to himself, "Jake and Ron and the UPS man...seize the moment...what's to discuss..."

Tim tried to imagine if he would ever be that free with Nick. When Tim was single he was always raring to go with anyone who turned him on at a moment's notice. But he couldn't picture himself doing something as spontaneous as Jake and Ron did without a lengthy discussion with Nick about it first. Maybe Jake had the right idea, though. Maybe it was just that simple.

Chapter 19

Buck stared at the phone while it rang four times. Then the answering machine picked up and he barked at Nick's familiar voice.

"Hey, Snowman, I thought I might catch you at home, but no such luck, so I'll have to leave a message. We're still in New York where it's nearly 10pm, so I guess that makes it almost seven in San Francisco. I can hardly keep track of the time zones anymore with all this traveling. The stem on my watch is about to fall out from resetting it so many times. I tried your cell, but you're probably at work or by the time you get this you'll have been out spending your tips in a bar someplace. I'm just calling to check in. Tomorrow there's an appearance at Barnes & Noble here and then on Tuesday we go to Cleveland. Then it's Detroit and guess what! We'll be in Minneapolis on the weekend. Is there anyone or any place you think I should see in your old stomping grounds? Let me know. I'm off to bed, so don't call me back tonight unless it's to talk dirty. Just kidding. Love you babe."

Tim decided against going South of Market when he got off work that night. The last rush of customers at the restaurant had been so intense that he even forgot about his sexual frustration…for a while. He stepped out onto the sidewalk and headed north on Castro Street slipping his arms into the sleeves of his leather jacket. He should have brought along a sweatshirt too because the fog was in thick. Home was just around the corner, a couple of blocks if you counted the downhill part and back up again, only about two blocks as the crow flies.

It occurred to him as he passed the Sausage Factory that maybe it wasn't really sex that he craved. He hadn't even thought about it since that hot guy in the tight gray shirt on table #5 had winked at him and brushed the back of his hand across Tim's crotch as he returned the dessert menu. Too bad he was with his husband. Tim gathered from the bits and pieces of conversation he overheard that they wouldn't have sex with each other tonight anyway. You didn't have to be psychic to feel the tension between them. The one in the gray shirt was a big flirt and the other one was really clingy, obsessing about every imagined slight, accusing him of fooling around when he wasn't but missing all the obvious signs when he was. Tim almost felt sorry for the guy because he reminded him of himself at his most neurotic. Maybe some of Tim's psychic ability did manifest itself when he was awake. He could foresee the jealous one moving back to Houston within a month.

No line at the ATMs outside the BofA was rare for a Saturday night. Tim reached into his jacket pocket and headed for the farthest one, lit the joint, took a deep hit and then matted it out against the stainless steel. He held the smoke as long as he could, like an abalone diver underwater going down for the biggest catch of the season.

"Kgh-ach-ckuh" he choked for breath. Nick's client's Humboldt County weed had done the job in one toke. Tim forgot all about the lovers and their quarrel. Any psychic tenderness he'd felt a moment ago was quickly healed over. Trouble was, now he felt the old familiar stirring in his groin again. Oh well...it was a constant. This was no better and no worse than usual. It wasn't just because of the grass. His realization earlier that he hadn't been horny was partly to

blame, too. *Don't think about a purple rhinoceros*! Trying not to
think about something was the same as thinking about it. Like
flying dreams, you just have to learn to let go.

Tim was cold now, too. The fog was pouring in and his
thin leather jacket wasn't much help He'd told Jake he might
meet him at the Edge, but the stoplight was red and if he
turned right instead of left he'd be that much closer to home
and central heating. The Mix was tempting, but the Midnight
Sun was even closer and on this side of the street. He could
have a drink and relax and try to turn off his conscious
thoughts with some mindless music videos and comedy clips.

Tim found an open bar stool and ordered a drink from
his favorite bartender, handsome Dan. He was always so
friendly that Tim thought it might be fun to spend some naked
time with him, but not if it meant waiting until after the bars
closed. Besides, Dan was probably already married and good
bartenders were always friendly. Tim stared up at the video
screen against the back wall. Shirtless men were dancing
around a woman in leather...or was it black Spandex? Tim
couldn't tell. The men on the video were far more impressive
than the music. The bar had a good crowd and Tim looked
around to see if he knew anyone. No. Then he looked harder
to see if there might be anyone he would *like* to know. He
didn't think so. He should have made plans to go South of
Market after work on a Saturday night or at least to the Edge,
but he had to work brunch in the morning. Maybe he'd finish
this drink and head over to Moby's.

Someone caught Tim's eye. The guy wasn't exactly
cruising him. He was looking at him with recognition, not
lust. He looked sort of familiar to Tim, but he couldn't place
him, even after he came over and said Hello. "Your name is
Tim, right? Hey, bartender...get my friend here another..."

"Yeah, I'm Tim...sorry..."

"What are you having?"

"Dan knows what I drink." They shook hands. "But I
don't know you, I don't think. Should I?"

"The name's Richard." He leaned his head back, struck a pose and did a slow turn all the way around. "Hello, Castro Street! It's so nice to be back here at Arts. You're always our favorite audience this side of Poughkeepsie. I'm Roxeanne and this is my partner in crime, the ever so lovely Rochelle."

"Oh my *God*! I never would have recognized you out of drag if you hadn't spoken to me first."

"That's what everyone says."

"It's really an amazing transformation!"

"Thanks."

"Where's the other one?"

"Back at the room," he glanced at his watch, "probably watching Perry Mason re-runs right about now if the cable is working again."

Tim was curious. "Are you two a couple off-stage too?"

"Oh, yes…"

"What's his real name?"

"Gary."

"I still can't believe it. How did you two ever…?"

"We met in New York," the one who played Roxeanne said. Tim thought he'd said he was Roxeanne. He could have been Rochelle. They looked so much alike in drag. Tim was sure that he said his name was Richard and the other one was Gary. Now at least Tim wasn't focused on sex anymore, but he was definitely stoned.

"I was trying to break into doing stand-up, but I wasn't out of the closet yet, so I wasn't all that funny. Gary was a singer, dancer, chorus boy, trying to work at anything that paid…TV commercials, modeling… We met in a bar called Ty's. Do you know New York?"

"Nope, never been…"

"It's on Christopher Street in the West Village…been there forever. Anyway, he stepped on my foot and we fell in love. Imagine that!"

"But how did you come up with the personas?"

"It was all Gary's idea. I'd never done drag in my life. He barely had either. He was a biker, belonged to a club and had all the leather and everything. He invited me along on a run with his bike club and one night they put on a show out in the middle of nowhere. We'd just started seeing each other and he somehow managed to volunteer the two of us to be in the show. We must have been on drugs. He just dragged me along on the run and then onto the stage. Pardon my choice of words…dragged…drag…get it?"

"So he was the…butch one?" Tim asked, not that it was any of his business, but he was on his second drink by now, on top of the grass.

"You mean the *top*? Richard asked. "Isn't it funny the conclusions people always want to jump to? You don't really want to know what all we're into, Tim. Trust me."

"Kinky, huh?" Tim returned Richard's sly smile. He really *did* want to know, but decided not to push it. "So how did the one-night show on the bike run turn into…?"

"It was Gary's idea all along that we work up some kind of act together. When we hit upon the drag thing it just clicked. We got gigs. We traveled. We found an audience. We made a little money. We're still not exactly your typical drag queens, whatever that means. It's made our relationship stronger than ever. Who knew that two guys could meet and fall in love and become a sensation as showgirls?"

"How long have you two been together?"

"Nearly eight years."

"Things change, I bet."

"They only get better, if you're lucky and if you're smart enough to work things through. Our relationship offstage has benefited from our act in one big way. You learn things, you know? Whenever the act starts getting hum-drum, we know we have to come up with something new, just like in real life, find a new gimmick, a new position, a new way of keeping it fresh and exciting."

"That's good to hear."

"Do you have a partner?"

"Yeah, sort of…well, I mean…. He's out of town for a while and we don't exactly live together full-time, but he's the only guy I've been serious about in…I can't even remember… ages." As Tim spoke he could picture Nick's face hovering over him on the kitchen floor that last night they were together before he left town. They were both naked except for their socks and dinner was nearly ready. Nick had come into the kitchen with his fly wide open, a drink in one hand and a hard-on in the other.

"How long?"

"Oh, it's been a couple of years since I met Nick, I guess. Where do you count back to, the first time you met or…?"

"That's an old joke. Do you celebrate the anniversary of the first time you met or the first time you had sex or when you moved in together? 'Yes, Mother, that's right.' I've always thought it was more applicable to lesbians, though. Guys don't usually move in together for a long time."

"You got that right," Tim said, "but lesbians have plenty of their own jokes."

"Right, you're a waiter…at least canoes tip, right?"

"Did things change in your relationship when you started doing an act together?"

"What do you want to know? Did we start having sex in garter belts and stilettos, is that what you mean? 'Blowjobs with lipstick, five cents extra!'" Richard struck another campy pose and it turned Tim off, especially now that he was out of drag.

"No, I'm serious! Did it change your sex life?"

"You are such an inquisitive boy! Shame on you!"

Tim even surprised himself with the things that came out of his mouth sometimes. "I'm sorry. I hope I'm not being rude. I'll shut up. I was just curious."

"That's okay, Tim. I like you. No, the drag didn't change things in bed, if that's what you mean. It's a costume, a character you put on. We don't live our lives in it. When it comes off it stays in the dressing room."

"I see."

"But it made things even better between us in another way. We got to put our creativity into a joint project, our act!

The energy was wild! When we're onstage together, I don't see Gary the way the audience does. I see the man I fell for and even though we're both turned on by our work and by the audience and even though we're both in these outrageous clothes, there are times I love him so much I just want to grab him and kiss him right then and there in front of everyone."

"That's great." Tim grinned. "You ought to try it sometime."

"Are you kidding? He'd kill me if I messed up our makeup and besides...I already told you...the drag stays in the dressing room. At home it's Richard and Gary, the butch leather men—Yee-hah!" He struck a pose with both hands on his hips. He was wearing designer jeans with intentionally faded legs, the kind people paid top dollar for because they looked used. It struck Tim as silly when you could find them that way at the thrift stores all up and down Mission Street. Richard also wore a white turtleneck sweater and a small gold hoop in one ear. No matter what Richard said about his life with Gary, Tim thought they must have been the nelliest leather men on the bike run.

Chapter 20

The next morning Tim realized that he hadn't looked at a newspaper in days. Sometimes the headlines depressed him so much he didn't even read Leah Garchik's column on the back page of the Datebook section. She covered everything from the opening night of the opera to the latest gossip in the Castro. The last three weekday Chronicles still lay on the stairs unopened. He spread them out on the kitchen table now along with the newest Bay Times and the B.A.R. from Thursday. It ought to be in at least one of them. He couldn't believe the armed robbery of a gay bar in the Castro—even if it *was* a tiny bit off the beaten path— wouldn't rate an article. There was nothing in the Garchik columns about it, but there were some funny comments about the new pope from a guy named Joe Mac.

Tim leafed through the *B.A.R.* from front to back twice, but he couldn't find it, not even in the crime column, which he came back to and read carefully:

100 block of Eureka / 2:15am Sunday / Resident returned home after night out drinking with friends in local bars discovered front door open and lights on. Hearing no sounds he proceeded inside to discover hidden wall safe emptied of jewelry and valuables. No sign of forced entry. Former domestic partner suspected due to victim's recognition of handwriting on Thank You note left on kitchen table. No charges filed.

MUNI underground / Friday morning / Elderly woman reported purse snatching on L Taraval inbound from Castro Station. No witnesses and the victim felt nothing. She reported the incident when she disembarked at Powell. Upon further investigation, purse was discovered in MUNI Lost & Found with all contents intact. It had been left atop turnstile at Castro Station.

Tim couldn't believe they wasted ink on this stuff and didn't mention the armed robbery at Last Call. He was sure that all the papers had covered the earlier hold-ups at Cliffs and Arts and Rossi's Deli. Or had they? Now he couldn't swear to it, but he figured they must have. The Bay Times didn't cover it either. Tim guessed someone had to either get killed or win another title to be featured in the gay rags these days. How many tiaras and leather vests and sashes did any queen really need?

The Chronicle might have it in local news in the Bay Area section. Tim started with the newest ones, but stopped. It wouldn't be in there, unless there was a follow-up. He needed to go back a little further. He spotted the stack of newspapers on the kitchen counter inside the back door. He'd meant to carry them down to the blue recycling bin at the foot of the stairs but he was in luck; he'd been lazy. What date would it be? Since Nick had left on his trip Tim paid little attention to what day of the week it was unless he was working or even cared when the weekends came. He was about to go and get a calendar and figure out the date of that day he'd gone to Last Call to meet CASTROSTUD, but here it was:

Another armed Castro robbery by stocking-covered bandits:
As the gentlemen clientele of this quaint Castro cocktail lounge settled into their after-work martinis and manhattans, the calm of the intimate hideaway was shaken when the Last Call at 3988 18th Street witnessed two armed men burst into the quiet

neighborhood bar with guns drawn and demand the take from the till.

In the ensuing scuffle, a customer took a shot to the shoulder and is still listed in satisfactory condition at CPMC Davies Medical Center on Castro Street.

"Took a shot?" Tim yelled out loud and Buck came running to see if someone else was there to sniff. No, it was just his city daddy. His country daddy had been gone a long time. Buck missed the country, especially the smells of the beach along the Sonoma Coast.

"How do you like that, Buck? They make it sound as if one of the robbers shot my potential date! They don't mention George Tavares at all! Tim was tempted to put in a call to every newspaper in the city and start shouting at anyone who answered. On second thought, he'd probably be stuck in voice mail limbo long past the time it took for him to calm down.

George Tavares wasn't Tim's concern, anyway. What he'd been looking for was some word about CASTROSTUD. He wasn't even sure why. A sense of guilt, maybe? The poor guy didn't even get to enjoy his drink before he hit the floor. And he wouldn't have been in that bar in the first place if it wasn't for Tim inviting him to meet there.

Neither would George Tavares, come to think of it. If Tim had taken George back to his place when George asked him to, they both would have been gone before any of it happened. CASTROSTUD would have finished his beer, waited around for Tim a while, cursed a little and chalked it up to another flake haunting the Internet sex sites. If he was like most guys, it wouldn't be the first time he made plans that fell through. Who knows, if things had turned out differently, CASTROSTUD might have stuck around for another drink at Last Call and ended up with someone else that afternoon after the stick-up. There'd been a decent crowd there with some good-looking guys.

How could Tim have known any of that, though? What kind of psychic ability did he have to show for himself? It was more a curse than a blessing, coming only in his dreams and even then, only rarely. Most of his dreams he'd gladly trade for a good night's sleep.

"Hi. Umm, I'm calling to find out about that guy who got shot? You know...the victim in that robbery on 18th Street at the bar called Last Call."

"Do you have a name, sir?"

"No, I don't know the patient's name."

"Then I'm sorry I can't help you."

Tim hung up the phone and wondered how else he could reach the guy he knew only as CASTROSTUD. Maybe flowers would do it. If he brought flowers in person to a patient in the hospital they could hardly turn him away. He might be just the delivery man. What reason could they have not to let him in?

Tim looked through his closet for something that said *Florist* or better yet *Floral Delivery.* He wouldn't have to pretend to know anything but how to drive a van. He wanted to look as inconspicuous as possible, maybe white khaki trousers and a white polo shirt. If only Nick were in town he'd be able to answer most of the questions that were spinning through Tim's head. If Nick were in town, Tim wouldn't have to buy flowers retail, either. But if Nick were here, Tim probably wouldn't have had the time or the inclination to consider tracking down his ill-fated sex date.

He found an Army jump-suit he'd worn to the Folsom Street Fair one year. It was olive drab with a dozen zippers that provided easy access to all his erogenous zones when it came to that time of day at the fair. A couple of joints and a few beers, plus the sexual energy of so many people outdoors on a sunny day always loosened him up enough to really want to play. Tim held the jumpsuit to his nose. It was a little musty from being folded up on the closet shelf for so long, but it wasn't stained. And it sure did look like something a person might wear while delivering bouquets to party-givers, mourners, the super-rich or the ailing.

He could even take Nick's nursery truck out of the driveway. It would be a good idea to start it up anyway. No one was apt to notice what he was driving when he arrived at the hospital, but the truck with the nursery decals on the doors might help Tim get into character.

Tim stopped on 18th Street for some flowers and now he carried them in front of his face as if it mattered whether anyone recognized him. "Excuse me," he said to the receptionist behind the desk at Davies Hospital, "I can't seem to find the order slip for these and I hate to open the card. They're for the guy that got shot the other day…"

"Third floor," the woman behind the counter said. If any more information would have been forthcoming, she was cut off by a ringing telephone.

Tim was alone on the elevator. When he stepped off onto the third floor it all came back to him, that winter he'd been driving Nick's truck when the brakes failed and he crashed into a redwood tree. They'd finally moved him here to be closer to home when he was well enough to leave the hospital in Sebastopol, but not well enough to be released.

Beep, beep, hummm…beep, beep, hummm. The sounds must be the same in every hospital. Tim wondered if the smells were all the same too. It was almost a *lack of* smell he first noticed when he held the flowers at arms' length away…then medical solutions, coffee and chemicals, cleaning supplies inside the open door of a nearby janitors' closet.

Alone on the elevator, Tim realized that the last time he'd been in this particular hospital was to visit his nasty "cousin" Dianne, who turned out to have been adopted as an infant by his Aunt Ruth and was therefore no blood relation to Tim at all, much to his relief. Tim would never disparage the bonds that formed between some adopted children and their parents—he and Nick might want to adopt a kid someday (if they could ever get their rules ironed out)—but Tim certainly felt no familial bond with Dianne. She was a bitch!

As he stepped off the elevator, Tim had a flash of sensory overload. Maybe it was the smell that triggered it, a whiff of cleaning solution, a chemical disinfectant combined with the human bodily smells of stale sweat and urine. These all combined with the sweetness of the flowers in his hands to make him dizzy. Tim stood still in the hallway, closed his eyes and took a deep breath. He felt transported back in time to a foreign battlefield, a huge canvas tent under the hot sun. Tim couldn't remember having watched any old broadcasts of *MASH* on television lately. He heard helicopter blades slapping at the stagnant air, the deafening roar of the motor, shouts of men, cries of pain and someone barking orders. Was this Vietnam? Iraq? Afghanistan? Tim had never been anywhere near any war. It didn't make sense.

He opened his eyes and it was quiet now. The smell had dissipated too. A male nurse around his age appeared, dressed in green scrubs with 5-o'clock shadow, cute...touched Tim's shoulder, "Are you alright? Do you need some help?"

Tim blinked a couple of times and looked into the young man's deep green eyes. "I'm looking for CASTROSsss..." he started to say.

"Castro Street is that way," the nurse pointed to the west.

"No. I meant...I'm here to deliver these flowers for a patient, but I lost the sales slip and there was no name on the outside of the card. Do you know the guy who took a bullet in the shoulder?"

"The third room down on your right."

"Thanks."

Tim stood in the doorway a minute. The patient appeared to be sleeping. That was okay. He was hot, though, even unshaven in a hospital gown with an oxygen tube running under his nose. Tim looked at the name on the door—GREG HOLT—and took another step inside to set the flowers down. He would leave them there, but he'd lied about a card. There was none. He looked around for a pen and something to write a note on...

"Hello?" a groggy voice said.

"Oh hi. Sorry, I didn't mean to wake you."

"Do I know you?"

"I'm Tim...SFTimS...from online...dudesurfer? You're CASTROSTUD, right? I see your real name is Greg, huh? We met online and then we were supposed to hook up in person at Last Call and then...this happened. I thought the least I could do was come by and see how you're doing. I'm really sorry about everything."

"Tim?"

"Yeah, Tim Snow. That's what the extra S stands for... Snow. That's my last name. I'm not into powder." Tim was more nervous than he'd expected to be. Greg Holt looked back at the television set over the bed where a baseball game held his attention. "How are the Giants doing? Ahead?"

"Nah, they're behind by three runs, four to one. They won't even make the playoffs this year if they don't start shaping up pretty soon."

"Well, they've had two Superbowl wins in the last three years. Whadya want?"

"Superbowl is football. What are you talking about?"

"Sorry. I don't follow sports that much."

"Obviously. They had two World Series wins in the last three years. The World Series is baseball."

"I knew that. Well, it looks like you're really into the game. Sorry to interrupt. I should probably go. I just wanted to say hi and...you know."

"Yeah, well...thanks for the flowers."

Tim started to leave. He was outside the door when he heard, "Hey, come back here. This game sucks, anyway."

"Uh...okay," Tim stepped inside the doorway but kept his distance.

"It wasn't your fault I got shot, you know."

"I know, but you wouldn't even have been in there if..."

"Come over here where I can get a better look at you." Tim stepped up beside the hospital bed again and Greg pressed the button to raise the bed and sit himself up a little.

"You're kinda cute. Do you hang out at that bar, the Last Call? Maybe I should start going there more often."

"No, not really...too close to home, I guess. I walk by there all the time, though."

"Me too."

"So how long are you stuck in here?"

"I should have gone home by now, but I got an infection so they had to put me on these antibiotics." He pointed to the IV drip. "At least a couple more days, they tell me."

"Hospitals are full of staph."

"I guess. My fever shot way up. At least the IV is on the same side as the bullet hole so I get to have one hand free to flip the channels and stuff."

"That's good," Tim grinned and their eyes locked for a moment, both thinking the same thing, or so Tim imagined. He had a name now, besides CASTROSTUD—Greg—and he really was hot, even with all the tubes. His hospital gown was off the left shoulder where the bandages stuck to the flesh. That arm was in a sling.

"You have to keep your arm in that all the time?" Tim's eyes moved across the fine black hairs peeking out from Greg's left armpit and the even pattern of hair across his chest. Greg moved his right arm to scratch his forearm above the IV and one fleshy brown nipple worked its way out into the sunlight. Tim let out his breath and Greg squinted. "Do you want me to close that curtain for you?"

"A little, yeah...thanks. The sun is awfully bright."

Tim rounded the foot of the bed and on his way back he brushed the bare sole of Greg's foot sticking out from under the sheets. "Sorry."

"That's okay."

Tim took the foot in his fingers and gave it a squeeze. "I'm glad you're not really mad at me."

"Course not."

"Well, maybe I'll see you on Dudesurfer after you get out of here. I'd better be going, unless you can think of anything else you need."

"Well, there *is* one thing…"

"Yeah?"

"Like I said, I can move my right hand just fine," Greg flexed and wiggled his fingers to prove it, then pulled the sheet down a ways and pushed his hospital gown upward, "but I'm left-handed." Tim had watched a porn film just the other night that took place in a hospital. He couldn't remember the name of it now, as hard as he tried, but he thought it had "male nurse" in the title.

That didn't matter at all now. Tim's eyes were glued to the monument under the pale blue fabric as the sheet slid down to unveil a human obelisk, fleshy and hard and uncut. Tim pulled the curtain closed behind him and leaned forward to perform a mission of mercy that made him feel just like a modern-day Florence Nightingale.

Chapter 21

As soon as Tim pulled a swimsuit out of the dresser drawer, Buck started yapping and jumping up and down. This must mean they were heading to the country where his other daddy lived, the one who had been gone for so long. It was about time. Dolores Park was okay for the city, but Buck was tired of being cooped up without a long run on the beach or under the redwoods in the rich country smells.

"Don't get so excited, Buck." Tim reached down and scratched between the dog's ears. "We're not going far and we won't be gone long. Aunt Ruth wants to see you today."

Buck was smart enough to know that "Aunt Ruth" meant lots of attention and maybe some good treats, too, as long as that stupid cat stayed out of his way. Bartholomew was a thorn in Buck's side, but he was still excited to be going someplace…anyplace.

"And stop that scratching! You're getting dog hair all over the place. One of these days I'm going to teach you how to run the vacuum cleaner. Then I can leave you home to clean house while I go to work. Or out for cocktails. Or cruising the Castro. Or downtown shopping… Buck, how rude!" Tim could have sworn that his dog had just looked up at him and yawned.

In Hillsborough, Tim and Buck played fetch with a Frisbee in and out of the pool while Ruth put the finishing touches on lunch. "What are you making? Do you need any help? I'm starving!"

"Not a bit of help, dear. It's all coming along nicely. You just enjoy yourself." She emerged from the kitchen with a tray that she carried across the patio. It held two glasses, a pitcher of something green and two bowls, the contents of which Tim could only guess. They were too big for lime and salt. Tim had a craving for a margarita, but whatever was in the pitcher was the wrong shade of green. He hoped his Aunt Ruth hadn't stopped serving alcohol now that she'd retired from bartending.

"What's for lunch?"

"Hold your horses. You'll find out soon enough. It's so nice to see Buck enjoying himself. Sam and I have talked about getting a dog, you know, with all this room for one to roam around, but Bartholomew would probably hate us for it. He always hides when Buck's around and besides; Sam is out of town so much. Cats are more independent and I don't guess I'd want to be tied down with a dog, either."

"It's like having a child...not that I'd know from experience, thank God."

"Come and dry off now and sit at the table. Everything's almost ready."

Tim climbed out of the pool and dried himself with a huge white towel. Buck knew what that meant; playtime was over. He climbed out of the water too, shook himself and ran off to explore the grounds, but he was back in no time with a tennis ball in his mouth. He looked up at Tim pleadingly as if a new piece of sporting equipment might convince him to continue the game.

"Been to the tennis courts already, eh Buck? Who was out practicing today, Andy Roddick?" Tim picked up the ball and tossed it to the far end of the patio where it bounced back and landed in the pool, so the game was on again. "If you see James Blake or Roger Federer, tell them I wanna see *their* balls."

"Tim! Don't talk dirty to your dog!"

"Buck has heard it all in the Castro. Besides, I was only talking about tennis balls. You're the one with the dirty mind." Tim pulled his T-shirt over his head and Buck was back with the wet tennis ball right away. This time Tim threw it over the fence and Buck was out the gate in a flash. "Go and fetch me the balls of Billie Jean King!"

"Come to the table before things get cold." Ruth was already seated and filling their glasses from the pitcher.

"Mmmm…what is that?"

"Lime Kool-Aid, your favorite."

"You're joking…please, be joking."

"Midori daiquiris, but I remember when you used to love lime Kool-Aid."

"I don't. Cherry, maybe, but not lime."

"You were just a little boy. I thought it would be fun to remember your favorite summer lunch when you were little, when you used to come and visit your Uncle Dan and me, years before you came to live with us full time."

"Grilled cheese sandwiches?" Tim did remember that much.

"Yes, but I made them on sourdough baguettes with a combination of sharp cheddar and gruyère. I was trying to copy the entire lunch, but sort of California-style. Instead of plain old macaroni salad, I did a lovely pasta primavera."

"And tomato soup?"

"Yes. You must remember Delia, Sam's old cook?"

"And the mother of his only son…how *is* Adam?" Tim remembered trying to seduce Sam's gorgeous fashion model son before he discovered that Adam was straight.

"Just fine. Adam is fine. Alex is fine, too and their little baby is darling. After lunch, remind me to show you the pictures they sent from Chicago. But don't change the subject. I ran across Delia's gazpacho recipe. I'm sure you and Nick had it here one time before Sam and I were even married. I followed the directions to the letter, but it wasn't quite the same. I'll ask Sam to give it a taste when he gets back tonight. I'll bet he can tell me what it's missing."

"Where is Sam?"

"Phoenix...on business. It's just the two of us here unless the gardener comes back to finish mowing in the orchard. I asked him not to run that noisy mower while we were having our visit and he said he had some chores to do anyway, a trip to the hardware store and then home for his own lunch, I would imagine."

"Maybe I should taste the gazpacho, Aunt Ruth. I might be able to tell you what it needs."

"Maybe later. Sit still. I made you the real thing, instead." She lifted the lid off a steaming tureen.

"Campbell's?"

"Right out of the can! I'll bet you haven't had this in years."

"I'll bet you're right." Tim grinned at his dear Aunt Ruth, his closest family member, the *only* relation that mattered to him anymore. His mother was dead and his father might as well be. The soup was saltier than Tim remembered, but it was delicious when he dipped in the crusty bread and caught the cheese on his tongue as it dripped all golden and gooey and drenched in Campbell's tomato soup right out of the can and steaming hot.

After lunch they took their drinks and the rest of the pitcher to a pair of chaise lounges where Tim had left his towel. They were still discussing Internet dating as Tim had been trying to tell his aunt about selected bits of his recent adventures. "Do you mean that people allow total strangers into their homes to perform sex acts? Isn't that dangerous?"

"Buck! No! We have to wait at least thirty minutes after we eat before we can go back in the water." Tim took the ball away and put it inside the Frisbee on the table outside of Buck's reach. "Does that old rule apply to dogs, too?"

"I don't think so, Tim. Let him be. If he gets a cramp in one of his paws we can go in and save him. He sure has grown, hasn't he? Remember when you first brought him here we could have fished him out with that long-handled tool the pool man uses to skim out the leaves and things."

"I hope he doesn't get any bigger."

"But you changed the subject again. Tell me more about this on-line dating business. I thought gay men had become much less promiscuous since AIDS came along."

"Many have. I have, but that has more to do with meeting Nick than it has to do with AIDS."

"It must be difficult having him be away for so long, but I'm sure it's good for you, dear. Look at it this way—it builds character."

"Easy for you to say...how long has Sam been in Phoenix?"

"Since yesterday."

"And when does he get back?"

"Tonight."

"I rest my case."

"Seriously, Tim, this Internet business sounds frightening..."

"Haven't you ever been tempted by another man... come on, tell me the truth?"

"There you go changing the subject again."

"Weren't you?"

"When? With Sam?"

"With Sam, with Uncle Dan, with your kindergarten sweetheart, who cares? No matter how much you love someone, you can also have physical needs."

"I never went to kindergarten."

"Now who's changing the subject?"

"I don't know. I guess I've always been a one-man woman. One at a time, anyway."

"Sing it to me, Judy Garland...*the road gets rougher, stormier and tougher...with hope you'll burn up, tomorrow he may turn up...*"

"What's that?"

"A one-man woman looking for the man that got a-way..." Judy Garland at Carnegie Hall! Man-oh-man, Aunt Ruth, hasn't your time in the Castro taught you anything about gay camp? Artie even does that song in his act, sometimes."

"It's vaguely familiar, I guess. Artie has a much better singing voice than you do, I'm afraid."

"Thanks. So you've always been monogamous... practicing serial monogamy, at any rate. What about your mother? Was my psychic grandmother a one-man woman?"

"I don't know, Tim. I never thought about it, to tell you the truth. Your grandmother was the most free-spirited creature that I ever knew. And yet, I think she was so in love with Dad that there wasn't anyone who could turn her head. Lars Bergman was a striking man, you know."

"I know. He was hot. I've seen the pictures."

Tim lay back on the chaise lounge and closed his eyes. He might have fallen sound asleep but for his Aunt Ruth calling from the doorway of the kitchen. "Should I make us another pitcher of daiquiris, Tim?"

"Huh? Oh, no. I've gotta drive. Not for me. I must have dozed off, sorry."

"That's all right, dear. I just tidied up in the kitchen a little. It looks like Buck is napping, too." The dog was lying in Tim's shade on one corner of his towel that had slipped off the chair. "I was just thinking about what you said earlier. You've never actually used one of those web-sites, have you Tim?" She had a way of steering the conversation back to the most worrisome topics she could think of—always!

She was so good at disarming him with her questions that Tim knew he had to be careful. Soon he'd be telling her about Britlad, the supposedly eighteen-year-old kid from London. Or the twenty-four-year-old amputee Iraq war veteran who was looking for another young man to warm his stumps. Tim gave her his best look of wild-eyed exasperation, threw his hands in the air and shook his head.

"What?" She yelled in self-defense.

"Why do you ask me questions like that?"

"What do you mean why? Because I love you and I care about you and I'm concerned about you getting into trouble. Why shouldn't I ask you questions?"

"Oh, you can ask all the questions you want, I guess. I'm only trying to warn you that you need to be prepared for answers that you might not like if you're gonna ask questions like those."

"Why would you need to use one of those web-site thingies, anyway? Nick is only gone for a few weeks."

"I signed up for it years ago, long before I met Nick. Before he left town, I hadn't logged onto it in so long I was surprised my profile was still up there. And I hadn't aged a bit, fancy that! I hate it when guys try to pretend they still look like they did in college—full head of hair, not a wrinkle on their faces and one of those bushy moustaches that went out with disco and bell-bottom pants, whenever that was."

"But you're a good-looking guy? Why couldn't you meet new friends the normal way?"

Tim laughed out loud at that remark. "Normal! What a choice word! And the normal way would be…what, I wonder? Drunk on a barstool or maybe at the baths in Berkeley or San Jose, out cruising the windmills or Buena Vista Park? How about the t-rooms at Macy's? I've never checked them out personally, but I've heard rumors. The YMCA used to have quite a reputation, too."

"What about meeting people at work or at the gym or at the supermarket? I still can't see why you need to meet anyone new when Nick will be back home in another week or so."

"That's exactly why I don't want to meet someone in any of those places you deem normal. If I met someone at the gym I'd have to see him again, sooner or later. Someone at work would be even worse…what if they started coming in regularly and asking for me? People would talk. The Internet is more anonymous…or at least it can be. Some people are looking for husbands, but that's not the site I'm talking about. Besides, on the Internet sites you can be very specific. Say you're only interested in blond guys who are Capricorns with removable dentures or you're looking for double-jointed red-headed dwarfs with green eyes. You might have to buy a plane ticket to hook up with them in person, but eventually you'll find exactly what you're looking for, whether it's the man of your dreams or Mr. Right Now."

"I still don't get it, but maybe I never will. How's Artie?"

Tim almost called her attention to the fact that she was the one who'd changed the subject this time, but he was glad to get away from talk about sex and cruising and dating. "Artie is fine, I guess. We don't see him as often as we used to. This weekend he's performing in Denver, I think he said. Or was it Portland? When he's in town he really packs them in. One Sunday he actually had to do three shows at brunch— three different seatings—all of them sold out."

"And how is it when Artie and Arturo are out of town to have Scott in charge as manager?"

"Just the same as before…it's not like he has to do anything special but count the banks. We're all big boys, you know. We can keep the place running fine without anyone cracking the whip over us."

"I'm sure you can. How's Phil?"

"I don't know…okay, I guess. He travels with Artie, at least some of the time, so he's not around that much, either. Buck! Stop that! What's he gotten into now? Buck! You get over here *right this minute!*

"It's just an old piece of chamois. Sam was probably using it to polish one of the cars. Let Buck keep it. He probably thinks it's a leather chew-toy."

"My dog, the leather queen…or chamois queen, I should say. We'd better get going, anyway, Aunt Ruth. Thanks for lunch!"

"It was my pleasure to have you and Buck both here. Next time when Nick is home we'll have you all out for a day and I'll make something fancy. Maybe we can plan a time when Sam is free and we'll play doubles at tennis."

"Sounds good...call me."

"You call me as soon as Nick gets home."

"No telephone will be plugged in or turned on for at least 24-hours after Nick gets home, trust me!"

"Call me the next day, then."

"Maybe on hour twenty-five, if you're lucky..."

Chapter 22

"*G*et you and keep you in my arms evermore… leave all your lovers weeping on the faraway shore…*" The door clicked shut and Artie was alone in front of the mirror, singing softly to himself. This dressing room in Denver was bigger than most, not that he cared very much anymore. Artie prided himself on being a professional. He could pull it together anywhere, in a phone booth if he had to. Did phone booths still exist? Or in the back seat of a car, preferably a limousine. He'd actually had to do that a couple of times.

Arturo was off on an errand, looking for a tube of cherry frost lipstick. Artie used to wear a color called rose frost that was about three shades darker, but that was years ago. He wore darker wigs then, too. This one on the Styrofoam head on the table was almost blonde. Artie had discovered that as he got older he had to soften his colors in order not to look cheap.

"*Out on the briny with the moon big and shiny…melting your heart of coal…*" No! That wasn't right. Or was it? "*I'd love to get you on a slow boat to China…all to myself alone…*" It had to rhyme with alone, so it couldn't be coal! Artie had the lyrics written down on a sheet of paper, but he tried not to look. He ought to have them memorized by now. He was doing the song tonight.

"*Melting your heart of **stone**…*" That was it!

Artie had lost enough weight—and *kept* it off too this time, thank you very much—to fit into all his old gowns from the Finocchio's years. He only wore a few of them, though. Sequins seemed almost garish at Sunday brunch. What worked in a smoky nightclub with a follow-spot and pink gels on the lights was just too-too while his audience was trying to eat eggs. Artie never wanted to ruin their appetites by appearing in broad daylight looking like some old hooker the cat dragged in.

Tonight he was wearing a little glitz, though. "Give 'em glitz and glamour," that was Artie's motto in the old days… *but don't forget to act your age.* He'd tacked that last part on as he got older. When he first started out in show-business, Artie never thought about getting older, never dreamed he'd get to be this age and still be performing. Back in those days every night felt like opening night and Artie Glamóur was the belle of the ball. Tonight's appearance was for another benefit— this time it was for AIDS services here in Denver, Colorado. Tomorrow night he would be in Portland for a fundraiser for another good cause. It seemed like he did more benefits than paying gigs lately, but Arturo said they were worth it for all the good publicity and exposure. "The spike in album sales pays for every minute of your time, Artie," he could hear him saying. As if Arturo could walk in high heels and carry a tune!

"*A twist in the rudder and a rip in the sails…driftin' and dreamin'…honey throw the compass over the rail…*" Artie reached for a fresh tube of lipstick. Cherry frost. He'd only sent Arturo out to look for some in order to have some time alone to think. He hadn't done "Slow boat to China" in years. It wasn't on his album, but if Artie grew comfortable with it he'd make sure it went on the next one.

The nearest Walgreens was just around the corner from their hotel, but Artie had bought their last three tubes of cherry frost last night after dinner while Arturo was browsing through the magazine section. The girl behind the counter said they'd be getting more in on Wednesday and they'd be happy to let Artie know just the minute the shipment came in. "That's quite all right, dear," he told her. "I'll be out of town long before then, but thanks."

Artie was wearing blue sequins tonight. It was one of the first new gowns he'd ordered to be custom-made by Pat Montclaire back when Artie first started making money at performing. Blue sequins trimmed in silver bugle beads dazzled them every time when he stepped out into the light. He'd been torn between the blue sequins and a white taffeta number trimmed in red marabou feathers. He was thin enough for the white dress now, but taffeta didn't travel as well and there was no way that sequins and bugle beads were ever going to wrinkle.

Nope, this wasn't something he could ever wear at Sunday brunch at Arts. Sequins at brunch-time were like pearls before five. Or was it diamonds before dark? Artie couldn't remember all those old sayings. He knew not to wear white shoes after Labor Day, but how could he remember everything? He was trying to brush up on his lyrics. He couldn't be expected to remember all of Amy Vanderbilt's dos and don'ts at the same time, could he? Nowadays, of course, they had Miss Manners instead.

"Out on the ocean, far from all the commotion…melting your heart of stone…" Artie had also decided on the blue sequins because he knew the MC would be in green, a local Denver drag queen, Formica Dinette. Formica only, ever and always wore green, the Green Queen of the Rockies, "Miss Mile High City" or whatever her current title was. She'd been around forever!

The first time Artie had met her was in San Francisco, but it was after Finocchio's closed and Artie had stopped doing drag. Formica was in town for the Coronation of the new Emperor and Empress. She was with an enormous entourage from Denver and they'd come into the restaurant for brunch. Artie wasn't even working behind the bar that day.

It must have been back when Jason was still alive and tending bar. Artie had just stopped in to go over the staff schedule and he happened to be in the office when the Denver gang swept into the bar. You'd have thought the President was in town with the Secret Service! Artie had never even heard of Formica Dinette, but she'd heard of Artie from someone old enough to remember his reign in North Beach.

*"Melting your heart of stone...*not coal...*stone!"* Artie brushed a stray fleck of mascara off his cheek and smiled to remember that day. He had come crawling out of the office in an old sweatshirt and corduroys, but the thing was, *Miss Colorado Attitude* wasn't dressed, either! And she was even nellier in boy clothes than any drag queen Artie had ever met at Finocchio's in a dress! And demanding? Prissy queen was enough to shake a stick at, expecting free this and free that. Artie was polite, of course. A fan was a fan, but this queen started acting like Artie should bow and scrape to her! "Not in my own restaurant," Artie said under his breath and excused himself to go back to the office. But first he told the bartender to be careful not to over-pour—yes, it *was* Jason, he remembered now. And he told Tim to be sure not to comp them anything! The very *nerve*, throwing attitude like that!

"Honey I'd love to get you...on a slow boat to china... all by myself alone..." Artie was laughing to himself now, remembering how long ago that day was. *Miss Rocky Mountain High,* all right. Artie would have been surprised if she wasn't a mile high at sea level, or whatever the elevation was on the 500 block of Castro Street. Too many drugs were no doubt responsible for Miss Formica's arrogance and Artie wasn't tolerant of drugs, not even back in Vietnam. In more recent years he'd seen the devastation of too many people's lives in the Castro from that nasty stuff they called Tina. No, Miss Dinette probably didn't even remember that day on Castro Street, but Artie did. He had a moment of worry...what if that queen did remember? Would she give Artie a hard time on stage? All she had to do was introduce him. Artie would be a pro, no matter what happened out there.

Arturo should be back soon. Maybe he should ask Arturo if everything was going to be okay. Thank heaven for Arturo, but sometimes Artie just needed a little time alone to collect his thoughts. Thank heaven Arturo understood...as well as he understood how to take care of business. Artie would be lost if he had to handle the contracts and the bookings and the plane reservations. Arturo also did their personal taxes and the ones for the restaurant and now for Artie's performing career, too. He must write off these benefits, somehow. Artie wouldn't have a clue. He didn't know how to use the computer, even to make a plane reservation. In the old days you called a travel agent for that sort of thing. If Arturo wasn't around, Artie wouldn't know how to do a million things so many people take for granted.

"All to myself...alone..." No, that was for sure, Artie always said that Arturo had better outlive him or he'd be up a creek without a paddle. There was just no way Artie could go on without Arturo. He'd have to hire someone. For everything. That was that.

Artie felt a sudden pain in his chest, as if a horse had kicked him there. "Damned jalapenos!" he cursed. He'd just plucked that one big fat one off of Arturo's plate at dinner earlier. Arturo warned him not to eat it, too. He said, "Artie, you won't like that! I ate the other one and it was hot! If they're too hot for me, you know they're gonna be way too hot for you. Don't forget you've gotta sing tonight."

But Artie pooh-poohed him and put it in his mouth anyway. It was on fire, but he wouldn't give Arturo the satisfaction of being right, so he up and swallowed the damned thing whole. Arturo just shook his head.

"Out on the briny..." Artie's face was finished, so now he unpinned the wig from its stand and very carefully turned it around—his final piece of armor before going into battle—and pulled it down over his head. *"...with the moon big and shiny..."*

The second jolt came even harder than the first one. Artie's chest lurched forward and his head jerked back. Then the pain was all gone and there was nothing but a bright white light in the distance. He didn't remember walking from the dressing room to the stage and the white light seemed too bright to be his follow spot, but what else could it be? He was so very glad now that he'd worn the blue sequins.

"Artie, I had to go about six blocks out of my way to find another Walgreens. The one near our hotel was all sold out of that cherry frost color you wanted. You really ought to plan better. If you're starting to run low on something you should... Artie, are you napping? Artie! Are you listening to me? Artie?"

Artie lifted his chin and strode out onto the stage. This place was much bigger than he expected. Arturo should have warned him how vast it would be. He would have come early and done a sound check with the musicians. Now Artie was really impressed that these Denver queens had pulled out all the stops!

Wait a minute.... Where were the musicians? It was much too quiet. Formica Dinette was supposed to make a big introduction. They should be playing Artie's entrance music right now. Where was that big green Denver drag queen? Artie didn't hear his introduction at all. Did someone miss their cue? Was he too early? Did he forget something? This whole situation was wrong. Should he go back and wait and make another entrance? He couldn't see anything but that blasted white light. To hell with the musicians; where was the audience? They could at least put a gel on that light to soften it up a little if they were going to aim it in his eyes like that. His make-up would look washed out in such a glare.

This place was enormous! Artie couldn't see the ends of it, no walls, no ceiling in view. Then he thought he had it figured out. The white light must be focused on the aisle to lead him in. It was theatre in the round, like that place they used to go to south of San Francisco—the Circle Star Theatre. The last time he and Arturo went there was to see

Liza Minnelli years ago, but this place was even bigger than the Circle Star- a whole lot bigger.

Artie walked toward the light, a little nervous now, trying to concentrate on the lyrics to *Slow Boat to China*, but they were all a jumble in his brain. *"Something, something on the faraway shore…"*

Artie's eyes began to focus a little. Now he could see the audience—rows and rows of them—and the first person he recognized was Jason, their old bartender from Arts, sitting right there on the aisle, looking better than ever as he stood up. Artie thought Jason must be trying to encourage everyone else in the audience into giving him a standing ovation. That wasn't necessary. He hadn't sung a note yet.

Jason. How nice to see an old familiar face in the crowd. Jason was so handsome…always such a stud; it was no wonder Tim fell in love with him. Everyone did. Jason was one of those stellar figures in the Castro, a man that everyone noticed, everyone lusted after, but Artie had never seen him look as good as he did right now. He was positively radiant! Artie wanted to say something like, "Where the hell have you been hiding yourself, you naughty boy? I haven't seen you in ages! Come here and give old Artie a great big hug!"

But then Artie remembered something else…Jason's murder, and how Tim was the one who found Jason's near-lifeless body inside the kitchen door on Hancock Street… still breathing, still alive, but barely…and everything about that time. Those were hard days for all of them. Ruth had just arrived in town that morning. It was Ruth who found the knife in the grass beside Dolores Park that night. And then they had the memorial at Arts. And that was the day Tim found the busboy Jorge's body in the trunk of Arturo's old car. It was later on when they went to the reading of Jason's will and found out that he'd left the house to Tim and the red Thunderbird convertible. And Jason had arranged everything so that Artie and Arturo owned the restaurant outright after Jason's death.

Death? But Jason was here right now and looking fabulous! But Jason wasn't smiling. Maybe he was, but Artie couldn't tell. He had an expression that confused Artie. Jason looked so very beautiful, but he was shaking his head NO. Then Artie saw other people coming down the aisle, approaching him slowly, his parents and his grandparents and hundreds of other faces hovering around him, as if they had descended from the balcony. They were floating all around him, the faces of old friends, old neighbors, former employees at Arts, old customers—so many of the guys who had died of AIDS in the years since he and Arturo bought the restaurant on Castro Street.

"No, Artie," Jason finally opened his beautiful mouth to speak and the words came out distorted to Artie's ears. They sounded like Jason was speaking through water, but Artie could still make out some of the words. "It's not your time yet, Artie. It's not your time. You don't belong here. You have to go back."

"But my beautiful dress..." Artie protested, "...look at how the blue sequins catch the light! I don't want to go back. I haven't done my number yet. Go back to where?"

"Artie, can you hear me? It's me, Arturo. Can you hear me, Artie?" Artie looked up at an IV drip suspended from a metal hook above his head and Arturo's face came into focus. The light wasn't nearly as bright as it had been on the stage a moment ago and his sparkling blue dress was gone.

"Arturo? What are you doing here? I was just talking to Jason. He's still as handsome and sexy as ever. I can see why Tim fell so hard for him. What's going on, Arturo? Are you all right? Am I all right? Where am I?"

"You're in a hospital in Denver, Artie. You're going to be fine."

Chapter 23

Teresa stood in the ground-floor laundry room on Collingwood Street, where Arturo had installed two brand new washers and two spanking new dryers. Teresa was folding clothes out of one of the dryers—hers and Birdie's—cottons, mostly. Birdie liked thick socks under her police officer boots and thin little sleeveless undershirts on top. She didn't really need a bra with her boyish body and she rarely wore one. Teresa couldn't remember the last time she saw Birdie get dressed up for any reason.

Teresa was just glad to see Birdie back at work again. She came home happier these days. George Tavares was on suspension from the department after the drunken shooting "incident" at the Men's Room Bar and Birdie was working the Castro beat with another cop now, a straight woman she liked and respected.

Teresa tossed the heaviest socks back into the dryer and fished in her jeans pocket for another quarter. The damned things took forever to dry, even with the new dryer and especially on a day like this when the humidity must be close to 100%. She kept on folding the rest of the load, but stopped when she got to a purple t-shirt. She'd never seen this before. It was so bright she was surprised she'd missed it coming out of the washer unless it was wadded up. She held it to the light

174

and spread it out enough to see the bold lettering across the front—BOY BAR.

Teresa dropped the shirt on the table like it was something slimy. Then she picked it up again, turned it over and folded it with the logo showing and carried it across the hall to Ruth's old apartment. She knew that Ruth and Sam rarely used the place lately but the shirt must belong to someone she'd let stay there—most likely Jeff and Tony's guests, some cousin or other—or some boyfriend of somebody's cousin. It was all too much for Teresa to keep track of. She knocked, but there was no answer.

Finding the t-shirt upset her more than it should have. Teresa told herself it was none of her business who Ruth let stay in her apartment. She told herself to just let it go, but she didn't quite feel safe knowing strangers were coming and going in the building. It had always seemed like family here.

Things changed, of course. Ruth had moved in after Tim moved out. When the Larsons had their second baby they moved over to Tim's duplex on Hancock Street. And then Jeff and Tony moved in downstairs, but they always seemed like a nice young couple. They were rarely noisy. Once in a great while she might have to go down there on a Saturday night and ring their bell and ask them nicely to turn the bass on their speakers down a notch. The biggest change, of course, had been when Malcolm left town and came back as a girl, but Marcia was still part of the family—even more so now that she was happy in her own skin.

The big thing was that Birdie was back at work now. School was out and Teresa had a lot of time on her hands when she was home alone, long mornings or afternoons when everyone else was at work and she was the only one in the building—most of the time. At least when Birdie was home she had her gun. Teresa was about to head upstairs with a basket of laundry when she heard the front gate open. "Hiya Teresa!" It was Tim.

"Hey Tim, what are you doing here? Did you come to fetch something for your Aunt Ruth?"

"No, for Arturo. I just got to work and he called the restaurant from Denver and asked me to run over here for him. Artie had a heart attack last night."

"Heart attack!" Teresa dropped the laundry basket and sat back on the steps as if she'd been pushed. "He's not dead, is he? Oh my Lord, Tim, tell me he's not dead!.

"No, he's not dead—"

"Oh, thank you Jesus! How is he, then? Is he going to be okay?"

"Arturo said something about stents. And he asked me to find some insurance forms in his desk at home. Do you know where it is? I've hardly ever been in their apartment."

"The desk? It's in their bedroom, I guess. You got keys? I have a set. They could have called me."

"Arturo wasn't sure you'd be home but he knew I'd be at work."

"Of course I'm home! Where else would I be?" Teresa sounded put-out, but it was mostly the shock of the news that upset her.

"Arturo told me where to find a set of keys for their apartment in his desk at the restaurant, but you should come inside with me. You can help me search. He said the insurance papers are in a file in the desk drawer and I'm supposed to fax them to him in Denver right away."

"But it's Sunday!"

"I'm just doing what I'm told. He said he's got a fax machine on his desk here, too. Come on, you can help me look." Tim grabbed her laundry basket and Teresa followed him up the stairs.

"Who's performing for the brunch crowd with Artie out of town? Oh, Tim, I just can't believe he's lying in some hospital so far from home."

"Those other drag queens are performing—Roxeanne and Rochelle or whatever their names are. Today was supposed to be their last Sunday at Arts, but I don't know when Artie will be well enough to perform again, if at all." Tim opened the apartment door and led Teresa into Artie and

Arturo's bedroom. It felt strange to be in there without them home. He was glad to have Teresa with him.

"I'm sure there are plenty of other entertainers who would love to perform for that audience."

"Yeah, morning drunks and sloppy eaters, guys who have the shakes so bad they can barely pick up their first Bloody Mary—a double!"

"What about that one called Gladys Bumps? Artie likes her, I know."

"But she doesn't sing live, though."

"How about Donna Sachet? I heard her sing at a party once and I'm sure it wasn't lip-sync because she was talking during the song, cracking jokes and making comments to people in the audience. I saw her emceeing at the Christmas tree lighting in front of the bank at 18th and Castro, too. She was funny!"

"She already has a Sunday brunch show every week at Harry Denton's Starlight Room above Union Square."

"Maybe she'd like to take a break from that sometime and work closer to home. She must live in the neighborhood, right? I see her around all the time. What do I know? Here it is—Insurance." Teresa pulled the file folder out of the lower right hand desk drawer.

"Teresa, you're a genius!"

"No, I'm a school teacher and I know my alphabet. 'Insurance' starts with the letter 'I' so it was right after 'Household' and right before 'Jewelry'."

"Great. Do you know how to use a fax machine?"

"I think I can figure it out. We have one at school."

"Good. Here's the number." Tim unfolded a slip of paper in his own scrawled handwriting while she took his place in the desk chair.

"Read me the number, Tim."

While Teresa fed the pages into the fax machine, Tim knelt and continued flipping through the desk drawers. One of the largest folders was filed under "P" for "Photographs." He lifted it out onto the desk top and opened the flap. "Teresa, look! They're all old pictures of Artie in drag when he was young. These must have been taken at Finocchio's."

"Shame on you, Tim. Artie wouldn't want you snooping through there. Wait a minute. Let me see that. Woo-hoo! Look at the size of that thing on his head! Those rhinestones must have weighed a ton, even if it was mostly made of feathers!"

"Look, here's one of Artie with Carol Channing in the dressing room. Look at all the wigs and racks of dresses behind them. I wonder if that's really her or some other drag queen."

"Look on the back. Does it say?"

"It says it's Artie and Carol Channing. Look, here's another picture of the two of them with another drag queen who must have been doing her in the show. You can see the difference now. The real Carol Channing doesn't have an Adam's apple."

"Look, there's Artie with Bea Arthur," Teresa fed the last of the insurance papers into the fax machine. "Or do you think that's a drag queen too?"

Tim laughed. "No drag queen would try to do Bea Arthur, bless her heart!"

"Why not?"

"Think about it." Tim arranged the pictures in rows across the desk and then he realized that he was also placing them in neat vertical columns. An eerie feeling crept over him as the sun through the bedroom window disappeared under a cloud. Lining up these pictures reminded him of Jason's memorial gathering at the restaurant. Tim had lined up rows of old photographs on the bulletin board—Jason dressed for Halloween on Castro Street, Jason at the Folsom Street Fair, Jason at the beach, Jason working behind the bar at Arts. Now he was doing the same thing for Artie, as if he was dead now too.

"What's wrong? Why did you stop?"

"You're right, Teresa. Artie wouldn't want us snooping in here."

"Artie's going to be all right, isn't he Tim?"

"How should I know? Arturo said they're doing something for him in the hospital in Denver...something about stents, but it's too soon to say."

"But you can tell, can't you Tim? You're the one who's supposed to be able to see things. What good is it being psychic if you can't tell?"

"It doesn't work that way, Teresa."

"Well then, how does it work?"

"Sometimes it doesn't work at all and it's usually only when I'm sleeping and I have dreams about things. I'm not Sylvia Browne!"

"Well, just try it. Close your eyes for a minute and tell me what you see."

Tim closed his eyes tight to humor her, but he was getting impatient and he needed to get back to work. The other waiters would be setting up his tables for brunch and grumbling about it. He opened his eyes and said, "Nothing! I see nothing. It's like asking a dog to smell something for you, just because you've always heard they have such great sniffing abilities. How do you know what things smell like to a dog? Maybe he has a head cold. Maybe some smells hurt his nose. Maybe he just doesn't feel like smelling. I feel sorry for those poor dogs down at the police department. Couldn't one of them just be having a bad day?"

"I don't know. Birdie doesn't work in the canine unit." Teresa was quick to defend her life partner.

"Well, then it's like asking a blind person to listen for you. How do you be sure that they can hear something you can't? Sometimes I go for weeks without any of that psychic stuff even crossing my mind and those are usually the happiest times in my life, come to think of it."

"I'm sorry, Tim. I was just...worried about Artie, you know? I sure would miss that guy if anything happened to him."

"Me too, but I don't know any more than you do. Why don't you use your women's intuition? It's probably just as good as any old psychic powers of mine. Close your eyes and tell me what you see. Women's intuition should work for you too, even if you *are* a dyke."

"I don't like that word, Tim. Birdie calls herself a dyke all the time, so I'm kind of getting used to it, but I still don't like it—coming from a guy, especially. I don't call you a fag."

"Sorry, Teresa."

"Besides, I was married once, so I guess you could say I'm bi."

"All the more reason your women's intuition should work, less testosterone than the average dyke…I mean lesbi… gay…bi girl. Close your eyes and tell me what you see."

"Nothing."

"Now you see what I mean, okay? Me too. I see nothing. All we can do about Artie is hope for the best."

"And pray," Teresa added.

Tim thought she really was different than any other dyke he had ever known.

Chapter 24

"Hello, Castro Street! It's so nice to be here at Arts in front of our favorite audience this side of Poughkeepsie. I'm Roxeanne and this is my partner in crime, the ever so lovely Rochelle." Tim looked up from the table where he was pouring coffee. He thought about the night he met the one named Richard at the Midnight Sun. They looked so much alike he still wasn't sure if Richard was Rochelle and Gary was Roxeanne or if it was the other way around.

"Last Sunday was supposed to be our last week here at Arts, but as some of you may have already heard, your usual hostess, Artie Glamóur, has taken ill in Denver." Tim felt dizzy all of a sudden. Rochelle and Roxeanne started in on their next number and Tim felt Artie's presence there on stage with them. "So this one goes out to Artie and we all wish him a full and speedy recovery...

"Sisters, sisters
There were never such devoted sisters,
Never had to have a chaperone, No sir,
I'm there to keep my eye on her..."

Tim almost never saw things while he was awake, especially since Doctor Hamamoto changed his HIV medications. Tim closed his eyes like Teresa suggested earlier, and this time he really *could* see things. He saw twins. Artie was right there on the stage behind those other two drag queens and so was his twin...but Artie didn't have a twin. Artie was an only child, same as Tim. Maybe this was just a hangover, but why wouldn't he have felt it before now?

> *"All kinds of weather, we stick together*
> *The same in the rain and sun*
> *Two different faces, but in tight places*
> *We think and we act as one..."*

Tim hoped that seeing Artie didn't *mean* anything. He hoped this wasn't Artie's way of saying goodbye. Tim couldn't imagine Arts without Artie...without Arturo, maybe, but not Artie... Arturo was quietly working in the kitchen for so many years that you tended to forget about him even when he was there. The waiters saw him more than the public did, but he didn't say much when he worked. He usually had his old radio in the corner playing a Spanish language station with a lot of words Tim didn't understand and music that sounded like the mariachi bands on Mission Street. Arturo probably kept the radio turned on as much for the busboys and dishwashers to enjoy, his "nephews," he liked to call them. The only time he turned that radio off was when Artie was performing.

Tim remembered so many Artie stories. They flashed through his mind like a compilation of scenes from movies. Tim could no longer remember which stories Artie had told as part of his act and which ones he'd told at home or at parties.

Tim remembered when everyone was trying to get Artie to run for Empress, but he said he just didn't have time. Artie told about how all that got started, how some character named Joshua Norton in the mid 1800s had lost his fortune investing in Peruvian rice and declared himself the Emperor of San Francisco and Protector of Mexico. About a hundred years later in 1965, a drag entertainer named Jose Sarria declared herself Absolute Empress I, The Widow Norton.

The royal titles spread from there across the country through generations of Emperors and Emperors, Grand Dukes and Duchesses and various lower titles of the court system.

Artie was always glad to host events for the royalty candidates at Arts, but he turned down the efforts of those who wanted him to run for a title. Arturo always said, "Look at Gladys Bumps! She's about as glamorous as it gets and she was never an Empress. Neither was KC Dare." Arturo told him it would be a step down to go from being Artie Glamóur to a mere Empress and Artie just laughed. Artie loved all the other drag queens…

Tim opened his eyes and Artie had disappeared again, but he kept staring at these two drag queens that were filling in for Artie when he was traveling. They could be twins too, but only when they were dressed up like this, not when they were men. Tim thought it strange that they were singing a song called *Sisters* when they were male lovers in real life.

"Those who've seen us
know that not a thing could come between us…"

Tim looked around to see if his customers needed anything, but they all appeared to be transfixed by the show. No one had an empty drink or cold cup of coffee in front of him. No one was trying to get his attention, so he took a couple of steps backward and stood outside the swinging doors to the kitchen. He could see everything from here and he closed his eyes again. This time he saw the Olsen Twins from television; he wanted to change the channel! If he was going to picture celebrity twins on that formerly blank screen on the back of his eyeballs, why not male twins? Why not male fashion models or athletes? If Artie could appear with a twin, why not Marcus Schenkenberg or Brett Stewart? Why not those blond gay twins he saw in that porn movie a while back?

Rochelle and Roxeanne segued into "We Are Family," and Tim had a funny feeling they were doing something incestuous until he reminded himself that they were men and unrelated at that...unless they'd gotten married somewhere it was legal. Tim closed his eyes again and this time he saw the Brown twins, Marian and Vivian, the dowager bookends of Nob Hill and Union Square. They'd been around town for years and they always dressed so identically they'd become celebrities in their own right, appearing in television commercials and in ads on the sides of buses. Tim heard that one of them had died a while back. He thought it was Vivian, but he wasn't sure. How sad it must be for the other one to be all alone now. They were real women, not drag queens, even though they dressed as if they might have been. The Brown Twins had never set foot inside Arts, as far as Tim knew.

Artie once said that if Emperor Norton had never existed, someone would have had to make him up. Or maybe some latter-day drag queens would have emulated the Brown Twins and each year they would run a big campaign and crown the two drag queens who looked the most alike. Now Tim remembered. Artie was on stage talking about old times when he and Jose Sarria used to work together at Finocchio's. When Artie came up with that idea about present day drag queens impersonating the Brown twins he howled, "...but that would never work because they'd claw each others' eyes out!" and the audience laughed along too.

Tim could hear Artie's voice now, but he couldn't see him. This time it was only a memory of Artie on stage here a few weeks ago, a Sunday brunch show when Artie was rambling, but he had the audience in the palm of his hand. "And sooner or later, the queens who wouldn't be caught dead in a dress would want to get in on the action too, but instead of running for Emperor, they'd have a contest to crown the Brown twin *boys* every year, too. Their job would be to keep the girls from killing each other!"

Then the laughter faded and Tim saw his friend Rene and his twin brother Antoine, but Antoine must be back in New Orleans where he lived. Rene was the hairdresser who protected Tim's Aunt Ruth from slipping into middle-aged dowdiness, but he and Antoine were fraternal twins and they didn't look at all alike. Tim started seeing other pairs now—Gary and Richard out of drag, Jeff and Tony, the couple who lived in the building on Collingwood Street that Artie and Arturo owned, Tony's cousin Eddie and his partner Clay. Tim opened his eyes and looked at a couple who were holding hands at one of his tables. They both went to the same gym where Tim belonged. It used to be Gold's but now it had changed its name to Fitness SF. One leaned over to kiss the other and Tim felt a hunger pang for Nick. Nick would be back home next week and Tim was nearly beside himself.

The dizziness passed, but the next time Tim closed his eyes he saw the pair of armed robbers who had been holding up businesses in the Castro. They might as well be twins. Tim hadn't thought of them in a long time.

"Hey, Tim, are you all right?" asked James, the waiter who was working the section by the front windows.

"Yeah, I'm fine." Tim blinked a couple of times. "I must have got something in my eyes."

"Bummer. I hate when that happens."

"Yeah, you don't know the half of it."

Chapter 25

Nick was coming home next Sunday. Today was Tuesday and Tim realized it was time to start cleaning house. He didn't want Nick coming in from the airport to find dust bunnies everywhere. Tim was scheduled to work Thursday through Saturday nights this week and Sunday brunch, for which they might not even need three waiters. If Artie was still in the hospital and those other matching drag queens had performed their last show at Arts, there wouldn't be such a big brunch crowd. Still, there might be something else planned, some other act. Tim couldn't remember what was going on with the performers. He had enough trouble remembering his own work schedule from one week to the next, especially when there was any variation in it.

Tim stripped the sheets and pillowcases from his bed, even though he would change them again on Sunday before he left for the airport. He shoved them into the washing machine with the clothes from the hamper and they made a full load. At the rate things were going, his bed wouldn't see any more action in the next five nights than it had in the whole time Nick was gone. On Sunday, Nick's first night back, they would sleep on crisp fresh linens—maybe he'd buy new sheets just for the occasion. Tim doubted they would do much sleeping, but after they'd exhausted each other sexually, they would eventually curl up in bed together. It was going to be so delicious after all this time apart. Tim wanted it to be more than delicious; he wanted it to be perfect.

But Tim was still thinking about getting laid. He never actually wanted to *sleep* with anyone besides Nick. Maybe that could be one of their rules if they ever got around to establishing them—no overnights. Tim just wanted to get his rocks off with another guy. Even if he brought someone home for sex, chances were good that they wouldn't get around to pulling down the covers. Tim was more apt to toss an old sheet on top of the bed to catch any spills, if it came to that—*if* they even got as far as the bed.

Tim remembered many a night when he was single. He'd bring someone home and offer him a beer and they'd start carrying on right then and there, never making it past the kitchen—maybe the bathroom. Before he met Nick, when Tim lived in his old apartment on Collingwood Street, he sometimes brought guys home and they never got past the laundry room across the hall. If it was late enough at night and nobody was coming and going, they might just get it on in the front hallway, just inside the gate. That was exciting!

Why couldn't he just get laid? Was that asking for too much? He just wanted some friendly, frisky, frolicsome flesh exchange without bodily fluids—especially if the guy was HIV negative. It was so nice not to have to worry about all that with Nick.

Tim sat down at his computer and checked his email. Nothing looked urgent or promising. If he was going to get laid before Nick got home it had better be soon. Nothing had worked out so far and it wasn't for lack of trying. If there were one perfect man he could conjure up in his imagination, like picking all the parts out of a catalogue—hair, eyes, nose, lips, shoulders, chest—if he could choose the shapes of each and then fill them in with his ideas of hair color, eye color, skin tone, the contrast of the darkness of the nipples to the rest of the flesh, a hairy chest or smooth...hmmm...maybe a fuzzy vertical stripe of hair from just above the navel down to the crotch—Jake would call that a crab ladder—and then the cock and balls, of course.

In Tim's fantasy the genitals would be substantial, but not overly large, not freakish. Oh, why not? It was only a fantasy. And the ass would be firm and full and smooth as marble until you got right up close enough and turned it to the light, maybe sunlight. Yes, but only in broad daylight at a nude beach would you notice that the ass cheeks were coated in the finest softest hairs like velvet, almost feathery and nearly invisible. And the calves and thighs would be lithe, but solid—no, not just solid but as firm and muscular as an Olympic runner and the feet—Tim could hardly begin to choose which sort of feet. There were so many possibilities with feet, but they would have to be large enough to hold up a statue and as agile as a dancer and as beautiful as any creature in the forest of his dreams.

And even if that perfect man appeared in Tim's bed right now—naked—and if Nick were coming up the stairs at the very same moment, after having been away so long, Tim would rather have Nick in his arms…Nick with the tiny gap between his teeth, Nick with his thinning hair, Nick with all his perfect imperfections.

Still, Tim might ask that perfect man he'd dreamt up if he would mind waiting in the kitchen for a while. "Help yourself to a beer or whatever you'd like…" Nick might enjoy meeting the perfect man, too. Tim supposed that their talk of rules, when it came, would also include a thorough discussion of the possibilities of someday having a three-way.

Tim pulled the vacuum cleaner out of the hall closet and Buck made a dash for the back door. He hated the sound of it. Tim slid open the sliding glass panel and let him outside. "How are you ever going to learn to vacuum if you can't get past the noise, Buck? I'm going to buy you some tiny earplugs one of these days and give you cleaning lessons. You can keep this place in tip-top shape while I'm gone at work. It's about time you did something to earn your keep around here." Buck

was already in the driveway chewing at an old toy one of the
Larson kids downstairs had abandoned.

Tim looked at the clock before he turned on the vacuum.
Tuesday morning at 11am the noise shouldn't disturb anyone
downstairs. Ben would be at work and Tim hadn't heard Jane
and the kids at all this morning. Maybe this was the week that
Ben's parents were taking their grandkids to Disneyland.

After he finished vacuuming Tim went back to the
computer and clicked on dudesurfer.com. There was another
message from Britlad. Tim had almost forgotten what it was
that the kid had done to piss him off last time. He thought of
him as "the kid" now, since he claimed to be eighteen. Was
anyone really eighteen? Oh yeah…now Tim remembered: the
kid had pissed him off when he asked for a picture of Nick.

This wasn't about Nick. How had Nick even come into
this conversation? This whole thing had started out to be
about Tim and his needs, not about Nick. Tim was angry at
Nick for being away so long. That was it. He didn't want to be
angry and he hated to admit it to himself because that made
him feel weak, somehow, but it was the truth.

Britlad had written: <I want you when I come to San
Francisco.>

Tim glanced at the note—same old, same old, but
there was a new picture this time. The kid was hanging from
a chin-up bar by one hand, naked and either halfway erect
or he was extremely well-endowed. He must be a gymnast,
Tim thought. He had an amazing body and maybe he really
was eighteen. This picture was much clearer than the others
and the kid's face was almost child-like. Tim had no taste for
children whatsoever, but he could appreciate beauty when he
saw it, whether in a gorgeous woman or a work of art. A green
light appeared in one corner of the screen that meant Britlad
was on-line.

<Tim, ru there?>

Tim stared at the picture again and typed back: <Are
you really 18?>

<glad to see ur online.>

<Answer me! How old are you? Don't lie.>

<B 18 next week. Coming to SF for birthday & want you for my present.>

Tim had a funny feeling about all this and it didn't take any psychic ability to smell something fishy. Why couldn't a kid like him find someone his own age to mess around with? There must be loads of strapping young guys in London who'd be eager to give him a tumble. Then Tim remembered what his life was like when he was that age or even younger. Tim started having sex with his high school track coach before he'd turned sixteen and Dave Anderson must have been close to the same age Tim was now.

Tim typed: <Nice picture.>

<Thanks.>

<Are you into gymnastics?>

<Some & I swim a lot. Athletics, mostly.>

<Athletics?> Tim thought the kid was just being vague.

<I think u call it track & field in the States.>

<I did track in high school too, but that was a long time ago.> Ahh, the boys' locker room flashed in Tim's memory. The smell of bleach was still a turn-on to this day.

<Ur still really hot.>

Thanks? Tim thought. Sheesh, only a teenager could turn a compliment into an insult. <What day's your birthday?>

<Monday. I land at SFO b4 sunset on Sunday>

Tim thought again about what a small world it was, an inflatable beach ball globe of earth, the seven continents printed on the plastic, a nozzle marked "North Pole" where you blew it up and "Made in China" on the seam in Antarctica. And someone must have pricked the world with a needle because nowadays it was shrinking into itself until the Atlantic Ocean disappeared into its plastic folds. Tim remembered that old expression "There are no accidents" and wondered why God or fate or karma or his dead psychic grandmother had sent this boy with the sculpted body into Tim's realm of awareness. And why was he arriving in San Francisco on the same day that Nick came home?

<U still there? Can I call u? Give me your number? I just want to see u when u have time. I won't be any trouble, promise.>

<Are you positive?> Tim asked. He had misunderstood that question the first time when the kid asked him the same thing. This time he realized what Britlad had meant—*are you HIV positive?* And the kid knew what Tim meant too.

<No, but u r, right? That's why I want u. To convert me. I need your poz load for my birthday present. You and your bf can both do it.>

Tim's hands leapt from the keyboard as if it were on fire. If only Nick were here now. Nick would know what to do, what to say, how to handle this. Nick would stay calm and sensible. Nick wouldn't freak out.

This kid wanted to become infected with HIV as a birthday present?!

Tim was shocked at the pure insanity of the idea. This stupid kid needed to get smacked in the head instead of slammed in the ass. Maybe he should agree to meet the kid. That would give him time to think. He had from now until Sunday to come up with a way to talk some sense to him. How could he make him change his mind? Tim knew that if he didn't do it, the kid would find someone else out there who was willing. San Francisco was full of guys who were HIV positive and would love to bareback an eighteen-year-old with a big dick and an athlete's body, whether they cared if the kid was negative or not.

Tim stood up and walked away from the computer. He'd rather say nothing than say the wrong thing. He stared out the window facing downtown. It was fixing to be one of those rare hot days, he could tell. There was rich blue sky directly above, but the air surrounding the tallest buildings had already turned to haze and the Transamerica Pyramid shimmered like a rocket ship during its final countdown.

When Tim turned back to the computer the green light was off. Had the kid gotten tired of waiting for Tim's answer? Or had he already found someone else?

Chapter 26

Arturo and Artie were seated in the front row of the first class seats on the flight back from Denver to SFO. Artie always preferred the window seat. He felt like a movie star whenever one of his fans recognized him in public. He secretly loved the attention, even though he tried to pretend he didn't, acting like he needed Arturo on the aisle seat to protect him from his adoring public. Tonight he was glad to have the buffer of Arturo between him and the world, but it wasn't because he felt glamorous. He was pale and exhausted from his hospital stay and he was sure he looked like hell, especially without the wig and the make-up and the dress. Nobody would recognize him as Artie Glamóur; that was for sure. He felt and looked like the sickly old man that he was.

"Do they serve dinner on this flight or is it too late for that?" he asked Arturo.

"I'm not sure, Artie. I didn't hear them make an announcement about it. Does anyone serve food on airlines any more?"

"They must still serve dinner in first class!" Artie harrumphed. "And I need a drink whenever you see that cute flight attendant again. Where did he go? He was a doll!"

"Artie…" Arturo didn't want to start playing the role of cop, but he knew it had to happen. "You don't *need* a drink. You don't need a lot of things you take for granted, like bacon and ice cream and well-marbled filet mignons and three martini lunches and…"

"Just kill me now!"

"Your heart attack was a wake-up call, Artie. It could have killed you, you know. It was just lucky that nightclub was close to a good hospital. And what if I hadn't found you in time? It must have happened just before I walked in the door to your dressing room."

"It felt like I was gone a long time, Arturo."

"The doctor didn't think so, Artie. And he said you were darned lucky to get away with stents, so they didn't have to open you up and do a bypass."

"I saw Jason in heaven, Arturo. He's the one who told me I had to go back. It simply wasn't my time yet. It just wasn't meant to be."

"That's what you already said, Artie." Arturo was raised Catholic, long-ago lapsed, at least in terms of practicing. And yet, when talk turned to matters of the afterlife, it was hard for Arturo not to revert to his childhood reverence for the church. If Artie had claimed that he'd been met by St. Peter or the blessed Virgin Mother it might have seemed more plausible that he'd had a glimpse of heaven, but Jason? That wasn't at all likely.

Even in life, Jason had seemed to exist on a plane that was about as far from organized religion as anyone—gay or straight—that Arturo ever knew. In death…well, he hated to think about where Jason ended up. If Jason was the first person Artie saw, could it really have been heaven? Come to think of it, Artie was never much of a churchgoer, either. All these years in the restaurant business, both of them always worked Sunday mornings. Arturo wondered if the Most Holy Redeemer Catholic Church in the Castro had any services that weren't during brunch hours. Maybe they needed to make a bigger change in life than just Artie's diet, but that was going to be a good start.

"And no more potato chips, either."

"What are you talking about?"

"Potato chips and Pringles and Fritos and fried pork rinds and all those salty snacks—you've got to cut them out. From now on, we're reading every label when we shop at the store. Better yet, you should eat all your meals at the restaurant from now on. I'll make sure they're healthy. We'll do a whole new menu and feature heart-healthy entrées. Everyone should eat better."

"Sure, Arturo, whatever you say...oh, young man! Yoo-hoo!" Artie waved at the flight attendant. "Is there food service on this flight? No? Well then, could you bring me a scotch, please? Just a couple of cubes of ice to cool it down, thanks."

"Liquor, too, Artie. You've got to cut way back on it. The doctor said a glass of red wine with dinner is healthy, but... no, nothing for me, thanks...maybe I'll have a cup of coffee with cream, please. No, skip the cream. I'll drink it black. It's better for me that way."

"No cream? No drinks? Just kill me now! I mean it, Arturo. Just pull the plug and leave my stretcher in the hallway."

"What if it wasn't heaven you saw, Artie?"

"Who said it *was*?"

"You did."

"Well, what else was I gonna call it, what with all the white light and the music?"

"I thought you said it was silent there."

"My intro music wasn't playing like I expected, that's all, but there were harps and things later on, I'm almost sure of it."

"All I'm saying is...you're not exactly a religious person, Artie. Neither was Jason. So maybe it wasn't heaven."

"So what if I'm not? So what if it wasn't? All I said was there was a bright white light and Jason was there. At first

I thought I was on stage in Denver, but then I saw so many people I hadn't seen in years. There were old customers and friends and family and then I realized they were all dead. Why do you have to go and make something religious out of it, Arturo?"

"You're the one who called it heaven."

Artie thought again about what he'd seen. Was there music or not? Maybe it was only playing in his head. He was trying to remember the lyrics to *Slow Boat to China* at the time... Maybe it *wasn't* heaven. What difference did it make, unless...didn't Artie remember the smell of smoke? It was a nasty chemical smell. Did one of those Denver drag queens try to revive him with a bottle of poppers? Now he wasn't sure if the smell was from then or if he could smell something burning right now. Maybe the heart attack had thrown off his sniffer. Artie just hoped the smell wasn't coming from the cockpit. Where was that boy with his scotch?!

Tim tossed and turned that night. He had his recurring nightmare about being on the airplane. It had been a while since he'd had this dream and he always forgot about it in the meantime, sometimes for months or years, but he'd had the same dream since childhood, maybe since the first time he flew on a plane. That was the summer his father took him to Chicago to see the Minnesota Twins play the Cubs. Nothing memorable happened on that flight. Nothing happened with his father, either—what did he expect? Male bonding? Not then, not ever...and his father never tried it again.

Why had they gone all the way to Chicago instead of to a home game? Tim had a vague recollection of stopping to visit some distant relative in a dark brownstone and his father's talk of an inheritance, but Tim was just a little boy then. He couldn't remember. At the ballpark, Tim was only interested in the food. He spent more time staring at the crowds of people in the stands than watching the game on the field. Bud Snow looked at his son with regret that grew into disinterest over the years of Tim's childhood and finally disgust when Tim turned into a teenage pervert who seduced his high school track coach.

In this dream, Tim was surrounded by his crowded fellow-passengers, strangers on a plane flying low, just off the ground, only inches above the asphalt that resembled tarmac...almost *like* a runway, but more like a highway. That's what it was, an interstate highway filled with cars and trucks pulling boats and campers and trailers, semi trailers hauling prime beef cattle to the slaughterhouse and shiny silver tankers full of gasoline. Tim could see the shadow of the airplane's wings on the ground. Then there were tall trees on both sides of the road and an overpass up ahead. The cars and trucks tried to get out of the way of the plane but they couldn't move fast enough, crashing into one another and rolling over, spilling livestock and fire and blood.

The plane made that *ping-whoosh* sound that meant the landing gear had dropped and locked into place. Flaps lowered but did nothing to slow them down. Even if the body of the plane could fit through the tunnel of the overpass, the wings would shear off. Or would they? Tim wasn't sure. Maybe the wings would catch the side embankments and cause a huge explosion, ripping out the overpass, the on-ramps and the whole damned thing.

Tim woke up sweating. Was it happening right now? Was this dream in the future or in the past? Did he know anyone who was on an airplane right now? Nick wasn't flying home until Sunday. Tim wanted to call him and hear his voice sounding calm and reassuring but it was four o'clock in the morning. What could Tim say? "Don't fly home, Nick. It's not safe. I had that dream again. I'm scared."

Tim wanted Nick home more than anything and Nick wasn't on the plane in the dream; Tim was. Tim was always on the plane and looking down on the plane at the same time. He always woke up just before whatever happened was going to happen.

Tim heard once that you can never die in your dreams. You can get close to dying, so close you think you will die. Or you might wish you were dead. Or you might hope you don't die, but you're sure that you will any minute and you just want to get the experience over and done with, whatever it is. Then you wake up in a cold sweat. Tim knew night sweats from the first time he went on HIV medication. It took a while for his body to adjust and then the sweating stopped. He used to wake up in a pool of his own sweat, every layer of his bed linens soaked through.

This was different.

Tim had heard once that if you died in your dreams you would really be dead. But how could anyone know that?

When Tim woke up again it was dawn and the dream lingered like a hangover headache but the sweating had stopped. He'd rolled over to the dry side of the bed, Nick's side, the empty side. He dragged his feet around and plopped them down onto the floor, shuffled slump-shouldered to the kitchen, turned on the coffee, turned on the morning TV news, went to the bathroom, turned the news off again. He carried his 49ers mug of coffee out onto the deck. Maybe his dad should have taken him to a football game instead of baseball. The Twins had lost that game, as Tim remembered. Nah, he doubted it would have made any difference.

Downtown San Francisco was barely an outline through the haze. Was it smoke or fog this time of year? Who knew? It didn't smell quite the same as when distant wildfires blazed on smoky summer days and California seemed to teeter on the brink of existence. Tim envisioned a map of North America without California and the Baja Peninsula, high school classes in which San Francisco and Los Angeles only existed in history textbooks…or geography…or geology…would they still have textbooks that far in the future? Maybe it wouldn't be that far. Maybe an earthquake would roll under him this afternoon and break off the west coast with a rumbling crack followed by violent hissing while the cold Pacific waters swallowed the flames.

Tim never worried about earthquakes or wildfires. Right now he was worried about last night's dream. Elements of it came back to him as he sipped his coffee. Too hot! He blew on it. Nick would fly home on Sunday. Arturo and Artie would be flying home from Denver at some point, no doubt. Or would Artie need an ambulance to bring him back? Tim had no idea how those things went. He couldn't remember anyone he knew personally who'd had a heart attack. Tim had never had a dream about a heart attack.

He had watched his mother's suicide in a dream once, but that dream was in wild Technicolor like a cartoon. At least that's how he remembered it now. It was real, but it didn't seem real. And it was true. Tim knew it was true when it was happening and he didn't much care, not nearly as much as he thought he should, not as much as he cared right now about a plane crash.

Jason had appeared to Tim in a dream—alive and in full leather—cracking a whip and cracking wise a few days after his own murder. That dream only happened once, like the dream about his mother. They were one-shot deals, unlike this plane-crash dream that never actually crashed but he knew the crash was imminent. He'd had the airplane dream lots of times and always woke up just in time.

What did it mean? Planes crashed somewhere every day, didn't they? People must have heart attacks every day too, but Tim didn't dream about heart attacks. Maybe his recurring airplane dream meant nothing. It never did before. Tim made up his mind then and there that he wasn't going to worry about it.

Besides earthquakes and wildfires, Tim tried not to worry about global warming and the mysterious disappearance of honey bees. Why worry about things he couldn't control? Why even think about them? Nick worried about wildfires in Sonoma County if they came close to his nursery. Nick must have been the one who'd told Tim about the honey bees disappearing, too. Tim hadn't paid much attention. Were they on the endangered species list yet? Nick had said something about the danger to the crops and how California was still an agricultural economy. Nick grew plants for a living, though not crops so much. What did Tim care about bees and propagation? Tim had always believed whole-heartedly in the value of *sex* without propagation.

Tim supposed that Nick must sell fruit trees at the nursery. And tomato plants...did they rely on bees? Tim remembered seeing the rack of garden seeds for vegetables. It stood near the cash register beside a section with gardening books and hummingbird feeders. Nick had always lived closer to the earth than Tim did. That was part of what made him so lovable.

Nick thought Tim had his head in the clouds sometimes and Tim never argued the point. Nick could call it what he liked. Tim knew it wasn't as far as the clouds, even when the clouds were low to the ground and sweeping through the neighborhood, whipping white wisps of moisture with cardboard and newspapers across the intersection of 18th and Castro in the mid-afternoon of a summer's day.

Tim's head was somewhere else, somewhere that he kept trying to figure out. He wanted not to worry about anything he couldn't control, whether it was plane crashes or wildfires or sex. Sex was always on his mind and that was rarely something he had much control over, either. He sipped his coffee and watched the steam rise from the mug as the fog burned back around the Bay Bridge and the sun shone down on the deep waters beneath it. Yes, sex was *always* on his mind.

Chapter 27

"Did you bring it, Ruthie? Give it here! I don't need a bowl or a spoon. I can use my fingers. Hurry up! Give it to me…"

"Of course I brought it, Artie, but first give me a minute to take off my jacket and set down my purse and let me get a good look at you. How are you feeling?"

"I feel like a prisoner in my own home!" It was Artie's third day back in San Francisco after being hospitalized in Denver for a few days and he was tired of being a patient. He lunged for the Mollie Stone's grocery bag and hustled it into the kitchen of their apartment on Collingwood. "Arturo won't let me do anything. I might as well be tied to the bed. He acts just like Kathy Bates in *Misery!* What else did you buy at the store? This had better not all be health-food!"

"Don't tear that bag, Artie! They charge ten cents for them now, you know. And not everything in there is for you. I picked up a couple of things I needed, too. The milk and the meat need to go in the refrigerator if I'm here very long. I parked the car in the sun. I'm making Swiss steak for Sam's dinner tonight. Where is Arturo now?"

"Swiss steak sounds so good. Make me some? I'm starved!"

"I thought Arturo kept you well-fed. You didn't answer me. Where is he?"

"I sent him out to Walgreens with a shopping list just to get rid of him for a while. He's keeping me fed, all right, but I might as well be eating hospital food."

"Arturo is a wonderful chef! How can you say that?"

"No salt, no fat, no fried foods, no red meat...he won't let me have anything I really want. That's why I asked you to bring me the ice cream, silly. Where is it?"

"It must be in the bottom of the bag. Let me find it. Here!"

"Fat-free frozen yogurt! This isn't ice cream! Ruth, how could you be so mean?!"

Tim cleaned his apartment all week. He wanted to figure out what to do about Britlad, but instead he kept thinking about a scene from a movie he couldn't remember the name of or even who starred in it. There was something about a guy getting ready to go out on a date with a girl and he was nervous. Nick's coming home reminded Tim of that movie. Having Nick back after such a long separation would be almost like a date and Tim knew he shouldn't put such heavy expectations on it, but it was hard not to. In the movie the nervous guy's buddy gave him some sage advice before his big date with the girl of his dreams so that he wouldn't do something awkward when he was out with the girl and Tim knew it had to do with sex, but what didn't these days?

Maybe Nick would be tired and wouldn't want to have sex right away. Tim had stopped at Walgreens on Castro Street for candles and the store next to Harvey's for bath salts. Maybe Nick would want a long hot soak in the bathtub first. Tim had also looked in the windows of the other two stores in that stretch, Phantom and Rock Hard, the ones that sold lubricants and porn and poppers, but he didn't go inside. He'd rather shop for that stuff when he had Nick with him, not that they needed any more sex toys.

Maybe Nick just would want to get undressed, put on his bathrobe, sit down in the living room and have a drink in front of the fire. Tim got the fireplace all ready so that all he needed to do was strike a match to it when the time came. He'd also bought a bottle of 12-year-old scotch and pulled Nick's bathrobe off the hook in the bedroom closet. It was his "city robe" and Tim had one just like it. They had matching robes at Nick's place at the Russian River, too. This one smelled like Nick, but the smell had pretty much worn off by now, so Tim put it through the wash and got it all fluffed up in the dryer.

Tim had even slept in that robe right after Nick left on his trip. He pretended to himself that he'd grabbed Nick's robe by mistake and slipped his arms into it and pulled the collar up around his nose and took a deep breath of Nick. Then he told himself that he might as well keep it on, even though it was a little too big for him. He wore it to bed and fell asleep in it. Tim played this charade a couple of times, as if he were fooling someone besides himself.

Tim thought the movie he was trying to remember starred some hot young actors, but it had to have been made at least a decade ago. He tried to picture Reese Witherspoon and Adam Sandler as the stars, but he knew that wasn't right. It didn't matter who was in it, but what they said. There was some reason in the back of his mind, some lesson he was trying to remember. He and Nick had rented it and watched it together a few months ago and it had one of the funniest scenes in any movie. They'd even stopped it, backed it up and watched that part again because they were laughing so hard. The guy's friend had told him he should masturbate before the date so that he wouldn't be horny when he was out with the girl. So he did, but just at that moment the doorbell rang. The girl was early and he didn't have anything to wipe his hands on, so he used his hair. The title had something to do with the girl's name. Mary…that was it! "There's Something About Mary!" Tim said it out loud and Buck came running.

Tim was so proud of himself for remembering the name of the movie that he decided to clean the oven. He hadn't even used it lately, but everything had to be spotless before Nick got back. The oven cleaner reminded him of mousse. The reason the girl's hair stood straight up was because she thought the boy had mousse in his hair—too much of it—so she took some with her fingers and rubbed it through her own hair. That was what was so funny, the girl's hair sticking straight up.

Tim could never understand why he could see things sometimes that other people couldn't see—especially in his dreams—but it was still hard for him to remember things he wanted to call to mind, like the details of a movie. It should be easier for a psychic, shouldn't it? If Tim couldn't figure out what his dreams meant, he sure didn't hold out much hope for solving the clues that came into his waking thoughts. He couldn't help anyone catch the armed robbers in the Castro and he sure didn't have a clue as to what he should do about *Britlad*. What good was his psychic-ness? It was just a nuisance!

He left the oven cleaner to do its job and moved on to the bathroom. The shower tiles were already so clean the grout was about to sparkle but Tim sprayed them again. Then it snapped into his head. The movie starred Cameron Diaz and Ben Stiller...and the other guy who played the friend was Matt Dillon. He was the one who told him not to go off on a date before he'd "spanked the monkey" or "flogged the dolphin" or "gotten the baby batter off the brain." He told him he had to...in other words...masturbate before the date. Tim could picture the scene in his mind now. Mary arrived early, before he'd finished cleaning up. He panicked and lifted his cum-filled hand to his head.

Tim closed the toilet seat cover and sat down. His eyes wandered to a stack of porn in the magazine rack on the floor beside him. That would have to go back in the drawer before Nick got home. Masturbation wasn't the answer. Tim had been doing that nearly every day since Nick left town, sometimes twice. He could do it before he left for the airport on Sunday and be ready to go again by the time he and Nick got back to the car in the parking lot. Now he wondered whether he should park or just wait for Nick at the curb. He didn't want to make a big scene in front of a crowd of travelers, but if he parked the car in a quiet section of the parking lots where there weren't a lot of people around, he could already imagine what their reunion might be like. Maybe he should take Nick's van to the airport and they could get it on in the back.

Tim tried to remember something else about masturbation, something he'd heard a long time ago. It had nothing to do with hairy palms or blindness and it wasn't from a movie, either. Someone gave him advice—as if Tim knew nothing at all about sex—and Tim resented it…but only for a minute

Tim couldn't remember now who had talked to him about masturbation. It couldn't have been his father. Was it Dave Anderson, his high school track coach, his first lover? Tim didn't think so. Dave thought he knew everything, but Tim couldn't imagine him having anything practical to pass along to him.

It was more likely he was thinking of Jason, Tim's last serious boyfriend before Nick. It was serious to Tim, anyway. Jason never showed himself to be serious about any other man, but he did like to give advice. When Jason got into one of his professorial moods there was nothing to do but tune it out or let it soak in. Tim sometimes thought that Jason could have been a teacher, a good one, if he hadn't chosen to spend his life as a bartender and all-around slut!

Tim sighed.

He had to stop this train of thought. He knew better than to replay the past in his head, especially if he was going to pause at each regret. But it *was* Jason who had told him, "Never stop masturbating! No matter what else is going on in your life, no matter what…I don't care if you're getting laid five times a day and you don't think you have the time or any spunk left in you. Never lose touch with the ability to make love to yourself."

Tim could hear him now. And Jason had always loved himself. That was for damn sure. And so did everyone else in town. Oh well...he must have felt something for Tim to leave him the duplex on Hancock Street and the '65 red Thunderbird convertible.

As if Tim would ever lose touch with masturbation! He didn't ever need Jason to tell him that, but as Tim was hearing Jason's words in his head, he also began to remember Jason's face and then the rest of him took shape and came into view. He was naked. They both were. Jason had that wicked sexy smile on his face and he and Tim were masturbating each other. Tim had completely forgotten about the one time they did that, how hot it was. They were downstairs in Jason's apartment, in the kitchen, drinking beer on a Sunday afternoon after both of them had finished work at Arts. They came back to Jason's place where Tim had left a change of clothes and they both got out of their work clothes, but they didn't put their other clothes on right away. They both paused for a minute and Jason offered Tim a beer so they both went into the kitchen naked and they moved closer together and then stepped back, then closer again and they circled each other as if they were doing a dance. It was one of the hottest memories Tim had of Jason, but he had forgotten all about it until now. And then they never did it again.

It wasn't masturbation that Tim needed right now, but he'd brought Jason back to mind so clearly that Tim could almost smell him. Now Tim wondered what would happen if he got off while fantasizing about Jason. Should he feel guilty? Would jacking off to the memory of Jason be like cheating on Nick or what? This went beyond the concept of rules and Tim didn't want to think about rules right now. Once Nick got home, there would be plenty of time for the two of them to figure all that out together—*when* they were together. Still, having that talk with Nick was just about the only thing Tim wasn't really looking forward to about Nick coming home.

What Tim really needed was to get laid...maybe just once before Nick got home. If only he could find someone he would never see again, someone whose name he would never have to know. That was what anonymous meant, after all. There had to be someone else out there in a similar situation. It could be a friendly encounter, just a couple of guys helping each other out, no biggie. And then they would each go on their own merry way.

The more Tim thought about it, the more rationalizations he could find. He figured that at this point, with Nick's return so near, making love with any other man would be making love with Nick too, as if every other man were EVERYMAN. At the moment of climax wasn't every man the same? When Tim thought about it some more, he realized that it was the moment *after* climax that worried him. That's when things could get sticky, in more ways than one.

If Tim was going to do anything about this, it had to be before Sunday, before Nick's flight got in. If Tim got laid before Sunday, he would be doing Nick a favor. Otherwise, he'd put too much of a burden on him, have too many expectations. Tim needed to prove to himself that he could take matters into his own hands—but not literally. That's what he was already doing, masturbating too much. That hadn't worked out very well for Ben Stiller's character in that movie about Mary, either. Tim needed to get laid in order to prove his independence. He thought about it a while longer. All this thinking was giving him a headache!

Tim packed some pot in the little wooden pipe, stepped out onto the deck for a couple of deep hits and decided that it wouldn't hurt to check out that dudesurfer web-site one more time. He was relieved that there was no further word from the young British bug-chaser.

"What does the doctor say, Artie? Did he tell you when you could return to performing again? How are things at the restaurant these days?"

Ruth and Artie were sitting on the little back deck off the kitchen. Ruth had a tall glass of iced tea in front of her and Artie was eating Haagen-Dazs vanilla raspberry swirl frozen yogurt right out of the carton. "Hmmm...this stuff isn't half-bad, Ruth. If it's really not all that bad for me, maybe I can get Arturo to buy me some next time. I'm still mad at you, though, for not getting what I asked for."

"Don't change the subject, Artie! What did the doctor say?"

"I have an appointment on Thursday morning with a cardiologist at UC. It's a woman doctor. The one in Denver who put my stents in recommended her and called and set everything up, sent over my files. I think these specialists must be like drag queens—they all know each other."

Ruth laughed and said, "They must have known each other if they were classmates in medical school."

"I guess...hey, if the doctor gives me the okay, I have a little plan that you might be able to help me with, Ruth. Are you doing anything this Sunday afternoon?"

"I don't think we have any plans. I'd have to double check with Sam to make sure, but what do you have in mind?"

"Well, as you may know, the girls that have been filling in for me, Rochelle and Roxeanne are doing their last shows at Arts on Sunday."

"Where are they going?"

"I don't know...back to New York, maybe. We asked them if they'd like to come and fill in from time to time, but they said they thought they'd done all they could do here. How was it they put it? I don't remember now...something about not wanting to wear out their welcome, but those weren't the exact words. They just felt like it was time to move on, I guess. But I have a plan for a big surprise in mind for their last show on Sunday and I need you to help me and swear to keep it a secret, Ruthie!"

A dozen messages for Tim popped up on dudesurfer, but none of the guys who had written them were on-line at the moment. Tim read each of the messages and looked at all the pictures. Some were from guys in faraway cities, listing the dates of their upcoming visit to San Francisco. They wouldn't do Tim any good. Nick would be home by then. Tim rarely liked to plan things that far in advance, anyway. There were plenty of other hot guys out there looking for now, as evidenced by the number who were on-line right this minute.

Tim's eyes were drawn to a motion in the corner of the computer screen. <RU there, Tim?> Damn, it was Britlad. Tim had tried to keep the young Londoner out of his thoughts, but he was back now. Dudesurfer provided a dialogue box in the upper left-hand corner where you could converse with someone while keeping his pictures in view and double-checking what he had listed as "likes" and "dislikes" in his profile. <I was waiting 4U to come on.>

<Yeah, I'm here.> Tim typed back. <What time is it in London? Don't you ever sleep?>

<I'm 2 excited about my trip. Counting on ur b'day gift in SF>

Tim had grown used to hearing people call his psychic ability a "gift" when most of the time he considered it a burden. The *gift* of HIV infection would be a much worse one to give somebody. <About that...I've been thinking.> Tim wrote.

<If u don't someone else will. Why not u?>

<I know that. I've thought about all that, but it's still a bad idea. You're healthy, right?>

<I'm neg...so? U & ur BF don't use rubbers, right?> Britlad had an irritating way of asking more questions than he answered.

<No. Not anymore. We tried to at first, but we're both positive.>

<Do U use them with other guys?>

<Yes, especially if they're negative!> Tim tried hard to remember the last time he had actually needed to put on a condom and he couldn't.

<But not if ther poz, right?> Britlad asked.

<There are lots of STDs out there besides HIV, you know. And there might be other strains of the virus.>

<But I don't want to deal w/ frigging rubbers. I want 2b free like ur.>

<But HIV is no picnic.>

<Ur not sick ru? U just take a pill.>

<I'm doing okay right now, yes, but it's still a lot better to be healthy.>

<Britain has good health care. Pill is easier than rubbers to get on with a bloke. Me mum takes a pill not 2 have more babies. What's the dif?"

<There's a big difference! Even if you find a pill that works for you, nobody knows about the long-term side-effects. And some people never do find a drug they can tolerate. Some people still die from AIDS, you know!> Tim was knocked off balance for a moment by the fact that he was conversing about sex with someone whose mother was still young enough to bear children.

<Me mum says her pills can have side-effects 2, but better than getting knocked up>

Tim shook his head and tried to think for a minute. He typed back: <You're just a kid!>

<18 next week. Legal is 16 here & I started fucking b4 then>

<So you've thought it all out, huh?>

<Yes.>

<I don't like this, but I don't know how to talk you out of it. Please don't go looking for someone else. I want to meet you, regardless. There's a drug you might be able to take so you can have unprotected sex and not get infected. Truvada, but I think you have to be on it for a while first.>

<But I want your disease. Like Lady Gaga's song. Turn me poz and get it over with.>

<We'll talk, okay? I'm not promising you anything. My boyfriend comes home on Sunday, too.>

<U told me. I can take U both on.>

"Fat chance," Tim said out loud, but he typed: <Call me on Monday, after you get settled at your hotel, okay?>

Then the dialogue box in the corner went blank. Tim wasn't ready to sign off yet, but he still didn't know what to do about Britlad. The boy was determined to infect himself and Tim didn't even know his name but still he felt somehow responsible. And he felt like he'd only made things worse with his answer about not using condoms with Nick, but he couldn't lie to the kid. Tim could almost put himself in the boy's shoes. Would he and Nick be having safe sex if one of them were negative? Tim didn't honestly know.

At least he should have kept him talking longer, asked him what time his flight got into SFO on Sunday. He'd said before sunset, that was all. Tim could have asked the name of his hotel or if he needed a ride in from the airport. No, Tim wouldn't have offered that much. Not even Buck was going along on this trip to the airport, as much as Nick would want to see their dog when he got home. That reunion would have to wait.

Tim sat back in his desk chair and wondered at the frustrations of the gay men who didn't live in San Francisco in the 21st century. At least they had the Internet all around the world, now. He could only imagine an ancient time when someone would scribble a note on the wall of a public toilet and come back to it again and again to see if there was anyone else like him out there in the world.

The computer age had certainly turned the world upside down for gay men. Tim remembered a graffiti-covered toilet stall somewhere in Minnesota when he was a kid, barely old enough to read. The graffiti was the standard scrawling about Kilroy being there with a few dirty jokes. Tim's family was having a picnic nearby, but his thoughts were captured by something inside here. Maybe it was his first psychic experience, feeling the energy of hungry need. He picked up the emotional turmoil of men looking for anonymous sex. These were the scary people, the ones society warned about, the ones he didn't want to become. Tim was only a child then, but he was intrigued by and fearful of the desires spelled out among the cob-webs and buzzing horseflies. He was disgusted and fascinated at the same time. Nowadays technology and acceptance had changed all of that, at least in most of the civilized world. Technology had also blessed janitors with modern graffiti-proof materials for restroom walls and gay men could find like-minded others at the click of a mouse.

Tim stared at Britlad's newest photograph, still up on the screen, the perfect skin, the gymnast's body. The boy was fully erect in this picture too. He wore leather arm-bands above his thick biceps and boots to his knees, a chain harness and a visored cap with mirrored sunglasses. Tim shook his head. Kids grew up so fast these days.

Chapter 28

Neither Teresa nor Birdie felt like cooking dinner on Saturday night. They sat in front of the six o'clock news on TV while Birdie sipped a tall glass of iced tea and Teresa lapped at the fumes of a dry martini before she slid the top layer of gin across her tongue. "You wanna call out for pizza?" Birdie asked.

"How's your foot?"

"Whattaya mean, how's my foot? My foot's fine. I've been back on foot patrol full time for a week now with no problem. You can't even notice the scar where I took the bullet anymore. The doctor says it's fine, too. I'm a textbook case."

"That's good, honey, cause I don't feel like pizza."

"What's my foot got to do with pizza? You wanna order Chinese instead?"

"No, I thought we could go out to eat, as long as your foot's okay. I thought if you'd been on your feet too much you wouldn't want to, but I've been inside all day. I'd like to go out, if you don't mind."

"Sure, Teresa, as long as my foot has nothing to do with pizza."

A half hour later they were sitting at a window table at Arts. Birdie sipped at another glass of iced tea while Teresa had another martini. Their waiter James brought warm bread and offered fresh cracked pepper for their Caesar salads. Birdie declined, wanting nothing to do with the oversized phallic pepper mill. Teresa said, "Sure, James, honey...bring it on!"

A couple of minutes later, Teresa poked at the last lettuce leaf on her salad plate and asked birdie, "Do you hear anything from George these days?"

"George who?"

"Yeah, right! Who! Who do you think I mean? You sound like a hoot-owl. George Tavares, your old partner."

"Nah, I haven't heard much. He's still on leave, I guess. I just wonder if it's *paid* leave. Maybe I should go shoot up the Last Call during Happy Hour the next time I need a vacation."

"Speak of the devil." Teresa dropped her fork and gestured with a tip of her head toward the sidewalk. "There he is, coming this way, jaywalking across Castro Street. And he's supposed to be a cop...what an example!"

George waved and smiled as he walked by, headed north a few more steps and apparently changed his mind. He turned back and came inside to say hello. "Hey, Teresa. How's it going, Birdie? How's the foot?"

"My foot's fine, George. Why is everyone so interested in my damn foot? How the heck are you doing these days? Are you coming back to the force?"

"Eventually, I hope..." George looked sheepish. Teresa noticed that he wasn't alone. A young man in tight jeans and a bomber jacket was pacing on the sidewalk, a date, Teresa figured. "I'm in rehab now, you know...going to my meetings. My sponsor is waiting for me, so I'd better get going. Good to see you both."

"James, another martini, please." Teresa always got a little nervous when people made references to not drinking.

"You too, George. Take it easy." Birdie waved as George left and said to Teresa, "For as big a dope as he is, I'm still glad to hear he's getting with the program, stopped drinking and all. I hope his sponsor helps him stay out of trouble and get his job back, eventually. He's not such a bad guy, really—"

"Sponsor, my foot," Teresa snorted after the two men were out of sight. "I'll bet he's George's trick for tonight."

"We're talking about *your* foot now, huh? At least we're off the subject of mine."

"They're both too good-looking not to be fucking."

"You really *are* bi, aren't you, Teresa?"

"Don't you worry, Birdie. George isn't. He's as gay as a gander and he wouldn't be interested in me, anyway. I was always a little too full-figured for most guys."

"You still like guys, though. I can tell. You'd dump me in a minute if the right guy came along, wouldn't you?"

"You're nuts!"

"If you like guys so much, how come you ever decided to settle down with me, anyway?"

"Other than being trapped into it? Hmmm, I don't know. It must have been the uniform, darlin'. I've always liked a man in a uniform, so why not a woman in a uniform, huh?"

The following morning Arts' was packed for Roxeanne and Rochelle's final performances. Seating for both brunch shows was sold out with an SRO crowd along the bar. Tim was too excited about picking up Nick at the airport later to think much about anything else. And he was too busy taking care of his customers—all the ring-side seats and then some—to pay much attention to the show.

"Sisters...sisters...there were never such devoted sisters..."

Tim was tired of their act anyway, especially this song. When they brought out the big fans from behind the piano, some of the feathers always flew loose and landed in people's plates and drinks. The audience never complained, though. They must have felt more included in the show by ingesting part of it, Tim thought, so he just kept smiling.

Their act was basically the same every time except for the patter between songs. Sometimes the two drag queens

got into a funny confrontation if an audience member tried
to provoke them. When the second show finally came to an
end, they had a special closing number, since this was their
last appearance at Arts. "Thank you so much, ladies and
gentlemen. You've been a wonderful audience week after
week and you've made us feel so very welcome, but the time
has come for us to move on. Another encore? Do we know
anything else?"

Rochelle picked it up from there, Tim thought it was,
but he still couldn't remember which was which. "Yes, we
have to catch a flight in a few hours, but before we go, we'd
like to do a special number to say good-bye and thank you to
your lovely city of San Francisco."

They spoke in unison now, "Thank you San Francisco,
thank you Castro Street, and thank you Arts!" Tim didn't
bother to look up when whichever one said, "This song was
made famous by a local gal, I believe. Is that right?"

The other one glanced at their playlist and the notes on
top of the piano. "A former local, we're told she's legendary
here in San Francisco, now lives down in La-la Land, but
you all know her. The song is by a fella named Michael Reno
and the singer is right here in our audience this afternoon.
Ladies and gentlemen, give a warm welcome to Miss Sharon
McNight! Let's all give her a big hand!"

Tim knew who Sharon McNight was, of course, but
he hadn't seen her come in and hadn't realized that she was
seated in Jake's section. Artie adored Sharon McNight. What
a shame he wasn't here! All the waiters had heard a million
stories about the "olden days" when he was still performing
at Finocchio's. He'd gone to hear Sharon sing at places like
Sutter's Mill and the Plush Room and Fanny's. Arturo still
talked about when they flew to New York to see Sharon
McNight on Broadway and how she was "simply robbed"
of that Tony Award. Sharon stood up briefly while everyone
applauded and then the drag queens began the song. If these
two kept doing encores, Tim would never get out of here.

"You've been one hell of a town, even when you let me down,
San Francisco
    With your nose up city class, full of vinegar and sass, San
Francisco
    To the nobs on Nob Hill, to the top of the Mark,
    to Chinatown, downtown, and to Golden Gate Park
    It's been fun, San Francisco, so long, San Francisco, bye-bye.

Tim was totaling up his checks at the waiters station, desperate for this shift to end so that he could go home and get ready to pick up Nick. When the drag queens mentioned catching a flight, his first instinct was to offer them a ride to the airport, but he quickly nixed that idea. Getting Nick from the airport was something he'd been looking forward to so long that he didn't want any company. Not Buck and certainly not these two drag queens. Besides, they must have a ton of luggage to hold all the costumes for their act.

    "To your bars, your cafés, to the straights, to the gays
    To MUNI, to Bart, and to Tony Bennett's heart…
    It's been fun San Francisco, so long San Francisco Bye–
bye…"

When the song ended the crowd gave Rochelle and Roxeanne a standing ovation until they were off-stage and out of sight in the dressing room/office. Tim was scanning credit cards when he heard some commotion at the front door. Most of the audience had sat back down, but now they stood up again and were clapping harder than ever. Artie Glamóur appeared at the front door in a white gown and matching hat. Hoots and hollers mixed with the applause and the noise was deafening. Artie strode through the restaurant like he owned the place, since he and Arturo did, in fact. Tim was amazed to see his Aunt Ruth and Sam coming in the front door right behind Artie. They must have known about this all along.

    Artie reached the stage, took the microphone off its stand and gestured for everyone to sit back down. Phil appeared in a tux and slid into a smooth arpeggio on the piano. Artie said, "What? You were expecting Norma Desmond, maybe?" and broke into his own rendition of a song from the musical version of *Sunset Boulevard*:

> *"I don't know why you're frightened*
> *I know my way around here*
> *The tacky queens, the salad greens, the cheap beer...*
> *Yes a world to rediscover*
> *But I'm not in any hurry*
> *And I need a moment..."*

Tim had already settled up most of his customers' tabs and now they wanted to reopen them. He could strangle Artie for pulling a stunt like this, but had to admit it was great to see him back on stage and looking pretty good, considering the heart attack and all.

Artie let Phil play the next verse while he joked with the audience. "Are you surprised to see me, kids? You thought I was dead, didn't ya'? And you've never seen an entrance like that before, I'll bet. I decided that if Donna Sachet can strut right down Castro Street in a red dress and high heels in broad daylight—and *broad* is the key word, my darlings—you've all seen her do it! Then I should at least be able to toddle over here from Collingwood in white with sensible pumps on such a lovely Sunday afternoon. Big thanks to Ruth for coming by to help me get dressed. Arturo told me Sharon McNight was here. Where are you, Sharon? There you are. Stand up. Take a bow. You look fabulous!" Sharon briefly rose to her feet again and waved. Artie joined in the applause for a moment. "But not as good as me, so sit back down!

> *So much to say not just today but always*
> *We'll have early morning madness*
> *We'll have magic in the making*
> *Yes, everything's as if we never said goodbye..."*

Artie took his bows and headed down the steps, but the audience refused to let him leave, so he grabbed the mike again. "I'm not doing a whole show today. You already had one! How did you like Rochelle and Roxeanne? Let's bring them back out here one more time."

Since Tim was closest, he ran to the office, but there was no one inside. They must have slipped out the same way Phil had come in, through the kitchen. Tim made a neck-slashing motion with his fingers to let Artie know they wouldn't be coming back for another encore.

Artie sat back down on the stool beside the piano. "I guess they've already taken off their faces and slipped into something more comfortable, so they can't come out and bid you adieu. You'll just have to come back next Sunday if you want to see more of me or anyone else. Oh, all right, all right! Twist my arm clear off, why don't you? Maybe I can do one more number, but that's it! I'm under a doctor's care these days, you know. Maestro, if you please?

It's a most unusual day,
Feel like throwing my worries away;
As an old native born Californian would say,
It's a most unusual day..."

Chapter 29

Tim pulled into short-term parking at the airport and drove around until he found a spot near an elevator. He had plenty of time to kill. Even after he took Buck for a long walk, changed the bed linens and spent a long time getting cleaned up after work, he was plenty early for Nick's flight. He wanted to be waiting for him right outside the secured area. He'd even considered buying a ticket on a flight to the cheapest possible place just so that he could get inside security and surprise Nick at the gate, but where would that be? Oakland?

"Tim!" Someone yelled at him and he turned around. It was Roxeanne and Rochelle out of drag as Gary and Richard. They were just heading toward the line for security clearance with their carry-ons. Tim still couldn't remember which was which when they were in drag, but he knew that the one he'd met and talked to a while back at the Midnight Sun was named Richard, so the other one had to be Gary.

"Hey guys, great show today. So you're really leaving town this time, huh? You should have told me and I would have given you a ride to the airport," Tim lied.

"No problem, "Richard said. "Our hotel had a shuttle. Where are you off to?"

"No place, I'm picking up my...um...boyfriend."

"Ah, romance," said Gary.

"Yeah," Tim grinned at the thought of seeing Nick again in a few minutes and started to blush. He glanced down at his watch and realized it would be nearly a half hour before the plane landed and then they'd have to wait for Nick's bags and then walk to the car and drive back into the city and climb the stairs. He wasn't sure he could wait that long. Maybe they should check into a hotel right there at the airport, at least for a couple of hours.

"You're blushing, aren't you Tim?" Richard asked.

"Well, he's been gone a long time." Now Tim was thoroughly embarrassed and desperate to change the subject "You know...as different as you two look right now, I still can't tell you apart when you're doing your act. Tell me again...which one is Rachel and..."

"I am," they both said at once, "I mean...she is." They pointed at each other and laughed.

"Oops. You caught us, Tim. We both are!" Richard said. "Remember that night at the Midnight Sun, I told you not to ask. You don't want to know all the things we do to keep things exciting and fresh in our relationship."

Tim remembered that conversation, but right now he was more interested in his relationship with Nick.

"We switch positions...in more ways than one," Gary said. "Hey, it was nice to see you again before we leave town. Look at those long lines. We'd better get going."

"Yeah, we'd better go," Richard agreed.

"Aren't you coming back?" Tim asked.

"Nah, we've pretty much played out San Francisco. It's time to move on. Besides, with Artie back in town, there's really no place for us to do our act."

"Come on, Gary. It's time to go play nice for the security people. We have to go take off our shoes and empty our pockets. *Everybody do what you're told and nobody gets hurt...*" Gary let out a roar of laughter and Tim realized that he was waiting in the wrong place. Nick was flying in on United and the guys were flying out on Delta. It was lucky Tim had allowed plenty of time. This was the wrong terminal!

"Have a safe trip, guys!"

Tim spotted the top of Nick's head near the baggage carousel above a sea of blue-haired little old ladies who must have been on the same flight. All Tim wanted was to jump on Nick and tear off his clothes, not wait for the baggage to spin around and around and make small talk all the way back into the city, gather Nick's belongings out of the back of the Thunderbird, climb the stairs on Hancock Street and THEN tear off each other's clothes. But that's exactly what they had to do. If Tim had planned better, he would have been waiting for Nick at home—already naked with music playing and candles lit.

They *did* get to kiss, at least. The minute their eyes met, Nick started running. They kissed and wrapped their arms around each other and squeezed as if they could absorb one another's entire being and turn into one ecstatic entity. The kiss was torture because it couldn't continue. Several of the blue-haired ladies' pacemakers must have kicked into high gear as it was.

Once they were on Highway 101 headed into the city, they tried to talk about Nick's flight, how the Thunderbird was running, how were Aunt Ruth and Sam, how was Nick's grandmother doing after her long book tour, business at the restaurant, business at the nursery, the Larsons and their kids who lived downstairs from Tim on Hancock Street.

They tried to talk, but at one point Tim was telling Nick about how Artie surprised everyone by showing up in drag at the restaurant today. "Those other two drag queens, Rochelle and Roxeanne had just finished up their last set. Sharon McNight was in for brunch, so they introduced her and ended their show with an old song of hers about saying goodbye to San Francisco. My tables were almost all paid up and I was so ready to bolt out of there, go home and get in the bathroom and get ready for you—I already had these clothes I'm wearing laid out on the bed to wear to the airport…"

Tim looked over to see if Nick was even listening and saw a huge grin on his face. "What's so funny?"

Nick's jacket was across his lap, but under it, he had unzipped his pants and now he pulled his jacket away slowly. "Someone else misses you too, Snowman."

"Jeez, Nick! Put that away! You're gonna make us have an accident on the freeway!"

Buck was overjoyed to see both his dads together again. If he weren't already fixed he might have enjoyed the sights and sounds they created in bed, but the dog soon understood there was nothing in it for him. Within five or ten minutes Buck gave up on getting any more attention and went back to the kitchen for a drink of water.

After a half hour, Nick said, "Gee, a person might think you hadn't gotten laid the whole time I was gone."

"I haven't, really…" Oh-oh! Was it time for this conversation already? Couldn't it wait a while? Nick's first night at home and they were already going to delve into *the rules* they had never established? Tim had hoped to keep the sex heavy and the conversation light.

Nick rolled onto his side and propped his chin in one hand. "Not really, huh?"

Tim forced a half-hearted laugh, "Ha…well…not for lack of trying on my part. I mean…I figured I *should*…while you were off in Europe, doing everything with anybody whenever you got the chance, right?"

"I'll tell you anything you want to know, Snowman…"

That was just the trouble; Nick *would* tell him everything and Tim didn't want to know. Didn't someone tell Tim that his relationship with his partner had rules like the military under "don't ask; don't tell?" But those policies were a relic of the Clinton and Bush administrations weren't they? Times were changing.

"...but you go first. What does 'not really' mean? Really!"

"Well...let me think how to put this. You roll us another joint and I'll go grab a couple more beers. Besides, I need to go to the bathroom and touch up."

"Okay, I'm rolling...hurry back!"

The topic of their sexual adventures while they were apart didn't come up again until morning. They were drinking coffee on Tim's deck, watching the fog burn away from the downtown buildings. Nick said, "God, it's good to be back in San Francisco. I hate to think of going back to work, but..."

"Do you have to?" Tim hadn't planned for this. He had just gotten Nick back; he couldn't be leaving again so soon. Tim would rather talk about *the rules* than talk about another separation so soon.

"Not today...tomorrow. I have a business to take care of, you know? You should drive up, too."

"You'll have so much work to get caught up at the nursery. I'd only get in the way."

"No, you wouldn't. I'll put you to work, too. My employees deserve a big bonus and some time off after doing such a good job while I was away. The time has come to pay the piper."

"I don't want to think about it," Tim said with a scowl. "Haven't I done a good job while you were away?"

"Um...uh...a good job of what, Tim?"

"Of keeping my sanity!"

"How about breakfast?" Nick changed the subject. "I'm gonna grab a quick shower and then I'll treat you to some of Orphan Andy's pancakes and sausages. How does that sound?"

"Yeah, okay..."

Tim was thrilled to have Nick back but it felt like a tease for him to return after all this time and disappear again. Maybe he would drive up to the river. He'd have to think about it. While Nick was in the shower, Tim sat down at the computer to check his email.

Sure, now that Nick was back in town, Tim had six messages from guys on dudesurfer.com and three of them were on-line right now. Why couldn't they have been interested last week? He had to log on to the site to read what they said and see their profiles. At least the pictures—of how they looked maybe several years and pounds ago under very flattering conditions—were hot. Tim always meant to have new ones taken of himself too, so he could hardly complain about anyone else's. His weren't exactly recent but they weren't all that flattering, either. Oh well… Tim thought it was better that his potential dates be pleasantly surprised to meet him in person, rather than disappointed that he didn't live up to Photo-Shop.

None of the messages were from Britlad. Tim had hardly thought of him in twenty-hour-hours what with all the excitement about Nick's return. The young bug-chaser should be here in San Francisco by now. His flight was due in last night sometime. Was his birthday today or tomorrow? Tim supposed he would have to find some way to broach this subject with Nick. But Nick might be the perfect person! This would give them an excuse to talk about sex with other guys in a more-or-less abstract way. Neither he nor Nick was into eighteen-year-olds—that was for sure. Nick might even have some ideas about how to talk sense into the boy.

Tim read the other messages, but didn't respond to any of them. Now that Nick was home, the prospect of hooking up with a stranger lost all its appeal. He logged out of the dudesurfer site and went back to his main page. That was when he glanced at the news. It didn't register at first… something about a plane crash. Tim thought back to his dream from a while ago when he woke up worried about Artie and Nick. That dream had faded into hazy black and white by now. Even though it was a recurring dream, Tim could only remember the highlights of it, the cold fear, the sense of time

stopping as the ground grew near and then time speeding up
again faster and faster.

Tim held the mouse in his hand and was hardly aware
of moving and clicking it until the screen changed and the
story got big and Tim said, "Oh. My. God!"

"What is it, Snowman?"

"I can't believe this! I had a dream about a plane crash,
but I've had that same dream lots of times and nothing ever
happened. If anything, I was worried about you or Artie
flying home, but this time it came true and I've never even
met the kid in person—"

"Let me see that." Nick leaned in over Tim's shoulder
and read the headline on the screen out loud:

"*'London flight to SFO crashes in Pacific at sunset.'* What
kid? You mean you knew someone on that plane? How can
you be sure?"

"I'm just sure, that's all. That was the time he was
arriving, at sunset."

"Who was arriving?"

"I don't know his real name. I met him on-line. He
was coming to San Francisco for his birthday, his eighteenth
fuckin' birthday and now he's at the bottom of the ocean.
Have you ever heard of bug-chasers, Nick?"

"Yeah, I read articles. Guys that want to get HIV like
they're pledging a fraternity or something."

"That was exactly how he made it sound. I tried to tell
him that the reality of it isn't like that at all."

"Who was he?"

"Britlad. That was his name on the website. He'd been
chatting me up for weeks—ever since you left town—on that
dudesurfer site, telling me he was coming to San Francisco for
his eighteenth birthday and he wanted us to infect him, like
it would be a souvenir of his trip and a birthday present all
rolled into one."

"Us? What do you mean *us*?"

"I told him I had a boyfriend and that you and I were
both HIV positive, that you were coming home the same day.

I think at the time I might have even thought you'd be on the same flight as him. You were in London when he started writing to me. I even thought at one point that maybe he *was* you, testing me somehow."

"Why would I do that?"

"I don't know. Anyway, he said we could both bareback him and double the chances. I figured if I turned him down he'd just find someone else. I didn't know what to say. You should have seen him, Nick. I could still show you the pictures on my computer, I guess. He was a gymnast—great body, big dick, really cute, if you're into teenagers. They're legal at sixteen in England. I was about his age when I started doing it with my track coach. Jeez, Nick, I just thought if I led him on enough maybe you could talk some sense into him when he got here."

"Me? What would I say that you couldn't? He was after you, not me."

"I told him how hot you are, that you're a better top than me, that you've been positive even longer than me…"

"Tim, they don't even consider us contagious at this stage. Haven't you heard? Studies show that when the virus is under control, like in our case, when there's no detectable viral load, the odds of us infecting someone else are virtually nil, even if we don't use condoms."

"Oh, yeah…I guess I've heard that. I just never run across anyone new who is negative, not usually anyway, not that it comes up very often. I don't think about it much. I should have done something, warned him not to fly, maybe."

"Would he have believed you? Did you tell him about your having psychic dreams and stuff?"

"No, he would have just thought I was crazy. I already told you, if I was gonna warn anyone not to fly, it would have been you or Artie. I was more worried about this Britlad kid getting AIDS."

"Well, I guess it doesn't matter now. The poor kid's already dead. I'm really sorry, Snowman. Do you wanna go out for breakfast? How about Orphan Andy's?"

They sat at the counter and the man at the next stool left his San Francisco Chronicle behind when he got up to pay his bill. Tim had the same newspaper at home, but he hadn't looked at it yet. The headline was the same as the on-line story, but this time there were more details:

London flight to SFO crashes in Pacific at sunset

British Airways non-stop from Heathrow to San Francisco reported trouble with landing gear while circling for final descent… diverted over the ocean to discharge fuel in preparation for emergency landing. Runway foamed…all other flights diverted. Pilot reported electrical trouble seconds before explosion over the water. All 287 passengers and crewmembers feared dead. Search is ongoing for black box. Terrorist plot suspected.

Tim pointed to the paper and said, "Just look at this! 287 *feared* dead, huh? Don't they know? How could anyone *not* be dead? Some of the passengers had parachutes or they executed a perfect swan dive from a burning ball of flames and swam over to the Farallon Islands where they're eating fresh sushi and waiting for a rescue helicopter to—"

"Hey…" Nick set down his fork and put one arm around Tim's shoulder. "Snowman, I'm really sorry about the kid, but headlines sell papers, you know. The Chronicle needs all the help it can get. It's too late to worry about it now."

That night in bed they got back to talking about their time apart. Words long held back unformed began to spill out. "I'll tell you anything you want to know, Snowman. I'll always be honest with you and I expect the same. I love you, Tim."

"I love you too, Nick…more than I want to sometimes."

"But if there's something you don't want to know, don't ask me about it, 'cause I'll always tell you the truth."

"Okay, tell me all about all the sex you had on your trip?" Tim pulled Nick close, face to face and wrapped their legs together. He placed both palms spread as wide as he could across Nick's bare chest. Their stomachs touched. Tim wanted as much shared surface space of flesh as possible without suffocating each other.

"Well, I went to a wild party in Amsterdam one night, but I really don't remember much about it. That was early in the trip. They have legal pot there, you know…coffee houses where you can buy joints and smoke them right there."

"You don't remember?"

"Well, I must have carried on at the party, judging by the looks of my clothes the next morning, but I don't think it counts if you can't remember what you did, not that we're *counting*…are we?"

"No, but that's still number one…what else?"

"I got a blowjob in a bookstore in Paris."

"That sounds fairly anonymous, I guess. I can't be too jealous of a glory hole thousands of miles away in some dirty bookstore in Paris, can I?"

Nick sensed that he could leave it at that, but he was the one who promised to be totally honest, so he explained. "It wasn't a dirty bookstore, Tim. It was a regular bookstore, the kind that sells travel guides and maps and dictionaries and… you know…books."

"A regular bookstore…with glory holes?"

"You *really* want to know, huh? There was no glory hole. The guy that ran the place…big sweet bear of a guy… he'd been to my grandmother's reading the night before and he was checking me out. She left her glasses there and the next morning she asked me to go back and get them while she finished packing. He was there working and he wanted to blow me so I let him."

"You're not really into bears at all, are you? I'm nowhere near being a bear, Nick. I can't compete with that, if you are. You were just horny, right?"

"No, but he was a nice guy and it just happened. I'm not into bears, particularly. It was just a situation with a couple of guys who would never see each other again, just helping each other out, you know?"

"I'm not into bears either, not really. What else?"

"Oh, this is the *best!* There was this guy on the ship coming back, a British guy, filthy rich, traveling on business with his wife. You should have seen her, dripping in jewelry and furs, even though her coat looked kind of ratty. I think they were both so eccentric that they probably would have paid me if I'd stuck around—"

"They?" Tim interrupted.

"She liked to watch her husband getting poled!"

"I don't believe this! Come on!"

"I swear to God! I told you I wouldn't lie to you, man!"

"You made this whole story up, just to tease me. I don't believe a word of it. And if you made up this one, I don't know what to believe about the others."

"Suit yourself, Tim. Now it's your turn, true confessions time. What did you do while I was gone? Will this take all night? Should I put on the coffee?"

Tim pulled away and used his open hands to give Nick a smack wherever they happened to land. "You act like you're going to enjoy hearing about what I did without you!"

"Why not live vicariously? You were in San Francisco the whole time. This should be good!" Nick grabbed Tim's wrists and wrestled him onto his back, pinning him down with the full weight of his body. "Ve haff vays to make you talk!"

"I can't breathe! I'll tell, I'll tell, just let me up a little!"

"Okay…"

"I didn't do much, really…"

"Sure, Tim."

"I didn't!"

"Just be honest."

"You won't care?"

"Not in a jealous way. It might be a turn-on."

Rules or no rules, Tim knew that Nick would always be honest. That's what he'd promised and Tim knew it was true. Nick would tell him anything he wanted to know and then some. Nick had told Tim about his brief encounters in Europe as if they were mere sight-seeing junkets. If that was the way Nick treated them, why couldn't Tim?

But he did! He started to realize that the cigar-chewing guy who followed him home from 440 and didn't bottom, the man he met at Walgreens whose partner came home early, the neighbor on Ford Street whom he planned to meet at Last Call and finally met at the hospital…none of them meant anything compared to what he and Nick had together. Wow! Maybe he and Nick didn't need a lot of complicated rules. Nick would just go on doing what he did, anyway. Tim wasn't really threatened and this way he didn't feel compelled to sneak around if he felt like doing something, which he didn't… usually. And besides, they weren't planning to be separated again for a long, long time, not in any foreseeable future.

"I don't know where to start. I guess the first one was that guy with the cigar. He never lit it; he just sucked on it like it was a pacifier or something."

"Where'd you meet him?"

"440—I saw him standing at the upstairs bar. Jake was looking for someone so I stopped in there with him for a drink after work."

"Jake, the one with all the tattoos and earrings? Was he looking with a metal detector or a magnet?"

"No…someone in particular. I didn't really meet the guy, either. He sure was cruising me, though. I lost sight of him and then later I was going home and got almost to the corner of Noe when I realized he was following me home like a lost puppy."

Buck growled at the word "puppy" but Tim ignored him. "The way he was sucking on that cigar I figured he just wanted to blow me."

"Then what happened?"

"He started grabbing my ass and insisted that he was a total top. Then I insulted him and his cigar."

"I see…"

"He's the one who got me thinking about rules, though. He asked me what our rules were and I didn't know what to say."

"Rule number one: *Don't let stray puppies follow you home.*" Buck let out another low growl and Nick patted the edge of the bed for the dog to jump up and join them. "I didn't mean you, boy. There's a good boy, that's right. I was talking about a different kind of stray. Okay, what else?"

"I really didn't do much at all while you were gone, Nick. See this hand? I got to know it all too well. I also wore out a couple of old porn videos. They just don't make them like they used to."

"I thought you had all your favorites converted to DVDs. What else?"

"I went up to the park one day."

"Up? You mean Buena Vista?"

"Yeah, I thought I'd see if the guys were still carrying on in the daytime. I barely got out of my car when I ran into someone who knew me from the restaurant. Howard, his name was, and his lover's name is Mickey, but he was out of town. I didn't even remember that guy Howard at first, but he called me by name."

"The world is so small you can't go anywhere these days. I ran into someone I knew from the Russian River in a bar in London."

"You didn't tell me about any adventures in London."

"That's because I didn't have any. It was a straight pub. My grandmother likes her Manhattan before a public appearance. Go on…"

"Well, I saw two other guys in the park that I did recognize, but they didn't see me right away. I don't know their names either, but I've always seen them around in the Castro and always with their partners in tow."

"Uh-oh!"

"They were the hottest guys there that day, too."

"They should have just done each other and gotten it over with."

"No, the park is so cleaned up these days that there's hardly any place left to get any privacy. They started talking instead and they suddenly turned into two big old queens. They were talking about London, too, come to think of it. One of them was bragging, 'When we were in London in this last trip, we only had five days and then Bradley had a client he had to see in Paris, so I went along and shopped for clothes.'"

"Woo-hoo!" Nick said. "Very grand."

"Yeah, but wait. Then the other one had to out-do him. He said, 'when we were in London, we ran the whole length of the Thames.' He was in great shape, but come on!"

"You're a runner, Tim. You should have told them you ran the whole length of the Nile or the Amazon or something." Nick laughed.

"The Mississippi! I'm from Minnesota!"

"There you go!" They both laughed now. Maybe this conversation that Tim had worried about for so long wouldn't turn out to be so bad after all. They still hadn't gotten very far, though.

Nick asked, "So what rule can we establish from that episode?"

"None. And these are supposed to be *our* rules, Nick— you and me, not what I did on your summer vacation."

"So what else *did* you do?"

"I met a guy at Walgreens, waiting for my prescription. We didn't talk until afterward, when he was waiting for me on the sidewalk by the newspaper kiosk. He lived on Seward. Man, it's quiet up there, just a few blocks up the hill west of Castro Street. I thought Hancock Street was quiet, but up there it's like a whole different world."

"So, how was that guy?"

"Fine. I mean, he would have been fine, I guess, but we were just getting going at it when his lover came home. That's why I remember how quiet it was. The sound of that garage door opening right under the bed was like an air raid siren. He nearly hit the ceiling and he made me run out the back door with my clothes in my hands and wait downstairs until the timing was right to sneak out."

"Bummer."

"Yeah, talk about paranoid. I could have been the cable guy or someone next door making noise or something."

"What else? What about the Internet?"

"That was how I got involved with Britlad, but there was one other guy I met, CASTROSTUD. We arranged to meet at the Men's Room, but that was the day of the stick-up. He was the guy that George Tavares shot. I told you about all that on the phone."

"You didn't say it was your date that got shot."

"Well, nothing happened between him and me, not that day, anyway. I went to see him once in the hospital. His name turned out to be Greg. I brought him some flowers, figured it was the least I could do."

"Right...flowers... I can't imagine anything he might have appreciated more but maybe a blowjob."

"How did you guess? His left arm was all bandaged up in a sling. His right arm was free, but it turned out he was left-handed."

"What else?"

"With him? That was it."

"With anyone?"

"That's all...yep, that was the extent of my adventures."

Nick burst out laughing. "Do you mean the entire time I was gone you never once even got your rocks off with another guy?"

"Only with guys that I could fast-forward and rewind. What's so funny?"

"I just can't believe it, that's all. You're right here in San Francisco and you hardly did anything. Some guys..."

"I'm not *some guys*, Nick. If you had been here I wouldn't have even done that much...*probably*... I missed you, that was all."

"Probably?"

"Hey, we still haven't talked about rules, Nick."

"Just be honest and I will be too. That's a promise. Isn't that enough?"

"Honesty is a virtue, not a rule. The next time you leave me alone for weeks I want to know what I can and cannot do so as not to make you angry or upset."

"Who said I'd be angry or upset? I don't feel threatened by any of the things you did. And I'm not planning on going anywhere for a long time…except back to work in the morning. Why don't you drive up and spend the next couple of nights at my place?"

"I have to go to the dentist tomorrow and my mouth will be all numb and sore."

"Then we won't use your mouth tomorrow." Nick bent down and kissed him hard for a long time.

"What's that for?"

"If it's gonna be out of commission tomorrow I want to get in some good mouth time tonight. We'll just have to use something else tomorrow."

"*If* I drive up—"

"See how you feel after you get through at the dentist."

"Okay, but what about our rules?"

"You go ahead and make a list of rules if you want to, Snowman. Write them all down if it'll make you feel better. Give me a copy and I'll sign it in blood or any bodily fluid you like. Whatever makes you happy, babe, you just let me know. I love you, man. No rules are ever gonna change that. No rules are gonna change anything."

"Maybe you're right, Nick. I love you too…"

Nick packed up his things the next morning and let Buck jump up into the front of the truck. "Don't slobber on me, boy! We'll get there when we get there."

The dog was excited to be out in the open again, to get away from the city noises and the confines of Tim's house on Hancock Street. He would be able to poke around inside the nursery again and chase rabbits and field mice through the surrounding woods. If there was time—most weeks, but not always—Nick would drive them out to the coast south of Jenner and let him explore the exotic smells of rotting kelp and empty shells and salt air. This particular dog's life was heaven.

Tim had an hour to kill before the dentist. He checked his email and emptied the SPAM folder. Then he noticed that he had a message on the dudesurfer site. Tim almost deleted it without looking. Now that Nick was back from his travels, Tim wouldn't need to seek out any sexual rendezvous with strangers. He clicked on the link and thought someone was playing some kind of a sick joke on him. The message said it was from Britlad: <Tim—I got a new lap-top from me mum for my birthday, so I can write to you in proper English. You must have heard about the accident by now. I saw it on the telly here. When I heard that the aeroplane crashed I thought I must be dreaming. I would have been on that flight but for the taxicab getting into an altercation just outside of Heathrow. To be honest, I was running late as it was, so there wasn't a moment to spare.

Maybe I didn't really fancy going anyway. It was almost like I had a premonition that I shouldn't. And of course I'm scared to get on another flight now. I don't think I'll be leaving terra firma again for a long while, mate. Life is too good here.

I've been thinking about that other thing, too. Maybe it can wait a while. I've got a cute new neighbor moving in next door to my apartment and he winked at me already. If he turns out to be negative, maybe I should see how it goes and stay healthy, like you suggested. But hey, it's my birthday, so raise a glass for me when you get a chance. And give my best to your handsome boyfriend. Cheers!>

Before he left for the dentist, Tim packed enough clothes for a couple of nights at Nick's house. Rules or no rules and no matter whether his mouth was numb or sore, he needed to spend more time with Nick after their long separation. The past two nights in the city weren't nearly enough.

Maybe the quiet of Monte Rio would crystallize his thoughts, put everything in harmony and focus, center him and restore balance to his life. Maybe the smells of the redwoods and the sound of the river below Nick's cabin would make all the rules fall into place. Maybe he would have a dream about Moses coming down old Cazadero Road with two stone tablets in his arms. Instead of the Ten Commandments, they would have *Tim and Nick's rules for a perfect modern gay relationship* carved into them.

"Asshole!" Someone was screaming at traffic from the middle of the intersection of Church and Market Streets. "You're not supposed to turn there! Can't you read the goddamn signs?"

Tim tried to relax as he settled into the dentist's chair. It was never easy, but this was such a small filling that he hardly needed anesthesia. Bette Midler's old song about Dr. Longjohn played in Tim's head:

"He said he wouldn't hurt me, but he filled my whole inside… you thrill me when you drill me, and I don't need no Novocain today…"

Dentists don't really use Novocain anymore, of course. They hadn't in years. Tim knew that, but he thought about the sensation of numbness with the song stuck in his head. He would love to have a shot of Novocain for his brain sometimes when his dreams were too frightening and too real…or for those painful mornings after any indulgence. There were times in his life when he could use a shot of Novocain for his heart…or his soul.

North on Van Ness from the dentist's office, west on Lombard and then the traffic started getting heavy on Doyle Drive. Tim thought he would beat the evening commute, but cars were already clogging the way to the Golden Gate Bridge, Marin County and everything north. At this rate there'd be no sense in stopping at the nursery. Nick would have already finished up for the day.

Tim finally got across the bridge and traffic thinned a bit north of the Sausalito exits. He glanced out the right side of the car at the domed blue roof of the Marin Civic Center. What a strange color; it must almost match the sky sometimes. Tim remembered the first time he saw it. Jason was driving the Thunderbird and it was Tim's first trip to the Russian River.

"It was Frank Lloyd Wright's last commissioned work...1957...wasn't finished until the 1960s, after he died," Jason could give a spiel as good as any tour guide. He prided himself on knowing the history of his surroundings. Jason would have been a killer at Trivial Pursuit.

Tim knew nothing of history until it was drilled into him by his elders, people like Jason and Artie and Arturo and his Aunt Ruth. Time meant something different to Tim since he could dream about things that hadn't happened yet and events in the distant past that he didn't remember. Tim was wide awake now, driving, but he was in that zoned-out state where the road was so familiar that the car almost seemed to drive itself.

Jason's voice was still in Tim's head, rattling on about some controversy between the architect and the estate and the county, was it? Tim couldn't remember the details of all that, but he could hear Jason's voice say, "The tower is the tallest man-made structure in Marin County..."

Then Jason's voice drifted off. Tim wondered what Jason would say about gay couples having rules. No, he didn't wonder. He knew. Jason would scoff at the idea. Nobody would ever tell Jason what he could and couldn't do. He wouldn't laugh at the idea; he would grunt, but Tim couldn't hear Jason's voice at all anymore, not at the moment.

Nick was such a good guy! Nick would do whatever he wanted, too, and he'd tell Tim all he wanted to know and trust that none of it mattered because he loved Tim so much. Nick was a lot like Jason in many wonderful ways, but one big difference was that Nick would take the time to humor Tim with the talk of rules, with talk of anything. Nick was willing to talk Tim through all his neuroses. Jason would have said, "It's none of your damned business!" Tim could hear his voice again now.

Tim wondered which of them had ever loved him more, Jason or Nick. Jason was a distant memory now and Nick was the present, the immediate past and the future for as far as Tim could see.

Traffic thinned some more as he continued north past the signs to Mt. Tamalpais and Muir Woods. Tourists in rental cars were turning off the main road to find parking lots where they could shut off their gas-eating combustion engines long enough to visit California's nature.

Now Tim heard other more recent voices in his head:

"Come on, Gary. It's time to go play nice for the security people. We have to go take off our shoes and empty our pockets. *Everybody do what you're told and nobody gets hurt…*" That was when Gary let out of roar of laughter and Tim realized that he was waiting for Nick at the wrong terminal.

"Have a safe trip, guys!" Tim had said. Now he almost slammed on the brakes. "…*and nobody gets hurt.*" Where had he heard that same voice say those very same words before? *"Everybody do what you're told and nobody gets hurt!"*

It was at Arts, the day the robbers came in and ripped them off. Gary and Richard had to be the guys with the stockings over their heads. They were drag queens, after all. They must have used their old pantyhose! Could committing armed robbery be one of the kicks they used to keep their relationship fresh?

Tim was tempted to pull off at the next exit at Petaluma and call the police. Would they believe him? Tim thought not. And there was no hurry, was there? They'd gotten away with it this long, if it really was them. But it had to be them. The voice, the same exact words!

Maybe he'd drive straight through Santa Rosa and west on River Road through Guerneville to Monte Rio. If he beat Nick home it didn't matter; Tim had his own key to Nick's house on the hill. Tim could call Arturo and Artie when he got to Nick's place. They could press charges. They ought to be warned if they ever planned to invite Roxeanne and Rochelle back to perform at Arts.

But come to think of it, Artie was back at Arts now. He was doing his Sunday brunch shows again and everyone was happy. They had filed, if not settled their insurance claims by now and so had everyone else in the Castro. Besides, the robbers never took anyone's tips. Tim liked that about them so much. It really demonstrated a lot about character. Maybe they were using the loot for some good cause—Robin Hoods in pantyhose. It never was that much money.

No one had gotten seriously hurt either, except for Birdie Fuller and she ended up with a new partner she liked better than George Tavares, so something good came out of it and besides, she got some time off work and now her foot was all healed. Tim thought some more about George, how he had been so quick to pull out his gun at the Last Call and shoot Greg Holt from across the room. It could just as easily have been George's gun that shot Birdie in the ankle. Maybe the drag queen robbers' guns weren't even real.

That woman who was waiting for the #35 MUNI bus broke her ankle, but Tim hadn't heard anything more about her. He tried to imagine what good might have come from her situation. Maybe her daughter, who had been doing drugs and running with a tough crowd of hoodlums from Mission High School, was so shocked at her mother's brush with death that she'd turned her life around. Or the woman's husband became so caring and attentive during her convalescence that she'd fallen in love with him all over again and decided not to leave him for the sexy neighbor down the block, who only would have hurt her more in the end.

There was CASTROSTUD—real name Greg Holt—but his taking a bullet at Last Call was George Tavares' fault, not really Gary and Richard's at all. Besides, maybe Greg Holt needed some time off work for his boss to fully appreciate all he did. And George was in a 90-day alcoholic rehab program now, because of the shooting in the bar. That was just what he needed. Tim still remembered the feel of George's cock in his hand. But Greg Holt been the closest Tim had come to having real sex with a real person during the whole time Nick was gone, but it wasn't really sex anyway, not according to the old Bill Clinton definition.

Maybe Tim would just tell Nick who the armed robbers were and they'd keep it between them. They could have a few laughs and chalk up one more crazy thing that happened during their long separation. Maybe he'd tell Nick all about it, how he'd finally figured it out without even needing to use any of his psychic ability, but probably not tonight. They wouldn't talk about their damned rules tonight either. They wouldn't need to talk much at all. Nick would come home from his first day back at work and want to forget about the nursery for a few hours. They would kick back under the knotty pine walls of Nick's cabin and they would have dinner and listen to the sounds of the river below them and watch the sunlight fade through the redwood trees and make love slowly while Buck slept on the floor beside the stove and they would have no need to talk much at all.

A sneak peek at
Chapter 1
from

Mark Abramson's

Seersucker

BOOK 8 OF THE BEACH READING SERIES

Chapter 1

"*Oh, give me land, lots of land, under starry skies above... Don't fence me in...*" Artie was trying out some new material in his act today. He had somewhere found a ridiculous-looking pink sequined cowgirl hat that he tossed onto the piano by the time he sang "On my cayuse, let me wander over yonder..."

Tim Snow wasn't paying much attention to the performance, but he noticed it was different from last Sunday's show and he couldn't remember if he'd ever heard the word "cayuse" used in a sentence before. The first seating this morning for Sunday brunch at Arts restaurant on Castro Street was difficult and getting worse. So far, most of the customers ranged from impatient to demanding to downright obnoxious.

"Hey waiter, when is our food coming?"

"Soon," Tim said with a forced smile. "Relax, the show just started."

"But they got theirs already and we were here first."

"That's because they ordered the special."

Tim had barely turned around when a woman at another table said, "I thought the sausages were gonna be patties, not links. I don't like links."

243

"*Just turn me loose, let me straddle my old saddle underneath the western skies…*" Artie sang louder.

"It says so right on the menu, ma-am…SAUSAGE LINKS. Do you want me to show it to you again?" Tim never used "ma-am" unless he was about to lose it. This particular "ma-am" was a very butch lesbian with a shaved head and a Harley tattoo on her bicep. Tim didn't think he'd be risking a big tip by being direct with her.

"Take them back and bring me bacon instead."

"There'll be an extra charge for that."

"Nevermind, then!"

It went on like that most of the shift. One guy sent back his Bloody Mary because it was too hot. "But you asked for it extra spicy," Tim told him.

"I wanted it spicier, not hotter! All they did was add Tabasco. I wanted more horseradish and celery salt."

Tim whisked the drink away and made a face as soon as his back was turned. Scott was bartending at the waiters' station. "What's wrong, Tim?"

"He wanted it '*spicier, not hotter!*'" Tim mimicked a whiny nasal voice. James stood behind him to wait his turn and Tim turned around enough to ask, "Hey James, do you know that jerk on table twelve…purple shirt, seersucker jacket?"

"Maybe…why do you ask?"

"He's a real pain in the ass!"

"Yeah, well, he's never been near *my* ass!"

"Have you seen him in here before?" Tim asked. "He looks kinda familiar."

"Sure, he's been in lots of times, but not lately. He used to ask for me all the time until I finally gave in and made a date with him once. You're right. He is a real jerk."

"Oh…sorry…I didn't mean to—"

"No need to be sorry, Tim. He's just got a thing for black guys. His ancestors must have owned slaves and he grew up with a deep-seated fantasy of being raped in the tool shed."

"James…how do you know?" Tim hadn't meant to step into a racial issue, but now he was curious.

"I can always tell his type. It's like gaydar for us black folk. You just know it when people are objectifying you…and why. Ever since then, he wouldn't give me the time of day, even if he was trying to show off his Rolex."

"I think he really has a Rolex."

"It's a fake, just like everything else about him."

"I'm just a girl who cain't say no…" Artie was wrapping up his opening country/show-tune medley and Tim just wanted to be back in bed with Nick. It was going to be a long day.

When the man in the purple shirt returned from the men's room he staggered and crashed into the new busboy Felipe, upsetting a heavy bus pan full of dirty dishes. He screamed at the boy, "You clumsy ass! Why don't you look where you're going?"

Everyone in the restaurant turned at sound of the crash and the outburst that came in the midst of the silence that followed, so there was no way they could miss a word of it. Artie Glamóur removed *her* fringed jacket before the next song and therefore wasn't at the mike when the man screamed at Felipe, "Fuckin' wetback!"

"Ooooh!" could be heard across the room now, along with grumbles of protest from several of the patrons. Some gays might *be* racists, but using that sort of language was far outside the realm of political correctness on Castro Street. Tim had witnessed the whole thing and he knew that the customer was entirely to blame for his collision with Felipe. This was the poor kid's first day and he seemed really nice and appeared to be a hard worker. Everyone felt sorry for him now.

Tim also knew from overhearing Arturo that Felipe grew up in the Mission district, just a few blocks from here, and needed a part-time job to help his family. His English was fine and he showed enormous restraint to say nothing back to the drunk. He no doubt wanted to keep his job. He looked up at Tim, who rushed over to help him. "Don't worry, Felipe. He'll get his. Go ask Arturo for a broom and a dust pan from the kitchen. I'll pick up the dirty dishes. You sweep up the broken ones. Deal?"

"Thanks, Tim."

"*He'll get his,*" Tim repeated out loud to no one in particular as he carried the bus pan through the swinging double doors to the dishwasher and thought: *Where did that come from? My voice sounded so ominous, like I was channeling Linda Blair or something?*

Tim and Nick had watched *The Exorcist* on TV the other night. Nick fell asleep before the end, but he'd already seen it a couple of times. Whenever Tim said something that sounded *extraterrestrial,* Nick told him he sounded like Linda Blair and to cut it out. "Extraterrestrial," that's what Nick had always called Tim's psychic gift. They both liked their old movies.

But that was more apt to happen early in their relationship. Nick had been with Tim through enough adventures to know that his psychic powers only came to him in dreams—*usually*—and even then they were too symbolic to do much good. They might as well be in some ancient alien code that Tim had never learned how to read.

That afternoon the second seating for Artie's show was friendlier, but some of the customers still seemed agitated. Tim wondered if it was a full moon. He hadn't checked the weather page of the Chronicle lately. Sometimes full moons were obvious and other times he'd swear there was a permanent full moon over Castro Street. Today the kitchen was backed up a couple of times. Felipe was thrown off by the incident with the jerk and Scott was training a new bartender who kept distracting him with questions, so the drinks were slow, too.

The dining room cleared out quickly after Artie's second show ended. James asked, "Whose turn is it to stay late today?"

"Mine, I think. You go ahead. I'll stick around…" The sound of Tim's voice was cut off by a squeal of brakes just outside the door and then a loud crash.

Arturo was sitting at the bar, still in his apron, talking to Scott about some problem with the soda guns. He had overheard the waiters and said, "James and Tim, you can both go home. The kitchen is closed! If people want to take drinks to their tables, they'll just have to carry them. The night crew should be filtering in pretty soon now anyway. Jake always shows up early on Sundays lately, for some reason."

"Thanks, Arturo," they both said at once. Sirens shrieked and grew louder; a fire truck and then an ambulance stopped right outside.

"I guess I'll go home and do some laundry," Tim said.

"Aren't you going up to Nick's place at the river?" Arturo asked.

"He's still at my house. We'll both drive up separately tomorrow."

Tim and James went into the office to count their tips. Artie Glamóur was turning himself back into plain old Artie so they each found a few inches of flat surface among the make-up, mirrors and boxes. James said, "Great show today, Artie."

"Yeah, they loved your new cowgirl bit," Tim added.

"Did you boys really think so? I'm still playing with it. We'll see…but who on earth was that loud-mouthed jerk in the seersucker jacket down in front? I almost went off on him, but I didn't have the strength to expend that kind of energy and still stay in character."

"James' old boyfriend," Tim told Artie.

"Was not! Damnit, Tim! Can't I tell you anything in private?"

"James' ex-*lover*!" Tim went on teasing.

"I told you it was only that one time."

They kept up their laughing banter all the way out the door to Castro Street where Felipe was standing in front of the restaurant. Tim had all but forgotten the noises of a few minutes ago. Sirens weren't unusual in San Francisco. "What happened, Felipe?" James asked.

"It was that same guy, the one that knocked the bus pan out of my hands and yelled at me earlier. He must have gone shopping after brunch 'cause his hands were full of bags. He started to jay-walk behind this car that was trying to back into that space when the van came around the corner from 19th Street. He got caught right between them."

Tim glimpsed a flash of the seersucker jacket and bloodied purple shirt as the EMTs slid the man's broken body into the back of the ambulance. "What was it that you said about him, Tim?" Felipe asked.

"That he was a jerk? I don't remember."

"No, Tim...you said, *'he'll get his'* and you sounded like you meant it, too." Felipe looked at Tim with a combination of admiration and fear. He knew nothing about Tim's past.

"I didn't mean anything by it," Tim insisted.

"Yes you did, Tim," James said. "I heard you say it too, and you meant it, all right."

Felipe's jaw dropped. "Wow!"

…to be continued

About the Author

Born and raised a Minnesota farm-boy, Mark Abramson has lived in San Francisco so long that he feels like a native. He is thrilled that the *Beach Reading* series, his first foray into fiction, has been so successful and he is deeply grateful for all the supportive emails from fans of Tim and Nick, Aunt Ruth, Artie and the rest of the cast of characters. He would also like to make clear that his mother, aside from being a Christian, is nothing like Betty Snow. She is smart and kind with a great sense of humor and she doesn't even drink.

400

CPSIA information can be obtained at www.ICGtesting.com
Printed in the USA
BVOW02s0032121015

421898BV00001B/10/P